PUCK DROP

DUSK BAY DEMONS

MAGGIE ALABASTER

JO BRADLEY

CHAPTER 1

ELENNA

I scoured my hands. Once. Twice. The blood wouldn't wash away.

I scrubbed at them until they were pink, rinsed off the soap and turned off the water.

Finger by finger, I dried them on the thick grey hand towel that hung beside the sink.

Hands raised in front of my face, I looked them over, scrutinising every centimetre of red, raw skin. Here and there, they'd started to peel from frequent washing.

Weeks had passed, but they still didn't feel clean. Weeks since I put a gun to a man's head and pulled the trigger. Weeks since Oscar Fiorelli's brains and blood were blown apart, flecks of both splattered on my fingers, my palms, my wrists.

He'd struggled, fought, tried to scream. Bound to a chair as he was, gagged with duct tape, he didn't stand a chance. He'd given up the right to one the moment he killed my brother, Ike.

Revenge. An eye for an eye. He deserved what he got, fear and death, but it was me who lived that moment over and over. It occupied my thoughts, my dreams.

Regrets? If I hadn't killed him, Aidan would have. Oscar's fate was decided the moment he put a gun to my brother's head and pulled the trigger. It didn't matter if he did it under orders, or for shits and giggles. The fact was, he did it and that couldn't, *didn't* go unpunished.

I stepped out of the relative quiet of the bathroom and into the chaos of the hockey arena. Arms wrapped around myself, I followed the sound of shouting and the clash of sticks, back to the rink. Eyes on the ice, I stepped through the open glass doors and back into my chair.

"What the fuck do you think you're doing?" Aidan roared. "You're supposed to be playing hockey, not tiddlywinks."

I scanned the rink, but wasn't sure which of the players he was yelling at. Possibly all of them.

Coast Riggs, the Dusk Bay Demons' first line centre, skated to a stop and turned around to grin. "Sorry, Coach. Javey is having a hard time telling the difference." He pointed a gloved hand at one of the other players.

Javey spluttered, but flipped him off, his thick glove

thickening and accentuating his finger. "I have no idea what tiddlywinks is."

Coast's grin undiminished, he skated backward toward the goal. He offered Phoenix DiMarco, the team's goalie, a fist bump.

Phoenix shook his head, but tapped his glove against Coast's before his attention was back on practice. He looked straight ahead, kneeling on his knee pads, legs apart, face focused.

Chuckling, Coast glided back to the centre circle, ready to face off against the second line centre.

Aidan glared at them and muttered something about fucking idiots.

I scooped up my laptop and opened it onto my current work in progress.

"Doing more research?" Finley Howard, equipment manager for the Demons, slipped into a chair beside me.

I glanced over at the redhead and smiled briefly. "Aidan wouldn't appreciate it if I put him in a book."

"You can put me in a book." Finley sat back and crossed his legs at his knees. "Don't forget to mention how handsome I am." The smile he gave me was warm, brilliant blue eyes shining. "Especially the part about abs a person could do all their washing on."

My eyes dipped.

His smile widened. "I'm glad you noticed."

I looked back up quickly. "Who says I'm writing a hockey romance anyway? I might be writing gridiron, or rugby. Or a book about a hot doctor who seduces his gorgeous patient."

"If you want hot, you've come to the right place." He rested his hands in his lap, but his gaze lingered on me. Blue eyes seemed to see right into my soul, warming me from the inside until my face heated too.

I swallowed, but I couldn't resist the tease. I gestured towards the rink. "Exactly."

He chuckled, knowing he walked right into that. "I guess some of them are okay. They'd do better if they won a game or two."

"You see that?" Aidan shouted. "That's called a puck. That thing in your hand, the stick, you're supposed to hit the puck with it."

I winced, but Finley snorted softly.

"Aidan is in a right mood today." His voice was brushed with a faint Irish lilt that both lulled me and made my skin tingle.

"When is he *not* in a right mood?" I asked.

"When the team wins?" Finley suggested. "Given they lost their last four games, not recently."

"They'll turn things around." Right now, the Dusk Bay Demons were the worst team in the AIHL, the Australian Hockey League. A fact none of them forgot, especially their head coach.

According to Aidan, the team's owner recently threw a bunch of money at them. Outwardly, to recruit new, better players and replace old, worn equipment. Given the owner's last name was Brantley, the injection of funds was likely aimed at better covering up some kind of criminal activity. Whether the team would see a cent was anyone's guess.

I tried to keep my nose out of Brantley business, having grown up in that lifestyle, but even I thought the team deserved better. The guys worked hard and Aidan was busting his ass, and their asses, to push them to succeed. Losing constantly as they were, that got the whole team noticed. Scrutiny wasn't ideal for smuggling guns and whatever other shit the Brantley family was into.

"That would make for a good book," Finley remarked. "The worst team in hockey, turning everything around and winning against all odds."

"With a smoking hot head coach and equipment manager?" I asked.

"And a stunning brunette who never misses a game or a practice." He looked me up and down meaningfully. "Just for research, of course."

We both knew why I was here so much. Sooner or later, the Fiorelli family would want revenge for me killing Oscar. The safest place for me was amongst people who worked for the Brantley family. People with the skills to help protect me if I wasn't able to protect myself.

I'd like to think I could. That if—when—they came after me, I'd be fine. Capable. Deadly.

The lingering feeling of blood on my hands suggested differently.

If I had to kill again, I might freeze. That moment of indecision might be all it took. My enemies wouldn't hesitate. They *would* kill me.

That thought sent shivers of fear up and down my spine. I wanted to run, to hide, but I'd done enough of that. Now all I could do was wait.

"Research, of course." I toyed with the ring on my right hand. It was a gift from my parents when I turned twenty-five a couple of years ago. A simple band of white gold, a pale sapphire embedded in the top. I rarely took it off. It reminded me how close we were, even though I didn't see them so much these days.

It also felt bloodstained.

"All right, take a break," Aidan shouted.

The guys skated to the edge of the rink and stepped off the ice, chatting and teasing each other.

Aidan stomped over to where Finley and I sat and stood with his back against the boards.

"Hard day?" Finley asked.

"It always is with these clowns," Aidan growled. "If they want to come together as a team, they need to smarten the fuck up. They have the talent, but they need to leave it all on the ice."

I closed my laptop. "I'm sure they're trying—"

"Not hard enough," Aidan snarled. He closed his eyes and rubbed the bridge of his nose with his thumb and forefinger.

"At least we know it's not their equipment," Finley remarked.

"I think half the problem is that they're too busy thinking with the equipment in their pants and not what's in their hands or on their feet," Aidan said without opening his eyes.

"You say they're thinking with their cocks like it's a bad thing, that you don't do," Finley said.

Aidan turned and opened his eyes just enough to glare at Finley.

Finley grinned unapologetically. No one else got away with speaking to Aidan like that. If any of the team did, they might only be found if the ice on the rink melted.

"I know how to keep mine under control," Aidan said. "My cock defers to the brain in my head when I tell it to."

Finley turned to me. "That's another way of saying he's getting so old, his cock doesn't work as well as it used to."

"Fuck off," Aidan told him. "Forty-two is not old." He scowled at Finley like he might dispose of him under the ice after all.

"Maybe the team should do one of those team building camps," I suggested, before any blood was shed. I wrung my hands, the sensation that they were coated in it renewed.

Aidan leaned over and grabbed my wrists, his grip warm and solid. "Don't. That little shit got what he deserved. You need to stop torturing yourself, Elenna. Do you think he would have thought twice about killing you?" His hazel eyes were intent on my face. "He murdered Ike. He probably laughed when he did it. He wore the blood on his hands like a badge of honour. Ike's blood." He frowned at my still-pink hands.

I looked back at him, contained a flinch, but I said, "I can't—"

"Yes, you can." His tone was firm, unyielding. He didn't give me any more slack than he did one of his players. "You're stronger than that, Elenna. Smart, beautiful and tough."

I dropped my gaze.

Just for me, Aidan's people found Oscar, so I could get my revenge. I never asked who, but I wouldn't have to look too far. Coast and Phoenix, in particular, did jobs for Aidan. They would have gotten a kick out of tying and gagging a Fiorelli.

And now… Now I heard that gunshot in my nightmares. That and the last sounds Oscar made before he died.

My stomach twisted. I should have left the room and let Aidan finish him. He would have done it without blinking and never afforded it another thought. Oscar who? No dark, pleading eyes would feature in his darkest dreams, both awake and asleep.

"It's easier to hide from someone else than it is to hide from yourself," I said softly.

Finley's response was immediate: "Don't hide from yourself." There were few secrets between him and

Aidan. They trusted each other as much as they trusted themselves.

"Elenna Christakos is a badass, from a family of badasses. Destined to continue the tradition of badasses. Own what you did. It wasn't a bad thing. Oscar was a shit who would have killed countless other people. Innocent and otherwise. It was a matter of time before he got a bullet in the head. You did the world a favour. You should be congratulating yourself, not condemning yourself."

"I hate to say Fin is right about anything, but he's right about this," Aidan said. He tightened his grip on my wrists. He'd leave bruises and he knew it. One of his favourite things was leaving bruises on me. He wasn't fucking me right if he didn't. One of the things I loved about him was that he never held back.

"Fin is right about a lot of things, including this," Finley said with a grin. "Aidan should listen to me more often."

"Not if you're going to refer to yourself in third person." Aidan grimaced. He turned back to me. "Put it behind you, Elenna. Do you think I dwell on every person I've killed?"

His voice was low, so only the three of us could hear. Not everyone on the team, or who worked at the arena, knew what he was like. Many saw him as the alphahole head coach and wondered what the fuck I was doing with him.

"To be fair, it gets easier every time," Finley said.

"After a while, they start blending together. But you never forget your first. It's like losing your virginity, you know?"

"I suppose so." I hadn't forgotten, although now I cringed, remembering who I lost it to. "If you're suggesting I go out and kill a bunch more people to numb myself…"

"We would one hundred percent support you," Finley said.

Aidan groaned. "He's right again. Can you stop fucking doing that?" He glanced over at Finley who chuckled in response.

"I can stop being right as easily as you can stop being an asshole."

"I'm not an asshole, I just don't tolerate dickheads," Aidan said. "With the exception of you."

Finley laughed louder now. "Ouch, *burn*. You tolerate me because we're more alike than you want to admit. And I know all your deepest, darkest secrets. You know what they say."

"Keep your friends close and your enemies closer?" Aidan asked.

"Something like that." Finley grinned. "Especially when they have more blackmail material on you than most people."

"Never forget the opposite is true." Aidan turned away from him, back to me. "I'll do whatever you need to help you get past this. Hell, you can kill half the team if it would make you feel better."

"That would be good for team morale," Finley said sarcastically.

"Yeah, but we could replace them with competent players." Aidan sighed. "Which they will be, once I lick them into shape."

"Go lick them," I said. "I'll be right here." I rubbed my wrists when he let them go and moved away.

CHAPTER 2

"I keep thinking about that meme." Aidan placed his hand on my lower back and led me into his office. "Something about the difference between knowing your shit and knowing you're shit. These guys know their shit, but they keep being caught up thinking they're shit." He closed the door behind us.

"Losing will do that to people." I turned to face him and pressed my palms lightly against his chest. "Plus you just offered to let me kill half of them."

"They don't know that." He gripped my wrists tight enough to add to the already faint bruising.

"They can probably guess. You were practically shooting lasers out your eyes at them." I cocked my head at him.

"Is this where you tell me I should be gentle with them?" His grip tightened. "That I should take them out for pizza and beer? Be their friend. Praise them when their stick actually connects with the puck? Maybe I should hand out chocolate every time they do the right thing."

"Lollipops," I corrected. "If you give anyone chocolate, it's me."

He barked a laugh. "You're right, I know better than to give away your chocolate. You'd have me skinned, tanned and made into a glove."

"We *are* talking about chocolate here," I said. "But I'd never tell you how to do your job. We know all you want is for them to start winning. And they will. They'll turn this season around and come out on top."

"They better," he growled.

His tone sent blood straight to my clit, like it always did since the day we met.

I'd come to watch Ike practice. My brother was new to the team, but enthusiastic. Watching the grin on his face the first time he stepped out on the ice was seared into my brain. I should have taken a photo of his joy, but I was quickly distracted.

The moment I heard Aidan yell at the players, I couldn't keep my eyes off him. An hour later, while the guys showered, he fucked me up against his office door.

We hadn't kept our hands off each other since.

"I always get you going don't I, Elenna?" His voice turned to a harsh purr, like an angry cat. He held my wrists in one hand and pulled me closer to him. With the other hand he gripped my hair and dragged my lips to his. "Who do you belong to?"

"You." Our mouths barely touched. We swallowed each other's breaths. I wanted to taste him, but he'd hold me like this until he was ready.

"Me," he agreed. "You know what it does to me when I see you talking to Fin?" He tangled his fingers tighter. "It turns me on. I see the way he looks at you. He undresses you with his eyes. He wants to fuck you so badly."

"I know he does," I whispered. Finley hadn't come out and said as much, he didn't need to. The looks he gave me spoke every word that didn't come out of his mouth.

"Do you know what I'd do if it was one of the guys on the team? I'd hand him over to Ice Miller to have fun with. You know he likes to see how long he can keep someone alive while he peels off their skin bit by bit."

I shivered, but my panties were drenched. Aidan would do exactly what he said, without hesitating and that was hotter than hell. He was a possessive, obsessive alphahole, but he was *my* possessive, obsessive alphahole.

Finley was the perfect counterweight. The eye of Aidan and my storm. The one who dared to call out Aidan when he was being too arrogant or hardheaded.

Okay, yes, I did too, but it always ended up with us fucking. When Finley did it, Aidan listened and sometimes changed his methods. Not enough to give Finley credit, but a little.

"What do you want to do with Fin?" He let my

wrists go and started to unbutton my blouse. He worked the last one loose and I let it slide down off my arms onto the floor. He tugged down the front of my bra and pinched my nipple between his thumb and forefinger. "Do you want him to touch you like this?"

I was already trembling with need. "Do you want me to let him?"

He pinched harder. Tears sprang to my eyes. If I was any wetter, my juices would be trickling down the inside of my legs.

"I asked what *you* want," he insisted. "Tell me. Tell me, Elenna."

How the fuck did I respond to that? The last thing I wanted was Aidan furious with me or Finley. But I knew Aidan, he wouldn't set me up like this. He had an unnerving way of knowing what I needed before I did. And making sure I got it.

"I want him to touch me like this," I said in a rush. "I want to feel his hands on me. I want him to fuck me."

Aidan undid the front of my jeans and shoved them down before spinning me around and leaning over the top of his desk.

I barely had time to kick them off before he tugged my panties to one side and drove a couple of fingers straight into my dripping wet pussy.

"I want you to go out with him," he said as he thrust his fingers in hard, over and over. "I want you to fuck each other, then I want you to come home and tell me every detail. Both of you. Can you do that for me, Elenna?"

I groaned. "Yes. Yes I can." The thought of him sitting at home waiting for Finley and I to return, knowing Finley would slam his cock into my pussy, that he'd touch me all over... My pussy throbbed desperately.

"I know you can," Aidan said. "Finley has wanted you almost as long as I have. I want to know he's fucking you." He finger-fucked me harder. "I want to know he's fucking my *wife*."

At the last word, I came, my face pressed against the worn timber of the desk. I screamed Aidan's name so loud they probably heard me all through the arena.

I was barely down when Aidan slid his fingers out, undid his pants and spread my legs wider. Before I could catch my breath, he slammed his cock into me.

I cried out with the suddenness of his penetration. It quickly turned to a moan of pleasure. He could pound into me with everything he had and I'd love every moment of it. The harder, the more painful, the better. I wanted every centimetre of him, thoroughly wrecking me. I wanted to feel him inside me for a week.

With one hand still tangled in my hair, and the other digging into my hip, he set a slow pace of deep, hard thrusts into my body.

"Fuck, you always feel so incredible, so tight. So *mine*. Fin is going to love fucking this pussy as much as I do." He slid his hand underneath me, over my stomach to grip my breast. He squeezed it hard. "I want to see the bruises he's left on your skin. I'll be sure to leave plenty for him to see."

I moaned. "Yes. Please…" Bruises from both of them — The thought drove me wild. Between that and Aidan's thrusting, I was close to coming again. "Just like that. Don't stop, Aidan, please."

He twisted my breast until I cried out. I blinked away tears of pain and bliss, and rocked my hips back onto his cock, pushing us both to the brink.

"Fuck, Elenna, yes, yes, yes." He ground himself against me hard as we both came. He pressed my head down into the desk, squashing his hand between that and my chest.

He pushed me down so hard I could barely breathe. My vision started to blur, but my orgasm was like the shattering of a thousand universes, and the birth of ten thousand more. Every nerve in my body was singing and tingling, on and on and on until it finally, gradually ebbed away.

He slumped down over me, releasing his grip and letting me breathe again. "Woman, you are…fucking everything," he said breathlessly. "Maybe if the whole team fucked you, we'd start winning."

I laughed from the back of my throat while still trying to catch my breath. "I don't think you'd tolerate sharing me with the whole team."

His laughter was a vibration against my back. "Maybe not the whole team. Just the ones we agree on."

He slid out of me and pulled me up straight by my hair. "I love seeing you like this. Face pink, hair a mess, my cum dripping down the inside of your thighs."

"And Fin's?" I looked him straight in the eyes. The heat of the moment was one thing. Whether he meant what he said was another. Aidan didn't play games, but he was the king of dirty talk. I loved that about him. He could turn me on with words as well as actions. Those two things combined and I was helpless to resist him.

"And his." He pressed his cock back into his pants and zipped himself up. He straightened my bra and leaned over to scoop up my jeans and blouse. "I wasn't joking. I'll make sure he understands that too. The only boundary of what he does to you is up to you. As long as you don't forget who you belong to."

His gaze bored into mine, as though he wanted to sear his words deep into my brain. He didn't need to, he'd all but tattooed my soul the day we met.

I stepped into my jeans and pulled them up over my hips. "How could I forget that?" I did them up and shrugged into my blouse. "I'll always be yours. No matter what happens."

"And I'll always be yours, but I want you to go out and explore and enjoy life. The attraction you and Fin have for each other… I'm not threatened by it. It doesn't diminish what we have and it never will. If anything, this should enhance what we have. I know I'll be in the back of your mind the entire time." He looked smug, but he wasn't wrong.

"You will, but," I started to do up the buttons on my blouse, "does this mean you intend to go out and fuck other women?" If I was going to kill anyone, it would be any woman who touched him. And Finley too, as irrational as that was. He owed me nothing, not yet.

Aidan cupped my cheeks. "Nothing could entice me to touch another woman. I'm not even tempted. Why would I be when I have you?" He scowled. "You're not going to ask me to go out and—"

"No," I said quickly, firmly. "Never."

"Good." He kissed my forehead. "Now, go out and make a date with Finley. Then I'm going to take you home so you can suck my cock."

CHAPTER 3

ELENNA

Wren's mouth dropped open. "Did I just hear you right? Aidan… Aidan wants you to go on a date with Finley?" She stared at me, her jaw hanging open.

Sinclair, on the other hand, sipped her coffee and looked unsurprised. "What's wrong with that? Aidan knows you two like each other and isn't threatened. How many men would do something like that?"

I'd struck up a friendship with her and Wren after I finished university and moved back to Dusk Bay. It was Sinclair who gave me a place to stay until I found a place of my own.

"Without them being there to watch, I don't know," Wren said. "No guy I've ever dated would have sent me off like that. Either they were the jealous kind, or they didn't last long enough to do anything like that. Now I think about it, that was pretty selfish of them." She pouted playfully.

"Would you go if they'd wanted you to?" Sinclair asked her. "If someone you were going out with, walked in here right now, and told you to go on a date with..." She waved her spare hand in the air. "Darren from the PR department, would you go?"

Wren glanced towards the door as though one of her exes might actually do just that. When none appeared, she sighed.

"Darren is kinda hot."

I wrinkled my nose. Darren seemed nice enough, but I wouldn't go as far as to say he was hot.

"You know who else is hot," Sinclair leaned forward. "The new left defenceman, Orion...something." She waved a hand again. "I saw him talking to Coast Riggs this morning. He's young but he's hot with a capital H." She fanned herself. "Not as hot as Coast..."

"Are you hoping Coast will take you out and fuck you?" Wren teased.

Sinclair sighed. "A girl can dream. Although, I'm not sure I can compete with his ego. Not to mention the thousands of other women who throw themselves at him on a daily basis."

I sipped my coffee and listened to their conversation. Sinclair, who worked for the Demons as a public relations manager, had a crush on Coast since she first saw him, but never acted on it. Not yet anyway.

"Are you going to do it?" Wren asked. She caught me off guard with the question, but I rallied quickly.

"I'd like to," I admitted. "I'm attracted to Fin, and

knowing that Aidan will be at home thinking about us..." Goosebumps popped up on my skin at the thought.

"That sounds like a yes to me," Sinclair drawled. "Personally, I think you should go for it. Everyone is consenting. What do you have to lose?"

"Assuming Fin agrees," I pointed out. "He may think Aidan has lost his mind."

"I've seen how Fin looks at you," Wren said with a grin. "He might think that about Aidan, but that won't stop him from doing it. The moment you say the word, he'll be all over you. Literally. He would have acted on it already if he didn't think Aidan would have put a bullet in his brain."

She embraced the lifestyle we all grew up in better than I did. Accepted it anyway. If she'd killed Oscar Fiorelli, she wouldn't dwell on it, much less feel the need to scrub her hands clean several times a day.

For half a second, I wondered if she was a better fit for Aidan, but the very idea of it made me want to strangle her with my bare hands. To me, she was like another one of my sisters, but if she touched him, I'd be furious.

This line of thinking was moot, because Aidan would never touch either of them anyway. He too saw them as my sisters. He might question their taste in men, but he wouldn't fuck either of them.

I decided against telling them Aidan suggested I kill half the team to make myself feel better. I had a sneaking suspicion they'd object to me doing that. Typically, that went both ways if they were inclined to commit mass murder. Which they weren't.

I hoped.

"Are you going to talk to Fin?" Sinclair asked.

"I think I will," I said slowly. "You're right, he's not going to say no to this. At least...I don't think he will. Unless he has some specific objection to fucking another man's legal wife."

Aidan and I both agreed that marriage was little more than a piece of paper, but we did it anyway. After a bottle or two of wine, it seems like a good idea. Neither of us regretted it, but it didn't automatically imply monogamy from either of us. His decision not to see other women was about our relationship, not our vows.

Of course, that also didn't automatically mean Finley would agree. Sexual attraction was one thing, crossing lines he didn't want to cross was another. I wouldn't push him and I knew Aidan wouldn't either. He wouldn't want to lose a friend because of a kink.

"If he does, he's crazy to miss out on the chance," Wren said. "If this is Aidan's thing, then another opportunity with another guy might arise. Pun intended." She grinned.

I shook my head at her and snorted. *Was* it Aidan's thing, or was this about Finley? I should have asked him. I was surprised he suggested it. So much so, I hadn't thought it all the way through. Not past what it would feel like to have Finley's hands all over me.

"Maybe with Aidan and some other guy," Sinclair said.

"Or a couple of them," Wren said. "You only live once and all."

"I don't really want to think about Aidan having sex with anyone, but Wren is right," Sinclair said. "There's nothing wrong with embracing your sexuality."

"I guess so," I said awkwardly.

Sharing me a little was one thing. Sharing me a *lot* was another. That was a conversation Aidan and I might have to have at some point. How far did his desire to have other men fuck me go? Not the whole team, that was more cocks than I knew how to handle. I only had three holes.

Although, I knew Abbie Hart, one of my favourite singers, had seven. Men, not holes. Six of them were members of the band Wolf Venom. The seventh was their manager. That was a lot of cocks. And a lot of egos. She must be something else to put up with all of them.

"If you get the chance," Wren said. "Go for it. I know you're not as…" She bit her lip, trying to find the words.

"Not as much of a horn bag as we are?" Sinclair suggested.

Wren choked on a laugh. "Something like that."

"Who says I'm not?" I'd fucked Aidan an hour after we met, didn't that count? A day didn't go past when we didn't fuck at least once, often several times. I decided I was probably as horny as they were. For all I knew, I was even hornier.

"Maybe you are and you're wearing Aidan out?" Wren ducked to the side when I threatened her with my spoon. "What? He is fifteen years older than you. It's only natural he'd slow down before you would. Maybe you should get yourself someone younger, just in case."

"You're making it sound like I have a series of boxes to tick." I counted them off my fingers. "Older guy who may or may not have anger issues." I ignored their snorts of laughter. "A guy who is between us in age and knows how to do laundry."

"That's a bonus right there," Wren said.

I ignored that too, even though she was right. A guy who knew how to use a washing machine was a keeper..

"And a younger guy to keep up with me when Aidan and Finley are old and decrepit. Should I wait a while? This younger guy might not have been born yet."

Predictably, they both made faces of disgust.

"I mean, if forty-seven-year-old you wants to date a twenty year old, you have my full support," Wren said. "But when you put it that way, it's icky." She shuddered dramatically.

I smiled. "That was the point."

"This certainly explains everything." Wren sipped on her coffee. "You and Aidan are both sadistic." She pointed a finger at me before I could say anything. "I'm only going on what the guys say. Aidan is driven. He doesn't cut the guys even a millimetre of slack."

"He shouldn't," Sinclair said. "The guys have lost the last five games. Someone has to kick them in the ass, or they're going to keep losing. Caleb Brantley isn't going to fund them forever."

"Are you sure about that?" I asked. "While they suit his purpose, he's going to keep doing what he's doing." I didn't elaborate. The coffee shop was small and fuck only knew who was listening. Plenty of people in Dusk Bay had no idea what went on virtually under their noses. I wasn't going to enlighten them.

Besides which, my friends both knew exactly what I was referring to. Many of the other wives and girl-friends also knew, but some were clueless. Sometimes I wished I was.

Subconsciously, I wrung my hands and glanced down at the table.

"It's not your fault," Sinclair said, as though she read my mind.

"I'm distracting Aidan." I sighed and looked back up at them. We both knew we were referring to Ike and Oscar, but it was easier to pretend we weren't.

"Sweetie, they were losing long before that," Sinclair reminded me. "Maybe not as badly, but still... Now with Lex on board as strength and conditioning coach, they can turn the season around. Personally, I'll be glad when they do. The PR department has its work cut out for it with the negative publicity." She sighed and toyed with the handle of her coffee cup.

"I'll bet it does," I said. "Aidan might let up on them a little." As if that would happen.

"Until then, Sinclair could offer Coast some pity sex." Wren grinned, even after Sinclair flicked cake crumbs at her.

"There's worse things than a pity fuck." Sinclair eyed her sideways.

"It's not as good as hate sex," Wren said. "Especially up against a wall." Her eyes glazed and she smiled, clearly thinking back.

"Hate sex is good too," Sinclair agreed. "Actually, everything but boring sex."

"That's a given," I said. No one would ever accuse Aidan of being boring. I frowned. "What if Fin is boring?"

They both grinned.

"If he is, we want to hear all the juicy details," Wren said. "And if he isn't, we still want to hear the details."

"Definitely." Sinclair nodded firmly before picking up her cup and drinking the last of her coffee.

"I don't know if you two are the best, or if you're just enabling me." I finished the last of my own coffee and pushed my chair back from the table..

They glanced at each other and spoke in unison.

"Both!"

CHAPTER 4

ELENNA

Crack.

Tiberius 'Tiger' Pennington whacked the puck so hard his stick broke. The blade almost splintered off from the shaft and dangled.

"Fuck yeah." Tiger looked impressed with himself. He shook the stick, making the blade swish back and forth. "Yep, it's fucked."

I thought Aidan might lose his shit, but he looked almost as impressed. "That, ladies and gentlemen, is how you hit a puck." He eyed the other players as though the rest of them didn't have a clue.

Some of them returned his gaze, a couple bordering on hostile. One muttered something about none of them being ladies.

Coast Riggs grinned. A few words wouldn't be enough to put a dent in his enormous ego.

"We're not gentlemen either," Phoenix DiMarco pointed out.

"Speak for yourself." Tiger gave him a narrowed-eyed glance and skated over to where Finley leaned over the boards, a new stick in hand. They swapped and Tiger skated off. He stopped near Bray, who clapped him on the back and grinned.

Finley hefted the stick in his hand, then started toward the exit. He got halfway there before he noticed me hovering in the doorway, trying to be as inconspicuous as possible.

"Hey." He glanced over his shoulder towards Aidan. All of his attention was on the players. Finley turned back, his eyes dark, expression attentive, like I was the only other person left on the face of the planet.

"Hey. Have you got a minute?" I forced my hands to stay down at my sides so I didn't wring them. In spite of his intent gaze, nerves threatened to swamp me and pull me under. I'd rehearsed this conversation in my mind, over and over, but speaking it out loud was something else.

Finley carried the stick like he might use it on someone's head. Was it wrong that I found that hot? Guys with an underlying edge of violence were both dangerous and addictive. If there was a support group, I didn't want to go. No, I'd embrace the throbbing in my clit, the damp in my panties.

"For you, sure." He lowered the stick and gestured towards the exit. "Is anything wrong?"

"No," I said quickly. "Everything is fine."

I glanced back to the rink to see one of the players watching me. Dark hair, dark eyes and a dark expression. He looked at me like he couldn't decide if he wanted to fuck me or kill me.

Judging by how panty-meltingly hot he was, this was Orion Scully-Evans, the new left defenceman. He glanced at Finley and his eyes narrowed further. It seemed to be a warning of some kind. Like maybe he'd take that stick from Finley's fingers and smash his face in if he harmed a hair on my head.

A chill passed through me and left my panties even wetter.

If Finley noticed, I couldn't tell. I turned to see him waiting expectantly near the exit.

"Sorry," I muttered.

"I might need to source a stick for Aidan to fight off the admirers. I'm thinking one twice the size of this." He hefted the one in his hand again.

So he *had* noticed. I should have known he would. It was Finley's job to watch everything and everyone here. Especially the players. He had to be ready with a fresh stick or clean glove at a moment's notice. Not to mention knowing every single player's size and preference. His attention to detail must be phenomenal.

"That was what I wanted to talk to you about," I said. "Maybe in your office."

"Of course." He eyed me speculatively.

No, I didn't miss the way the front of his pants tented. He wanted this as much as I did.

He led me to his office and closed the door behind us. He stashed the broken stick against the wall and picked up a book to scribble something inside. Presumably a record of the breakage and replacement.

He set the book aside and leaned back against his desk. "I'm all ears. Except my cock."

My gaze dipped to his groin before I forced my eyes back to his face. He was grinning.

I swallowed.

"This may sound strange…" I started tentatively.

He laughed slightly. "You might be underestimating the things I've heard in my time." He cocked his head at me. "I'm sorry, I don't mean to make fun. What's on your mind?"

"Aidan wants us to go out on a date with each other," I said in a rush. "You and me." My tongue darted over my lips. "He wants us to fuck each other."

Finley's eyebrows twitched upward. "Does he now?" He ran a hand over the light stubble on his chin.

"You don't have to, if you don't want to," I said quickly. "Like I said, it's strange."

"I'll do it," Finley said almost before the last sentence left my lips. "If this is something you want too? This isn't just Aidan being Aidan? If he's trying to push you into anything—"

"I want to," I said. "He's turned on by the idea, but… so am I."

My whole body was trembling. I wanted to taste Finley's mouth. I wanted to hear him shout my name in his soft, Irish lilt. El-Ehh-nah, rather than el-Enna. It was sexy as hell.

"Aidan is full of surprises," he mused softly. "I presume I wasn't as subtle as I thought I was. I've decided I have no regrets about that." He grinned, popping a dimple in his left cheek.

He was sweet, laced with violence, while Aidan was all hard edges, and acid tongue.

Also laced with violence.

Finley walked the three steps to close the gap between us, hooked a hand around the back of my head and slammed his lips down into mine.

It took me a moment to react, and then I was kissing him back. I placed my hands on his chest and gripped fistfuls of his shirt to hold him closer.

He tasted of coffee and something else that might have been cinnamon donut. Whatever it was, it was pure perfection. I couldn't get enough of it. I could have eaten all of him up here and now.

He pushed me until my back was pressed against the wall. He broke off from my mouth and kissed down my cheek and around my neck and throat. Between kisses he managed to say, "I wanted you from the moment I laid eyes on you. If I saw you first, I would have hidden you away from Aidan."

He might have tried, but Aidan would have seen me and, one way or another, found a way to claim me.

What we had was meant to be. So was this. I believed that with everything in me. Finley was claiming me as thoroughly as Aidan had. From now on, I belonged to both of them.

Finley undid the button of my jeans and pushed them down far enough to slide his hands down the front of my panties. He skated his fingers over my pussy until he found my clit and started to rub.

"You're so fucking wet," he said, his mouth near my ear. "Such a good girl."

No one ever said that to me before. I almost came, the blood rushed so hard into my clit just from his words.

I groaned. "Yes," I whispered. "I'm your good girl." Holy shit, that was so fucking hot. His praise made me want to sing and scream at the same time. I wanted more. Needed more.

"My good girl, Aidan's bad girl," he said. "Sounds fucking perfect to me. I might need a big stick to fight off other guys too." He slipped a couple of fingers inside me, working me harder. "Be a good girl and come for me."

I tilted my chin up and pressed my head against the wall. "I want to. I want to be good for you."

I was so close, I was teetering on the very brink. Finley's fingers were roughened to perfection, increasing the friction where he touched my clit.

"Then do it, Elenna, come for me like a good girl."

I came hard against his fingers, my body rocking in

time to his strokes. My vision blurred and all I knew was pleasure, and his hand drawing out my orgasm, milking it for every precious drop.

I finally slumped forward, using my hands on his chest to keep me upright. I leaned my head against his chest until I caught my breath.

"Wow, that was…" I shook my head. I couldn't articulate it. One of my hands wandered down his body, but he caught my wrist and held it hard.

"We can leave that for our date," he said. "The first time I slide my cock into your glorious pussy, I want to know Aidan is thinking of us. I want him to know when I fill your body with my cum. I want him to know when you're screaming my name when you come on my mouth like the good girl you are." His eyes got darker and darker with every word.

His balls must have been aching. He was making my pussy throb all over again.

"I want that too," I whispered. That was about the extent of my words right now.

"All of it." Did Aidan realise what a gift he'd given me? I'd have to make sure he understood the full extent of it. I was going to enjoy every minute of everything Finley did to me. The anticipation might drive me crazy.

"Of course you do." He slipped his hand out of my pussy and pressed his fingers to my lips. "Taste how delicious you are."

I opened my mouth and sucked on his fingers. The

combination of my release and the salt on his hands was delicious.

"You like that? I want to taste you too, but I can wait. You're going to love the taste of my cock. I'm going to come in your throat and in your pussy."

Yes please.

"Yes please." I always enjoyed sucking cock. I loved watching a man lose control and knowing it was my mouth doing that to him. I loved feeling cum squirt out into my mouth. Men loved watching me swirl it around in my mouth before I swallowed. I was sucking cock long before any guy ever slammed his into my pussy.

He chuckled softly. "Aidan might be lucky if I return you afterwards. You're hotter than under a goalie's cup." If anyone knew how hot players got under their equipment, apart from the players themselves, it was him. He would have handled enough of it.

"I don't know about that." I dropped my chin and glanced down at the floor. I was just…me.

I had a vivid imagination and shot a man in the head a few weeks ago, but I didn't see myself as sexy. Sinclair and Wren were cuter than me. They'd both argue otherwise, but it was true. Sinclair was striking with her golden blonde hair and blue eyes. Wren was adorable with her shorter stature, dark red hair and brown eyes. I had boring brown hair and a few extra kilos here and there.

He placed a finger under my chin and lifted it to

look at him. "You have us hot for you. You're the flame and we're the moths."

"You know what happens when you get too close to fire," I said, my voice low.

He smiled. "You melt. Personally, I can't wait." He kissed my forehead.

"We have an away game in Sydney on Saturday night. What about tomorrow night? That's a Thursday. That'll give me Friday to get all the equipment organised for the flight up."

"Tomorrow night sounds perfect," I said. My heart did a little skip and skated around the rink in my chest. If this was a dream, I didn't want to wake up from it.

CHAPTER 5

FINLEY

"I hope you like this place." I opened the door to the restaurant and gestured for Elenna to step in before me.

The air outside was frigid, making her cheeks pink and misting her breath. Wrapped tight in a charcoal grey winter coat, with a Demons' scarf wrapped around her neck, she was hotter than fuck. Especially with knee-high boots that laced all the way up the front. They were so sexy I might get her to leave them on while I fucked her.

"I'm sure I will." She stepped inside and turned back towards me. It wasn't until I was safely inside and the door closed behind us that she looked around and took in the place.

"Wow, this is incredible," she breathed.

"Gianna's is my favourite restaurant in town." I stood behind her and helped her to shrug off her coat and scarf. I draped them over my arm while the maître d' led us to a table by the window.

I pulled out her chair and nodded for her to sit before pushing the chair in.

She smiled her thanks and placed her hands in her lap. After the maître d' left, she leaned forward and said, "Doesn't it usually take a year to get a reservation here?"

I smiled slyly. "I know people. And Gianna owes me a favour or two."

Her eyes widened. She glanced around at the other customers who sat nearby, plates with artfully placed food in front of them.

"Isn't that—" she whispered.

"Daven Grey, star forward for the Dusk Bay Smashers," I finished for her. "And his latest girlfriend." I gave them both a wave which wasn't much more than a flick of my wrist and hand and nodded.

Daven smiled and nodded back.

"You know them?" Elenna asked, disbelieving.

I shrugged. "Daven is an old friend. We bump into each other every so often."

"So he's not..." She frowned.

"A violent criminal?" I suggested lightly. "No, the team's owner is as shifty as Caleb Brantley, but Daven is one of the good guys. There are some left in the city."

She sighed. "It must be nice not knowing what goes on around here."

I patted her hand. "There's a difference between one

of the good guys and not knowing what goes on. I'd be very surprised if he didn't at least suspect people like you and I existed. In every city all over the world, we're there, getting up to no good."

I could make no claim to being one of the good guys. As equipment manager, I knew more about what was smuggled in and out of Demons Arena than most people. The things I knew, could put Caleb and Reuben Brantley behind bars for the rest of their lives.

If I was inclined to tell anyone, that was. Which I wouldn't, for a variety of reasons, including the fact I was up to my eyeballs in all of it too.

Besides, if word got out, the Demons would be screwed. I wanted them to win, not get thrown out of the AIHL on their asses. If a few diamonds went missing from a delivery here or there, and found their way into and then out of my hands, where was the harm?

The Demons did a lot of good in the community with charity work and encouraging kids to take up hockey, or live their dreams or whatever. To me, that seemed more important than a few shiny lumps of rock. I had a harder time with the drugs that came my way, but as long as I was getting them out of Dusk Bay, then I could sleep at night.

"What would you be doing if you weren't one of them?" She picked up her menu and slid her gaze up and down the options.

I did the same, with only a fraction of my attention

on the page. The only thing I wanted to eat right now was her. My balls ached like the blazes, but I'd take my time.

When we went back to Aidan and told him what we did, I didn't want her to have to say it was over in a flash. I wanted him to know I seduced his wife, not just fucked her. I wanted her to want to do this again. If Aidan got off on her fucking me, I was on board with that. I was sure to get off on it too.

"Probably the same thing, but I wouldn't be making as much money," I replied finally. "I'm not saying the Demons don't pay well, but Caleb pays better for all the...on the side stuff. In fact," I leaned forward, "if you'd like to help me with some of that, I'm sure Aidan can get you a permanent position at the arena. One that allows you to go wherever you want, with no one asking questions."

Her eyebrows twitched upward, eyes widening in surprise. "I'd like that. As long as I have time to write on the side. Aidan keeps telling me I don't need to worry about money, but I like to make my own. My books do well enough, but a girl could always use more."

"In case you want to buy some of those diamonds?" I teased. "Or decide Dusk Bay is too crazy for you?"

She flinched slightly. "I promised Aidan I wouldn't leave. Wouldn't run away. Not unless it was something we planned." Her eyes twinkled and it took me a moment to realise what she was referring to.

"The bruises," I said slowly. "You really do like it rough." How rough did she like it, because I could be rough if that was what she wanted.

Her smile faded. "Do you think that's wrong?"

"Fuck no," I said as firmly as I could. "The last thing in the world I would ever do would be kink shame. I know for some that giving up control gives them *more* control. You set the boundaries. You decide exactly what happens to you. And then you roll with it."

She looked relieved. "That's exactly it. I know Aidan would never overstep when I tell him enough is enough. He feels powerful and that's hot as hell, but I'm in charge at the end of the day."

"What's hot as hell is a woman who knows what she wants," I said. "For the record, I'm all about safe words and stopping when you say them. But I like—" I stopped when a server came up to take our orders. I waited until he was gone to continue.

"I like to give praise," I said finally. "I like my partner to enjoy herself. The more you enjoy yourself, the bigger the turn on. I want you to come four or five times before I come even once."

"If you keep talking like that, I'm going to come right here," she said softly.

My eyebrows twitched. I propped my elbow on the table and rested my cheek against one finger. "Really? You're that turned on right now?"

Her eyes got darker. "I really am," she said softly.

"How wet are you?" I looked at her sideways.

"Very wet." She shifted in her chair.

"Interesting." I slipped a hand under the tablecloth and over to her lap. I grabbed a handful of her skirt and pulled it up until I was able to work my hand underneath the fabric and over her thigh. "How well can you contain yourself?"

She swallowed visibly. "I don't know."

"You're going to find out." I rubbed the tip of a couple of fingers over the gusset of her panties and smiled when she quivered against me. I pulled the fabric aside and ran them straight over her damp pussy.

"You really are wet." This woman was going to be the end of me and I was going to love every minute of it.

She hummed something semi-coherent and rocked herself just slightly against my hand. Her eyes were half opened as if she needed to remind herself we were in a restaurant full of people. Or maybe because she wanted to remember, because being finger fucked in public was something she enjoyed. Did Aidan do this to her? I hoped not. I wanted this to be our thing. She could be my good girl whom I fingered in places like this.

If it wouldn't go unnoticed, I'd ask her to kneel under the table and suck me off. I had a feeling she'd do it too. There was a boldness to this woman, even if she didn't know it yet. Between me and Aidan, we'd show her. We'd bring out every drop from her. If she wanted a third guy or a fourth, I'd make sure that was what she got. She deserved all of that and more.

"You're doing so well," I said as if making casual conversation. Like my fingers weren't stroking her clit while people around us ate their meals.

"Finley," she whispered.

"Good girl, come for me," I urged.

She chewed her lip, obviously trying to keep from bucking and screaming. The top of her body didn't move. Unless someone peeked under the tablecloth, they'd have no idea what I was doing to her. Unless her pink cheeks and dilated pupils gave her away.

She was so fucking gorgeous, she took my breath away. She genuinely didn't seem to have a clue. When she looked in the mirror, she saw an ordinary woman, not the goddess she really was.

Surrounded by enormous egos, as I usually was, she was refreshing. I admit to being more than a little turned on by the fact she was another man's wife. If they wanted to have an open relationship, I was here for it, but that little legality was as arousing as fuck. As though somehow we were doing something wrong, something taboo.

Ironic considering I had a hand in running guns and stolen diamonds on a more or less regular basis. This was much more exciting.

She pressed her lips together and groaned softly. She breathed harder out her nose a couple of times as her muscles clenched, shattering her around my fingers.

Feeling her come was almost enough to make me lose my load in my pants then and there. Since that would be embarrassing as hell, I contained myself and reminded my cock of where we were. He softened just enough. My balls became less tense. For now.

"Such a good girl," I said soothingly. "You might be the best fucking girl I ever met." I slipped my hand out of her panties and straightened her skirt just before a server came to place plates in front of us.

I looked up at him and smiled. "Thank you," as though nothing at all had happened.

In my line of work, or at least side hustle, you learn to master the art of the innocent facial expression. Everyone noticed the players and the coaches, but no one noticed the equipment manager who looked like butter wouldn't melt in his mouth.

Now I thought about it, I actually had a lot of practice as a kid. When you're the youngest of four boys, one of the most important lessons to learn is how to keep out of sight, and how to make sure your brothers were blamed for the shit you did. And how to avoid leaving evidence. They basically trained me for this existence. Ironic, since two were police officers and one was in the military.

The server nodded his acknowledgement before hurrying away.

"Are you hungry?" I asked Elenna.

"I am now." The pink was still in her cheeks. Her release must be virtually running down the insides of her thighs. Her panties were definitely drenched.

I fixed my gaze on her meaningfully. "Me too. I can't wait to eat. But first, food."

CHAPTER 6

ELENNA

Finley helped me back into my coat. While I pushed the buttons through the holes, he wound my scarf around my neck. Eyes on mine, he pulled it firmly around my throat, not enough to cut off my air, but enough to send another shot of hot blood straight to my pussy.

"Thank you," I said, my breath catching in my throat.

He shrugged into his black wool coat and brushed the back of his hand over my cheek. "You're welcome." I thought he might kiss me. Instead he took my hand.

"It's not far to walk from here. Unless you'd prefer me to call for a car?"

"I don't mind walking," I said. "It's a nice night out." The air was frigid, but the sky was clear. If we weren't in the middle of the city, we would have seen the stars glittering.

Instead, we'd enjoy the city lights, and the hum of

passing traffic. The feeling of life, the pulse of Dusk Bay.

"It's beautiful," he said, looking straight at me. "Romantic. I have a feeling you don't get enough of that."

"Romance?" I asked. "I suppose not." Aidan and I were lucky to eat dinner together most of the time, much less go on walks through the city at night.

"Then that's what I'll be," Finley said. "The one who does romantic gestures." He swung our hands between us.

"You don't have to do that," I told him.

"Maybe not, but I want to," he said. "It's been a long time since I had a woman to spoil."

"How long?" I asked without thinking. I quickly added, "I mean, you don't have to talk about it if you don't want to." The evening was going so well, I didn't want to screw it up by being nosy.

"No, it's okay." He glanced down at the footpath. "Four years. Siobhan and I were engaged. The plan was for us to live the rest of our lives together."

"What happened?" I asked gently.

"The Fiorelli family happened." He looked over at me. "I managed to get her involved in something she shouldn't have been. She was killed because of me. Not a single day passes when I don't want to put a bullet in the brain of anyone from that family."

My hands were drenched with blood and brain all over again. The gun was cool in my hand. Aidan stood behind me, holding me steady before I squeezed the trigger. I heard the gunshot, just one. Oscar Fiorelli was alive in one minute and the next... He was a corpse, slumped in the chair, his life blasted away by my hands.

"Why don't you?" I barely managed to keep my voice even, in spite of my racing thoughts. His death was the past. This, right here, was the present. Everyone was right, I needed to put it behind me. How could I, when everything reminded me of that night?

"Because if there's anything I'm good at, it's biding my time," Finley said. "Besides, the only way to avoid them coming back at me is to take them all out at once. For that, I'd need help."

"The Brantley brothers?" I guessed.

"Right. Reuben and Caleb at least. Possibly Hunter and Parker as well. The twins would be all for killing them, but Reuben and Caleb have their own agenda. One they don't share with the likes of me. Or Aidan."

Of course not. Men like that, with money and power, rarely felt the need to explain themselves to the people that worked for them. They expected people to do as they were ordered, and if they didn't, they'd be screwed. End of story.

"Four years is a long time to wait for justice," I said.

He grunted bitterly. "You've got that right. But Siobhan is cold in her grave and we aren't. In the interest of keeping it that way, don't look back. We're being followed."

Of course, the first urge following his words was to look back. Instead, I squeezed his hand tighter.

"Any idea who?" My tongue darted over my cold lips.

"I can't see any specifics, but I know they're there. If I had to guess, I'd say their last name starts with an F." He put an arm around me and pulled me closer.

"Fuck," I said softly.

"Different F, same meaning," he said with a grunt-laugh.

"I don't know how you can—" I started.

"Play it cool," he insisted. He tilted his chin back and laughed. "We're having a relaxing, romantic night out."

I swallowed. "Right, yes." I forced out a strained giggle. It was inevitable that sooner or later the Fiorellis would come after me or Aidan. They had no way of knowing who pulled the trigger, but they'd have a fair idea of who was responsible for Oscar's death.

Even if Aidan pinned it on someone else, they knew the minute Oscar killed Ike, one of us would want justice. For my brother, and for one of Aidan's players.

In spite of suggesting he'd let me kill half of the team, Aidan would go after anyone who fucked with any of them. The team was a dysfunctional family right now, but it was still a family.

"Gianna's really does have the best pasta I've ever had." My voice sounded more normal now, although I wondered if it might be my last meal.

"I told you they did." Finley grinned. "If you ever

want to go back, Gianna owes me lots of favours." His gaze flicked over to a shop window beside us. He drew us to a stop and pointed. "I'm no expert, but I've heard that's the best kind of vibrator you can get."

I peered into the shop. "I'm not saying I need a vibrator, but I've heard that too." I wasn't short on clit stimulation, but it was a nice shade of red, and the rose shape was pretty.

I saw no one but us in the reflection from the glass.

"My tongue is much better than a vibrator," Finley agreed. "Let's keep walking." Only the slightest twitch of his eyeballs suggested he was looking anywhere but *at* me, but his face was angled so the corner of his eyes could see behind me.

"How am I supposed to keep walking when you say things like that?" I teased. The effort to keep from turning around was driving me crazy.

"We could stop walking and give the whole road a show?" Finley teased. "They might learn something."

His suggestion sent a shiver through me. Part lust, part overwhelming desire not to be shot in the head while Finley's face was between my legs. With a healthy dash of 'it's fucking cold out.'

"Why don't we save it until we get to your place?" I suggested. "We wouldn't want your cum to freeze."

He chuckled. "I wouldn't want my cock to freeze either. Or your pussy." He let one hand drift across my stomach and down across the front of my skirt.

"Definitely not." If my voice was strained now,

blame it on the fire he sent coursing through my body. Not just because there was someone behind us who might very well want one or both of us dead.

Okay, maybe it was a combination of the two things. I seemed to thrive on fear and need, not necessarily in equal measure.

"Not far now," he said softly. "The anticipation is making my balls hard as hell. My cock is desperate to get inside you."

"I'm desperate to have you inside me." When I glanced over at him, it was with a meaningful expression on my face. Was he so sure we'd even reach his place alive and intact?

Whoever was tailing us would assume Finley had something up his sleeve. They'd expect us to pull out something once we knew they were there. They were likely biding their time, waiting for the right moment. The right place.

We might be screwed before we were fucked.

"I know you are." He returned the look, but his was with confidence. His head inclined slightly.

Trust me. I won't let anything happen to you. Because I won't allow it and because Aidan would tear my nuts off with his bare hands and shove them up my ass.

He said all of that with his eyes.

"Across the next set of traffic lights. My building is on the corner." He stopped before the curb and carefully looked both ways, as if the traffic was so heavy we'd have to wait, or watch carefully. One car slid past before we started across the road.

I knew where Finley's apartment was. I'd been there a bunch of times before, always with Aidan. His place was only a couple of minutes from Aidan's. Ours, technically, but it still felt like Aidan's apartment to me. The only thing I contributed to it was a bag full of clothes and myself. Everything else was his. He never made me feel like I wasn't welcome to change things around, but I hadn't. Instead, I was working up to the day when I suggested we move into our own place. That never seemed to be enough of a priority so far.

Now, I would have liked one of those mansions on the side of the cliff overlooking the bay, with more security than the average bank. Not that our place lacked security, but we shared the building with twenty other apartments. With neighbours always came risk, even if Aidan had anyone vetted thoroughly before they moved in.

"This is the place," Finley said lightly. "There's an elevator, but I prefer to take the stairs."

"A bit more exercise never hurt anyone." Plus we couldn't get stuck in an elevator if we didn't step into one.

"Not yet," Finley agreed. "It's a good place to meet my neighbours anyway. They're often coming down when I'm going up."

I got the message, loud and clear. He was expecting someone to be at the top of the stairs, waiting for us. If whoever was behind followed us, we'd be stuck between both of them. I mentally corrected myself. When they followed us. Presumably that was the plan all along. The question was, why? If they wanted us dead, they could have shot us outside Gianna's without anyone seeing a thing.

"I'm sure you have an interesting set of neighbours," I said.

"We get all sorts in here," Finley agreed. "Men, women and a few non-binary. Half a dozen different nationalities. A former nun. It's an eclectic mix."

So he didn't know who to look out for. We'd have to be careful not to make any assumptions, in case someone innocent got caught in the crossfire.

Assuming anyone innocent actually lived here.

"Don't tell anyone, but Danny from the band Blazing Violet lives in the building." Finley shoved open the door that led into the stairs and guided me inside.

"He's the drummer, right?" I asked.

"Yep." Finley flipped the back of his coat up and pulled a gun out of the back of his pants. He moved slowly towards the bottom step. "He's a nice guy." He kept an eye on the door we came through, while we made our way up the stairs.

I glanced up. If anyone was waiting for us, they weren't visible from here. They must be standing back from the edge of the stairs.

"I'm sure he is. He must be very talented," I said.

"You'd have to be pretty sharp to be a professional musician."

Finley nodded that he understood what I was trying to say. If anyone used a gun in here, it would be loud. A knife would be quieter.

"Sharp and dedicated," he agreed. "Not unlike being a professional hockey player. You have to want it very much. You have to want it more than anything or anyone else."

We reached the second floor landing as the ground floor door opened and closed. The sound of movement from a few floors above immediately followed.

"I'm sure you're just as dedicated as any of them," I said. "You want them to win."

Translation, 'you want to get out of here alive.' Although, the presumption he wanted the Demons to win was equally accurate. He worked his ass off as hard as them and Aidan, for exactly that goal. That was yet another very good reason we needed to deal with whoever thy were as quickly and quietly as possible.

"I want that very much," he agreed. His brow was creased in a frown, but he kept on moving, keeping me between himself and the wall.

"Is there anyone else interesting living here?" I asked.

"I'm not saying the rest aren't interesting, but the two of us are the most captivating." He slid a look my way and smiled. He actually seemed to be enjoying himself. And he neatly answered the question. As far as he could tell, there were only two of them in the stairs with us.

I almost wished I had a gun, but the same old fear lingered. When it came down to it, would I be able to use it? Would I freeze while someone lunged at me with a knife? What if they lunged at Finley instead? Could I react to protect him?

Too many thoughts rushed through my head, threatening to rise in a tsunami of panic. That would be the very worst thing I could do. For me, and for him.

"I think they know we're here," Finley said finally. He spoke loud enough for them to hear. "They know that we know."

We stopped.

Complete silence fell. The only sound was the pounding of blood in my ears. That was so loud I was sure it would give away exactly where we were. Finley was right though. We were moving too slowly to be unaware of their presence. If we'd trotted up, we might have appeared to be clueless.

He tilted his head back. "What do you want?"

The silence hung heavy for a few more moments.

"We want justice for Oscar," the voice below us replied.

"I know plenty of good movies have missed out on the award, but you might be taking it a bit too far," Finley quipped.

The voice, he sounded like a man about my age, chuckled. "That's cute. You know I mean Oscar Fiorelli.

He was murdered by you or someone you know. That either makes you a killer or an accessory."

"I'd make a cute handbag, but I have no idea what you're talking about," Finley said. "Whoever killed Oscar, and I mean the person not the awards, did the world a favour."

The voice growled and stepped up towards us. "Oscar was nothing more than a kid."

"He killed my brother," I said without thinking.

"He killed a lot of people's brothers." He stepped up the stairs and into view. Dark hair, dark eyes, long black coat over black patent leather shoes. He reeked of money, influence, confidence. "We've all done our share of that." He looked me up and down, like a lion might appraise a deer.

"Nicholas Fiorelli," Finley said as though greeting an old friend. "How are you not dead yet?"

I was wondering the same thing myself. Nicholas was Oscar's brother. A year or so older than me, he was as bad as Oscar. Worse. If anyone was going to step into the shoes of their father, Dante, it would be Nicholas. He was one of the few who might bring the family back together and back to strength. That made him dangerous as fuck.

"Finley Howard, Elenna Christakos-Draeger, I could ask you both the same question. Rumour has it you're as up to your eyeballs, just as Ike was."

I kept my gaze steady. "You shouldn't believe everything you hear. He was working with you, against the Brantley family, but you had him killed anyway."

Nicholas clicked his tongue. "We both know that's not what happened. The opposite, in fact. He was working *for* the Brantley family against us and we dealt with him. Was he reporting to you? It can't be a coincidence you married one of Caleb Brantley's lieutenants. That must have been very convenient for Ike and you. But here you are, with one of Aidan Draeger's underlings. I can't imagine he'd look favourably on you cheating on him."

"There you go, listening to gossip again," Finley said. "Elenna had nothing to do with whatever Ike was doing." He kept his eyes on Nicholas the whole time, his gun held loosely in his hand.

"That's what they all say." Nicholas' eyes narrowed. "I haven't believed it yet." He slipped out his gun, but held it the same way, like he wasn't prepared to use it in a heartbeat.

So much for using knives, and trying to be quiet. Even a silencer would be louder than thunder in the stairwell.

"What do you want?" Finley demanded. "If you've come here to kill us—"

"Believe it or not, I haven't," Nicholas said smoothly. "Instead, I've come with a warning. Stay the fuck away from us and our business. My stepmother, Geneva, doesn't want to start a war between us and the Brantley family."

Finley snorted. "You could have fooled me. Dante seemed hellbent on doing just that. Taking out the Brantley and Bell families and replacing them both."

"Dante is dead," Nicholas said flatly. "We don't want a war, but that's what you'll get if you don't stay out of our way. If you want to earn some points with my aunt, you could tell us exactly who murdered Oscar. Once we've dealt with them, we can all stay out of each other's way."

I managed to contain a flinch. "I have no idea," I lied. "I can promise you it wasn't Aidan or Finley."

Nicholas dipped his chin, his dark brown eyes sceptical. "How do you know?"

"Because they would have told me," I said quickly. "If they killed the person who killed my brother, they would have said so. They would have wanted to put my mind at ease."

Nicholas' shoulder jerked forward slightly. "Maybe, and maybe not. Either way, it's in your best interest to find out who it was and tell me. Things don't need to be ugly between us. I'm a reasonable man. And if you ever get tired of Aidan, you're welcome to spread your legs for me."

In the corner of my eye, I saw Finley's hand twitch. He was clearly tempted to shoot Nicholas in the head for that suggestion.

"I'll bear that in mind," I said dryly. He wasn't even on the list of people I'd like to fuck, given half a chance.

Footsteps headed down the stairs towards us. Celine

Fiorelli looked a lot like her brother Oscar, dark-haired and stunning. She looked at me like she'd just found me searching through the bargain rack at Target.

"Elenna," she said smoothly.

"Celine." I didn't bother to smile. The woman was as toxic as the rest of them. She'd probably shoot me if she had a bad day or broke a nail.

"We're done here," Nicholas said. He put his gun away and gave us both a nod.

Celine didn't look so convinced, but she followed him down the stairs and back out the door.

"Maybe they can text next time," Finley muttered. He put away his gun and took my hand to lead me to the door on the landing above us.

"Yeah," I replied. They wouldn't do that. Not when they knew this would leave us rattled.

CHAPTER 7

ELENNA

Finley pulled me into his apartment and closed the door behind us. He locked it and tapped on a screen set back in the wall.

"It's not as if I don't trust them or anything, but it's better to be safe than sorry."

"If they wanted to kill us, they would have done it on the stairs," I pointed out.

"Yeah, true, but I can't rule out the possibility Celine didn't come in here and rig up something funky. And by funky I don't mean in a good way."

"I didn't think you did." I stood back as he tapped at the security system.

The lights all flashed green before it beeped once and fell silent.

"According to this, no one stepped foot in here apart from us," he said. "They're good, but they'll not get past my security system. We should be safe in here."

"Should be," I echoed.

He stepped over to me, grabbed the ends of my scarf and pulled me to him. "I wouldn't let you stay here if it wasn't completely safe. I care about you and I'm very attached to my nuts. I'm all too aware of what Aidan would do if anything happened to you. However," he drew the word out, "it's nothing compared to what I'd do to myself."

We stood chest to chest, almost nose to nose, breathing each other's air.

"Are your nuts in danger from yourself?" I teased.

He grinned. "They might be. I guess I better work super hard to keep you safe and satisfied." He kissed me lightly, barely more than a brush of his lips over mine.

A jolt of lightning went right through me, from my mouth, down through my stomach and straight to my clit. Even after being finger fucked under the table at the restaurant, I was ready to climb the walls. Or better yet, climb *him*.

Instead of deepening our kiss, he let go of one end of my scarf and unwound it around my head. At the same time, he turned me around, so it unwound more and more. By the third turn, I was dizzy and laughing.

He twirled my scarf in the air like a lasso before tossing it onto the couch. Smiling, he undid the buttons of my coat, grabbed the shoulders and pushed it down my arms and over my hands. Before it could land on the floor, he grabbed it and tossed it on top of the scarf.

His coat followed before he pressed me down on the one side of the couch and worked the laces of my boots loose.

"These boots are fucking hot, but sweet baby puck, they're some work."

"You think so?" I asked.

He glanced up at me. "Definitely, but you're worth it." He loosened the laces all the way down to my ankle and eased one off before starting on the other. "I don't think I've ever seen anything cuter than socks with pink ice cream cones with smiley faces on them."

My face heated slightly. "I like cute socks. Usually no one can see them under my boots," I said.

"Remind me to keep you in cute socks then." He eased off my other boot before sliding his hands up my legs, up to the inside of my thighs.

I could keep myself in cute socks, but I laughed anyway. I'd never turn down a new pair. Especially when he was tracing circles around the gusset of my panties and trying very hard not to touch my clit.

"What am I going to keep you in then?" I asked.

"Dessert." He grabbed handfuls of skirt and the side of my panties and pulled them both off in one, swift motion, leaving the bottom half of me bare.

He kissed his way up from my knee to the top of one of my thighs. "Be a good girl and take off your blouse and bra. I want to see those gorgeous breasts."

I tingled all over, and hurried to do as he said. He

watched me carefully while I did it, blue eyes becoming darker when my bra slid down my arms, exposing my already hardened nipples.

"Well, aren't those just perfect," he said reverently. He rose from his crouch just high enough to take one of my nipples between his lips.

I quivered both from the sensation of his touch and the thought of Aidan wondering what we were doing right now. He'd be pissed we didn't tell him about Nicholas and Celine straight away, but he'd approve of this. Finley's red-brown stubble tickled the bare skin of my breast. His head bobbed slightly as he sucked.

"Such a fucking good girl," he said lifting his mouth and tracing circles around my nipple with his tongue. He gave both nipples over to the safe care of his hands and lowered his mouth down to my pussy.

He snaked his tongue around my clit, tasting everywhere but there. Teasing me with every deliberate touch.

"Please," I said breathlessly.

He looked up at me and one dark eyebrow raised questioningly.

"If you don't touch my clit, I'm going to go crazy," I said.

"When you put it that way." He went on teasing and avoiding my clit.

I growled slightly.

He chuckled. "No one ever said I wasn't a ruthless

bastard. I intend to thoroughly enjoy Aidan's wife." He grabbed my hand and kissed my wedding band.

"I'm starting to think you're naughty," I told him.

That had him laughing. "If you're only just starting to think it, then I must not have been trying hard enough." He regarded my finger. "I wonder how many more you can fit on there."

The ring I wore was narrow by choice. I had small hands and slender fingers, and my taste in jewellery ran to the dainty.

"At least another two or three," I said semi-jokingly. "Legally—"

"I don't need legally." He dropped his face back to my pussy and took pity on my aching clit.

The conversation was forgotten for now, while I revelled in the feeling of his lips, teeth and tongue lavishing all of his attention on my pussy.

I was completely naked, on his couch while he was still fully dressed. I wanted to see him naked too. I suspected I wouldn't get that until I came for him. Which was going to be soon, the way he was working me. His fingers didn't leave my breasts, he did all the work on my pussy with his mouth. At the same time, he tweaked and pinched my nipples.

"I'm going to come," I panted.

Between licks he said, "Come for me. Come for me like a good girl."

I came all right, hard and fast, rocking my hips and grinding my clit against his tongue. My whole body exploded into too many pieces to count, each piece a dedication to orgasmic bliss. I pressed my hands to either side of me, arched my back and cried out his name to the ceiling. If Nicholas and Celine were still lurking around, they would have heard me shout.

Finley went on licking and teasing until I came down, sagging and puffing lightly.

"Such a very good girl." He kissed his way down the inside of my thighs and down to my knees before leaning back and grabbing the hem of his shirt. He pulled it off over his head and tossed it to the side.

I drank in the look of him. He was as muscular as any of the players, with broad biceps and sculpted abs. His stomach was flat apart from a long scar which slanted across at an angle. His chest, covered in a light smattering of hair the same colour as on his head, was also crisscrossed with scars.

I leaned forward to trace my fingertips over the one on his stomach.

"That was from a knife," he told me. "The other man didn't survive."

"What about these others?" I touched the ones on his chest.

He shrugged as though they were nothing. "Various things. Knives, a shard of glass or two, a screwdriver."

"A bullet?" I touched a scar on his right shoulder.

He glanced down sideways at it. "Yeah. Didn't duck fast enough. I learned my lesson after that." He stood to take off his pants and black boxer briefs.

I half expected him to wear cartoon underpants. Or maybe superhero socks. Those were black too. He was a surprise. Not as surprising as the size of his cock. I didn't expect him to be so big. Or to have a piercing glittering from the top of his tip.

"Like what you see?" he teased.

"Definitely." I reached out to curl my fingers around his erect length. I pumped him a couple of times, enjoying the way he got even harder and leaned into me.

"As much as I like the feel of that..." He gripped my ass and pulled me to the edge of the couch. Kneeling in front of me, he guided me onto his cock and slid deep into me.

"Holy puck," he groaned. "You feel even better than I dared to dream." His eyes half closed. A faint smile graced his lips. "So fucking perfect for my cock." He cracked one eye all the way open and his smile broadened. "Be sure to tell Aidan that. My cock fits perfectly inside your pussy."

"I'll make sure he knows." I felt so full. His cock touched everywhere inside me. My body throbbed as if I hadn't already come twice already.

"If you don't, I will." His eye returned to half open. "I'm going to tell him every detail about how I fucked his wife and made you mine too. Be a good girl and tell me who you belong to." He slid out of me before slamming back in hard.

I moaned. "You," I said. "Aidan and you."

"That's right, both of us," he said. "Every centimetre of this gorgeous body of yours belongs to him and me. And mine belongs to you."

"Do you belong to him too?" I asked, half teasing.

His eyes widened and his face turned slightly pink. "That's a conversation for another time." He grabbed me tight and lay back down on the floor, pulling me with him so I was straddling him, his cock still deep inside me.

"Ride me hard, beautiful girl," he said. "Ride me until I come inside your body."

I placed my hands on his chest, muscle and scarred skin firm as I rose and fell on him, pushing him hard while my breasts bounced.

His eyes were open fully now, watching me, appreciating my body while he pushed his hips up, driving himself into me in a perfect, heated rhythm.

I got the impression he was memorising every moment of this so he could tell Aidan the details. Aidan was going to want to hear all of them too. Every groan, every drop of sweat and cum. Every thrust. Neither of us would hold anything back, not now, not later.

Finley moaned as he came inside me, hands still gripping my hips as he drove me, milking his cock for every single drop.

At the same time, I came for a third time, my muscles clenching around his throbbing erection.

"Yes, yes, fuck," he groaned. "Elenna, you are mine, mine, mine. Dear fucking puck…"

We kept pumping and rolling until we were both spent. We finally sagged on to the thick pile of the carpet, sweating and puffing.

"That was perfect for a start," Finley said. "Let's take this into my bedroom."

CHAPTER 8

ORION

I ignored the roar of the crowd. The cheering. The shouting. The jeers.

Everything.

My attention was laser focused on one thing; the ice. On the edge of my awareness was Tiger, the left defenceman. Phoenix behind us, ready to defend the goal. Javey and Bray, ready to provide offence. Coast, as cocky as always, looking like he was on holiday. That was a pretence. The moment his stick touched the ice behind the puck he was ready.

A nanosecond behind the opposition's centre, who took the face off advantage to slap the puck out of the centre circle, away from Coast.

Tiger moved to block it, but the Wattle Valley Dingoes winger got to it first, driving it deeper into our defensive zone.

My territory.

I growled under my breath. I didn't question why I ended up in a team of fucking losers, but how I was going to help turn them around. My father would have said the head coach was too hard on them, on us. I thought he was too fucking soft. He must be. We had the talent, but the team was a mess.

The winger drove the puck in front of him, his whole posture certain he was going to walk all over us. The Dingoes beat the Demons the last time they played. Handed them their asses.

That was before I was here.

I skated backward, keeping my eye on the puck, moving closer to the goal and waiting for the right moment. On cue, the winger tried to take a shot at goal. He thought I wasn't ready. That he'd get it past me while I was still occupied waiting for him to make a move. He was fast, but I was faster. I blocked his shot and sent the puck sailing back, right to Coast.

I almost caught the centre by surprise. Lucky for him, he managed to respond in time to smash the puck to Javey.

Javey took the puck all the way to the opposition's goal, but the goaltender blocked the shot at the last second.

I resisted the urge to smash my stick into the boards. We should have evened the score with that play.

I skated back to the blue line and waited again.

Coast managed to take control of the puck, but the Dingoes took it back less than a minute later. The

Dingoes' right winger crowded me as the left drove the puck back towards our goal. I shoved him with my elbow.

"Fuck off," I growled.

He turned around and grinned. "You might as well give up now, you're gonna lose anyway. The Demons always do."

"Fuck off," I growled again.

He laughed.

He stopped when I punched him in the face. He threw his stick aside and lunged at me. He swung, but I skated back, out of reach.

The Dingoes took the distraction as a chance to score, but Tiger was right there, blocking the shot again. The opposition tried to get around him but I managed to skate away from the asshole whose face was covered in blood, and whacked the puck away from the goal.

Coast regained possession of it and drove it to Bray who smashed it straight into the Dingoes' goal. That evened the score right before the half-time alarm sounded.

I skated off the ice, right past the winger who pulled off his helmet and was having his injury looked at by his team medic.

Nothing a couple of stitches wouldn't fix. I should have punched him harder.

"What the fuck was that?" Aidan snarled before I could even pull off my helmet and grab a water bottle.

He was tall. I was taller. My hair was darker than

his, my eyes brown where his were hazel. My skin was a shade or two darker. My soul was probably darker too.

I picked up a bottle, opened it and took a swig. "Just doing my job."

"Your job is to make sure the puck doesn't get past you." He pressed his fists to his hips and stared me down.

"That was exactly what I did," I said. "Did you miss me preventing them from scoring just now?"

He leaned in closer. "I don't miss a fucking thing."

I resisted the urge to lean back away from him. "What's that supposed to mean?"

"It means keeping an eye on you," he said. "And you're off for the second period."

"What the hell?" I would already have incurred a five minute penalty for punching that asshole in the face, but not the whole second period. "I'm the best right defence the Demons have, and you know it."

"And I'm the head coach. A fact you seem to have forgotten. If I say you're out, then you're out." He started to turn away.

I curled my lip at him. "You wanna know why I punched that dickhead? Because he assumed we're going to lose. That's what's going to happen if you keep me out of the rest of the game."

Yeah, I was as cocky as Coast, but I was also right. The team needed me. Aidan fucking Draeger knew it too. What was his problem? He couldn't even keep his own wife from straying. Maybe the other guys didn't notice what was going on with her and Finley Howard, but I did. I saw the way they looked at each other. If they weren't already fucking, they soon would be.

Why did I care? Because Elenna was smoking hot and if anyone was going to screw her, it should be me. Thinking about her made my cock want to split the seams of my pants to escape.

I hadn't even spoken to the woman. So what? She haunted my dreams. When I lay in bed with my hand wrapped around my dick, I thought of her. I imagined her mouth on me, licking and sucking. Taking my cum when I squirted it down her throat. On her hands and knees while I pounded into her pussy.

Aidan turned back to me, face full of thunder. Anyone else would have been intimidated, but I held my ground.

"You'll go back on if we need you. Until then, my decision stands. Save your fists for the right time. If you let some dumbass prick get to you, which was clearly what he was trying to do, we'll definitely lose. Pick your fucking fights." He gave me a long look before he turned away.

I wanted to hate him, but what I really hated was the fact he was right. That was exactly what happened. I let the prick get under my skin and distract me. That was stupid and unprofessional. I was pissed at myself and the opposition winger. The same winger who was grinning at me right now, even with an ice pack pressed to his face.

I ignored him, and dropped my stick before following the rest of the team into the dressing room and sinking down onto a seat.

I didn't notice who sat beside me until I caught the faint scent of something floral. Perfume or maybe nothing more than soap or shampoo. Whatever, the smell went straight to my cock, making me half hard in half a second.

I glanced sideways. She was even more gorgeous up close. Close enough that if I shifted a little, my thigh and shoulder would touch hers. If that happened, I might ignite, so I kept perfectly still.

"You have an impressive right hook," she said softly. Her voice was like a match to my already raging inferno. Husky and precise, never skimping on syllables.

Not fancy, but careful, every word and nuance chosen. As though if she got them wrong, she'd provoke a war.

Those first few words told me a thousand things about her. Including the fact she knew all about the dark side of Dusk Bay. In the shadows, the wrong words could, indeed, provoke a war. Look at someone the wrong way and you could start one without trying to be provocative. She *was* provocative, but in a different way.

I looked directly at her and nodded. "Thanks." I had

no particular, personal rule against smiling, it was something I rarely did. Not unless I had good reason to do it. She might give me a reason. My eyes lingered on her mouth. Her lips would be the perfect crown for my cock.

"If you're going to say I should have walked away," I started.

Her lips dropped apart slightly. "I don't think Aidan did the wrong thing in taking you off, but the Demons are playing better. Whenever people call the team losers, I want to punch them in the face too." She noticed where my gaze was and why. If she minded, she didn't show it. If anything, her eyes got slightly darker. Anyone might try to tell me I was imagining it, but I wasn't.

"And would you?" I raised my gaze. Her eyes were a shade or two lighter brown than mine. Deep enough to drown in.

She laughed softly.

My dick was promptly hard.

"I think I'd hurt my fist," she said.

I frowned. "Hasn't anyone taught you how to punch?" She was right, she might hurt her fist, but I got the impression she never tried. "Boxing, I mean. It's a good way to burn off excess."

"Excess what?" She cocked her head so her ponytail fell out to the side.

"Excess everything," I said. "Energy, anger, toxins. Fighting and sweating are two of my favourite things."

I definitely didn't imagine her eyes getting even darker.

"You box?" She seemed genuinely interested.

"Since I was twelve. I could have gone professional, but I chose hockey instead." I smirked. "And look how that turned out."

"So far, that's turned out with the Demons playing better than they have in months," she said. "Usually the score is much worse at this point of the game." She looked slightly embarrassed. "Which you probably know."

"Yeah, but I don't mind hearing it from you. It's good to be reminded the move from Sydney wasn't a complete waste of time." I stopped talking for a moment. "I want the Demons to win. Not just win. We should have been dominating by now."

The rest of the team was getting ready to go back on the ice. Tiger glanced at me but shrugged. He might argue with Aidan over his decision later, but right now his head was where it should be. In the game.

"You will be," she said. "The team's biggest problem was that they weren't playing as a team. You've been doing that all game. Maybe you should take them all for a boxing lesson."

"Do you want to be my guinea pig?" I asked. "I can teach them, but I've never taught before." It wasn't exactly true, but teaching kids wasn't the same as teaching adults. Kids wanted to learn. In my experience, adults thought they already knew everything. Except Elenna. She was different.

I wanted to get myself into her pussy, but I wanted to get to know her as a woman too.

"I..." She glanced in Aidan's direction. He was watching us both. I expected to see him looking angry or suspicious, but instead he looked curious. What did that mean?

"I'd love to," she said finally.

CHAPTER 9

ELENNA

"I think it's a good idea." Aidan paced the living room like a caged lion. The Demons beat the Dingoes by a point, but he was more agitated than usual.

Finley and I told him every detail about our date and night together, but he was fixated on our run in with Nicholas and Celine. That hadn't stopped him from waiting until Finley left before fucking me while I was still sticky with Finley's cum. He'd called me his best slut and made me come even though my body was tired and sore.

"I agree," Finley said. He sat on one chair with his feet propped on another. "Sooner or later, they'll work out who killed Oscar. The better Elenna can defend herself, the happier I'll be."

"Not that either of us is going to let her out of our sight for the foreseeable future," Aidan said. He gave

Finley an accusing look like the equipment manager might actually be suggesting that.

"You don't have to fawn over me," I said. "I kept myself safe for twenty-six years, remember? I know how to run and hide. I know how to shoot a gun."

I glanced down at the potato I'd stopped peeling. I reminded myself my hands were covered in juice and not blood. Still, I finished peeling quickly and sliced the potatoes before tossing them into a pot and thoroughly washing my hands.

"You know how to hold a knife," Aidan said. "But you might need to work on convincing the other person you intend to use it."

"I might have to surrender my badass card." I opened a packet of sausages and placed them in a row in the frying pan.

I wasn't much of a cook, but I could do sausages and mashed potatoes. I probably made too much, but I was used to cooking for one or two, not three.

Aidan invited Finley over for dinner the night after the game. I couldn't disagree over the necessity of the conversation the three of us had to have. So far, we'd skirted around it, talking about everything else. Nicholas and Celine gave us the perfect distraction.

Aidan stepped over behind me. He placed his hands on my shoulders and started to massage lightly.

"Your badass card is safe." He worked out a knot in my left shoulder. "All we want is for you to be safe. I've tried my best to give you the skills to do that. If Orion can help, then I want you to let him."

"You could come with me," I suggested. "It might be a good way for you to work off some rage."

He leaned in to nibble the side of my neck. "I already have a way to work my rage out. Fucking you is the best stress relief there is."

"What he said," Finley agreed.

I lifted my chin and our gazes connected.

That seemed to be the in he was looking for. He cleared his throat.

"About the other night..."

"I know you both enjoyed yourselves," Aidan said when Finley trailed off expectantly. "So did I. Imagining you together. It was everything I thought it would be. More."

"We can do it again?" Finley asked.

Aidan's hands went still on my shoulders. I thought he was angry until he spoke.

"What do you want, Elenna? Do you want to fuck Fin again?"

I licked my lips. "Yes." My voice was firm and unwavering, but I held my breath for his response. He was unpredictable. He was just as likely to be angry as he was aroused. And if he was angry, he knew where the knives and guns were. And how to use his words as a weapon. He could cut straight through anyone with his tongue.

His breath was hot on my neck. Silence hung in the air, heavy and tense.

"That's what I want too," he said finally. "He can give you something I can't. I don't do praise well. That's something you need, as much as you need what I can give you. I want you to get everything you crave. I know I'm a grumpy asshole sometimes—"

Finley snorted.

"Don't make me change my mind," Aidan growled. "This is about Elenna. Not you."

"It's about him too," I said softly. "I'd like to have both of you in my life." I hesitated, my heart racing. "Equally. Not just as a fuck now and again. I care about Fin."

Aidan's hands tightened on my shoulders. Hard enough to bring tears to my eyes, but not to tell him to stop.

"You care about her too?" he asked Finley.

"Very much." Finley nodded. He got to his feet and came around the island to us, slowly, carefully. Cautious of provoking Aidan. He also knew where the knives and guns were. Most of them anyway.

"She's a special woman. One who deserves all the good things. All the hot things. All the orgasms." He smiled at me. "You can give her things I can't. Between us, her needs would be better met. One man was never going to be enough. She needs a team."

He quickly added, "Not the *whole* team, but more than one."

"What if she needs more than two?" Aidan asked over the top of my head.

Finley held my gaze. "Then that's what she gets. I'm a mere planet moving in her orbit. Held in place by her heat and light." He leaned in and kissed my mouth.

When Aidan didn't go for a sharp implement, I deepened the kiss, my tongue sliding over his lips.

Aidan pressed himself into my back, his erection poking into my hip.

I startled when the sausages crackled in the pan.

"I should turn those." I reluctantly broke off the kiss and stepped away.

"We should set some boundaries," Finley said. "No one named Fiorelli."

Aidan grunted. "Obviously. Will you be moving in here?"

I glanced over to Finley before I picked up the tongs and turned the sausages one by one.

He grinned. "It would be my pleasure. That's another boundary."

"You have your own room and we'll work from there," Aidan said. Evidently he wasn't in a hurry to share his bed.

"Deal," Finley said lightly. "I can help with the cooking. My mother was a chef. I don't mind admitting I'm not too bad at it."

"It's all yours," I said. "It's a miracle we haven't poisoned each other."

"My cooking isn't that bad," Aidan protested.

"If you like ramen and baked beans." I shook the tongs at him.

"Which I do. I got by on those for years before we met." He checked the potatoes in the pot by stabbing them with a fork. That was another one of his few culinary skills.

"No wonder you're grumpy all the time," Finley told him. He opened the fridge and searched around for some vegetables. "That shit has to be bad for your indigestion."

"You're not going to put us on a diet of lentils and tofu are you?" Aidan looked disgusted. "Because there's a pizza place down the street."

"Get away with ya," Finley retorted. "Do I look like the kind of guy who eats tofu?" He looked almost offended. He found a knife to slice the vegetables with, but before he started, he wielded it at Aidan. "I'll make you a pizza that'll make you forget the place down the road or anywhere else you ever ate it."

"Put that down before you hurt someone," Aidan told him. "Never, ever wave a knife around my wife."

"Our wife." Finley grabbed a cutting board and started slicing.

Aidan froze. "What the fuck did you just say?"

"You heard me," Finley said. "We agreed Elenna is ours. That makes her our wife, not just yours."

Aidan's face turned pink. For a while, I thought he was going to grab the knife from Finley and drive it through his heart.

"Aidan," I said carefully.

For at least a full minute, he stood glaring at Finley.

Finley pretended like he was oblivious, but we all knew five percent of his attention was on the vegetables and ninety-five percent on Aidan. His survival instincts were too strong not to be alert for danger from a variety of angles. If Aidan made a move, Finley would be ready. This situation could turn very ugly in a heartbeat.

"Both of you," I said tentatively. "Please don't."

"Don't what?" Aidan asked. His eyes never left Finley. "What do you want me to do, Elenna? Do you want me to protect what's mine?"

"Not if it means hurting Fin." I felt like I was walking on the edge of that knife, ready to topple off at any moment.

"Do you want him instead of me?" Aidan's voice was low. Demanding honesty.

"Hell no," I replied immediately.

"Do you want Orion instead of either of us? I saw the way he was looking at you. He wants to own you and fuck you the way I do."

The only thing I could say to that was, "I know."

Aidan grabbed my upper arms and turned me to face him. "Do you want him?" he demanded.

"I don't know," I admitted. "I've had one conversation with him. I agreed to let him teach me how to box. That's all. I want you and I want Fin. Right now, that's all I know. Don't make me choose one over the other."

That would be difficult. My husband or my lover. If it was greedy to want both of them, I didn't care. I didn't want the whole frying pan full of sausages, just two of them.

Unless something developed between Orion and me. There was a distinct possibility nothing would grow between us. He seemed to have more anger issues than Aidan. Cold confidence and red-hot fury. Was it hot as fuck? Yes it was, but you can't build a relationship on a single conversation and physical attraction.

Then there was the fact he was a year or two younger than me. Finley was five years older and Aidan was fifteen. A year shouldn't be a big deal. Except Orion was the same age as my younger brother was when he was murdered. What would Ike have thought of this whole situation? He probably would have found it hilarious.

I looked up at Aidan and searched his face. He was difficult to read at the best of times. Always with anger and a biting remark bubbling just under the surface. Not directed at me. Never directed at me. But I was well aware that if I pushed him the wrong way, that could change.

"If I thought I'd put you in a position where you had to choose, I never would have let you anywhere near Fin," he said finally. "I'm not going to keep you from what you need. No matter what that is."

"Even if she fucks Orion?" Finley asked. He finished slicing vegetables and pulled the steamer out of the cupboard. He scooped up the slices in two hands and threw them in before placing the steamer on the stove.

"Even then," Aidan said. "If that happens, it doesn't happen behind my back. Or behind Fin's."

"Of course not," I said firmly. "This… All of this only works if we communicate."

"Agreed," Aidan said. "But if Orion thinks he's getting any preferential treatment—"

"It's only because he's good at his job," I finished for him. "Not because anything else happens."

"Half his problem is that he is good and he fucking knows it," Aidan said with a sigh. "Cocky prick."

I couldn't argue with that. Orion would give Coast a run for his money in the cocky department. What would he think if he knew we were talking about him like this?

Right, it would inflate his ego even further.

CHAPTER 10

ELENNA

"Keep your hands up. Like this." Orion demonstrated before grabbing my arms and raising them higher. "Not so tense. If you hit anything like that, you're going to hurt yourself."

He'd been nothing but focused since we started this lesson. He didn't say a word about Aidan, or the team. Only when he was correcting my posture, or how I held my hands, did he touch me or even get within a metre or two of me. He didn't need to. I was aware of him. His presence. The way he filled the room and seemed to steal the air from my lungs.

I shook out my wrists and tried to relax.

"Good. If it helps, pretend the punching bag is someone you don't like." He stepped behind it and nodded to me. His dark eyes watched, unsmiling. He was fitted into a snug, black singlet and black shorts that did nothing to hide his muscular arms and thighs, even half hidden by the bag.

I nodded and tried to imagine Nicholas Fiorelli. He'd shoot me long before I had the chance to punch him, but he was the first person who came to mind.

I pulled my arm back and punched the bag.

Orion held it to keep from swinging away. "Harder."

I punched harder, then with my left hand as well.

Orion snorted. "Is that the best you've got? The only thing you're going to do punching lightly like that is break a nail."

I caught and held his taunting gaze. He was trying to piss me off, to make me hit harder. It was working. I didn't want to break a nail. His nose, on the other hand…

I drove my fists into the punching bag.

"You're not trying. If you hit me that softly, you wouldn't even leave a bruise." He sounded bored, like he was regretting offering to teach me, because I was doing nothing but wasting his time. His *precious* time, by the expression on his face.

Forget Nicholas Fiorelli, it was Orion's face I wanted to punch now. I slammed my fists harder and harder. I'd wipe the smirk off his face.

"Better," he said finally. "Show that motherfucker who's boss." He was almost smiling, smug as fuck. He knew I was picturing him.

I was sweating lightly by now. Some people hated it, but I loved to sweat; it meant I was working hard. As a bonus, anything that made me sweat was usually a good way to release tension. Especially punching the shit out of something. It felt better than I'd imagined.

Over and over, I punched, grunting with exertion, and to help me hit that much harder. I even drove Orion back a couple of times.

"All right, take a break," he said finally. "Grab a drink.

"Do I get to punch you next?" I opened a bottle of water and took a big gulp.

He smirked. "You think you can?"

If he was Aidan or Finley, I would have flicked the water at him. I was tempted, but had no idea how he'd react. He was almost a foot taller than me, a lot wider and a lot fitter. If he wanted to come at me, I wouldn't stand a chance.

That should have deterred me, but it tempted me more. I pictured him pinning me to the mat, parting my thighs with his muscular legs. Kneeling between them, his cock erect and ready, glistening with pre-cum.

I took a few more sips before closing the bottle and placing it back beside the wall.

"You think I can't?" I stood with my hand on my hip and cocked my head at him.

"I think you'll hurt yourself." His dark eyes became darker. His expression was intense, his cock outlined in the front of his grey track pants, semi-hard.

I couldn't stop my eyes from dipping down. What he had in there was impressive.

"I might like a bit of pain." He could hurt me with that if he thrust hard enough into my body. The thought made the pulse in my clit throb relentlessly.

His cock went from semi-hard to tenting his pants.

"Really—" He took a step toward me.

The lights went out.

We were plunged into darkness.

"Fuck," he said. "Wait there."

For half a second, I thought this was his doing.

"Wait." I turned the light on my watch.

He turned away, but he snapped back now. "Turn it off," he snarled. "There are lights on outside."

I turned off the light and realised he was right. Across the street, the lights *were* still on. Through the front window of the Indian restaurant, people continued eating.

"The Fiorelli family—" I whispered.

"I know," he said bluntly. "One of them killed your brother, then he ended up dead. I'm guessing they assume Aidan did it."

"Oscar had a lot of enemies," I said evasively.

Orion snorted. "That's an understatement. I would have killed the prick myself, given half a chance. He's done the same to a couple of... It doesn't matter now." He grabbed my wrist and guided me towards the back of the gym.

I just made out his shape, crouching down, followed by the sound of a zipper.

"Here." He pressed something into my hand.

A handgun. Gripping it and placing my hand on the trigger was automatic. Trained by hours spent at the shooting range.

The thought I might have to use it threatened to give me hives. Every centimetre of skin on my body started to tingle and itch.

"Stay down and stay quiet," he whispered.

I crouched in the corner, where it was darkest, and listened.

At the other end of the building, a door opened. After a few moments, it closed again. They weren't doing anything to try to hide their presence.

"Orion Scully-Evans," a male voice called out. They sounded familiar, but I couldn't quite place them. It wasn't Nicholas.

Orion's response was to put his hand lightly on my lips. "It's me they want. I'll deal with this. You should get out the back door." He lowered his hand.

"There's probably someone out there waiting for us," I whispered.

He exhaled sharply. "Then stay where you are. I'll try to lead them away."

"Who are they?" I asked.

"Associates of the Fiorellis," he replied. "I might have disrupted some of their operations. The Brantley twins really hate human trafficking."

I'd heard that about Hunter and Parker, but no one could explain the reason for it. Neither of them had much in the way of a moral compass, so why did they care about that?

"I see why they'd be pissed off." Brantley, Bell or Fiorelli, none of them liked to lose money. I couldn't bring myself to sympathise with anyone who trafficked other people. Inanimate objects, yes; humans, no. As crimes went, it was the worst of the worst.

"Yeah, but there's a chance they don't know you're here, so shhh."

My phone vibrated in my back pocket. I couldn't risk taking it out without being seen, but I knew who it was and why.

"We could wait—" I started.

"Aidan would probably shoot me and pretend it was an accident," Orion said.

"He wouldn't do that." My phone vibrated again.

"No? I might." Orion's teeth flashed white in the darkness.

"If you do, I'll shoot you in the ass," I told him.

He actually laughed softly. "I believe you. I prefer you don't. I like my ass. I know you do too, I've seen you looking."

Before I could confirm or deny his claim, he moved away through the shadows.

Aidan was right, he was a cocky prick.

I slipped out of the corner and crawled behind the front desk of the gym.

When we arrived, a woman had stood behind it. Orion had assured her we'd lock up when we were done. She clearly knew him and must have believed him, because she wasn't here now. Unless she was hiding. I hadn't seen her leave.

Either way, there was no one behind the desk to see me pull out my phone and glance at the screen.

The first message was from Aidan.

What's going on there?

The second was from Finley.

Are you okay?

Worried face emoji.

I'm fine

I sent them both.

They're after Orion

I'd just hit send when I heard a tap at the back door. I jumped.

Another message flashed on the screen.

Let me in

I pushed my phone back into my pocket and crawled, careful not to squeeze the trigger as I went.

I glanced back at the shadows before unlocking the door and opening it a fraction.

"Come on," Aidan whispered.

"We can't leave Orion here alone." I peered out.

"I took care of them," Aidan said. "Fin is dealing with a couple more."

"Correction, Fin *dealt* with a couple more." Finley appeared out of the darkness. He slipped a knife back into his boot, not before I saw it glistening with blood. A few drops dripped off onto the floor.

"Get Elenna out of here," Aidan told him. "I'll help Orion."

"I can get myself out of here," I argued. "I'm even armed." I held up my hand with the gun in it.

"Unless you're prepared to use it—" Aidan started.

"I'm going to have to at some point," I said. Whether they were after me, Orion or Aidan and Finley, the Fiorellis were going to keep coming. It was increasingly unlikely I'd go for the rest of my life without killing one of them.

A gunshot rang out, followed by a cry of pain.

"Fine," Aidan said quickly. "But stay behind us." He and Finley crawled past me, guns in their hands.

I stayed low, back from them. My heart raced. I was sweating heavier than when I was punching the punching bag. My hands were so slick I had to grip the gun tighter to keep from dropping it.

What was I doing? I should have snuck out the back door and stayed the hell out here.

Aidan, Finley and Orion, they knew what they were doing. I was just as likely to get them killed when I panicked. None of them would blame me if I changed my mind and snuck away. They *wouldn't*.

I'd blame myself though. I couldn't abandon them, no matter how scared I was.

I heard a sound behind me.

I turned as a figure appeared in the doorway. They held the door open with one hand. In the other, they held a gun.

They raised their arm toward me.

I didn't have time to think or panic. I raised my gun, aimed and pulled the trigger.

The shot sounded loud in the silence.

My hand vibrated from the recoil. I gripped tighter to keep hold of the gun. In a flash, the bullet left the chamber and slammed straight into their face.

Time stopped. The only sound was blood in my ears and a cacophony of thoughts. None of which made sense right now.

The thud of the body dropping to the floor echoed louder in my ears than any of the gunshots.

I killed them.

I killed them.

I killed them.

Time resumed.

Another shot rang out at the front of the gym. A cry of pain was followed by another shot. Then silence that drew out for a minute, two minutes.

It was broken when the back door opened.

I barely had time to raise my gun before Aidan and Finley shot the first two dark figures who walked through. The next two were more cautious, stepping inside with guns in front of them, movements slow and deliberate.

"It's Orion we want," one said. "Hand him over and we'll be gone."

"You found him," Orion said from behind them. He shot one in the back of the head.

The other started to turn, gun ready.

Aidan shot them before they could squeeze the trigger.

"Let's get the fuck out of here," Aidan growled. "Orion, come with us. You have some explaining to do."

"Explain." I crossed my arms over my chest and glared at Orion. Typical of the cocky prick, he didn't look apologetic. Not even slightly. Instead, he met my gaze unwavering, stone cold.

"What is there to explain?" he asked. "Elenna and I had a practice session. It was interrupted. We dealt with it. For the record, I was doing fine before you showed up."

"Any other time, I would have left you to it." I matched his tone. "But not when Elenna was in your company."

For once, I didn't refer to her as my wife. Her involvement with Finley complicated things. They'd be complicated further if she got involved with Orion.

She was still my wife and she always would be, but I didn't need Finley correcting me right now. Not in front of Orion and not when Elenna was curled up next to Finley, his arm around her.

Her face was slightly pale, but she was dealing with her second time killing a man better than she dealt with the first. She acted on instinct. I was proud as hell of her. If she'd hesitated, even for a heartbeat, she'd be dead. They might as well kill me straight after. There was no life for me without her.

I'd barely functioned before we met. Finley would tell you I firmly had my asshole hat on most of the time. The team would tell you I had it on *all* the time, but I was worse before her.

"I was taking care of her," Orion declared. "Which she didn't need. She can take care of herself." He turned to her. "That was a perfect shot to the asshole's eyeball."

She gave a watery smile. "Thanks. I wasn't really aiming at his eyeball. I couldn't see much of anything in the dark. All I knew was they were going to shoot me if I didn't shoot them first."

Finley clicked his tongue. "Never tell anyone that. Own the eyeball shot like you meant it." He kissed her cheek.

I pictured them together, naked. Him sliding his cock in and out of her. Her with his cock down her throat. The mental porn turned me on so hard. Almost as much as being with her myself. I wanted to watch them fuck each other, but one step at a time.

The right defenceman was an arrogant pain in my

ass, but imagining him with her was as arousing. Unless he got her killed in the process.

"Fin is right," Orion said as if they were old friends. "Always own the eyeball shot. Or the ass shot." He didn't smile, but he and Elenna seemed to share something amusing.

"I'd definitely own the ass shot," she said. "And remind you that you deserve it."

If anyone deserved to be shot in the ass, it was Orion. I might even shoot him there myself.

"This is all very amusing," I said sarcastically. "But you haven't explained why you were interrupted. Why were they after you?"

"I'd suggest they were friends with the dickhead I punched at the game the other night, but we all know that's bullshit," Orion said.

"Along with most of what comes out of your mouth," I told him. "If you don't cut the shit, I'll make sure you never play hockey again as long as you live. I mean that as a head coach and as someone with a cricket bat that could break your fucking knees."

Orion rolled his eyes. "As I said to Elenna, I helped Hunter and Parker Brantley to disrupt the Fiorellis' human trafficking operation. They're tougher targets these days, so they came after me. Partly to get rid of me and partly to send a message to the twins. They don't like being fucked with."

I nodded. I used my well-practiced mask to hide the relief that the Fiorellis hadn't gone after Elenna. Not this time anyway. Trying to kill Orion was less likely to start a war. There wasn't much love lost between the older, more powerful Brantley brothers and their younger twins these days.

From what I understood, the guys who referred to themselves as the evil twins, were as likely to try to shut down Caleb's human trafficking as anyone else's. Ironic for people who probably received drug shipments the next day. If nothing else, people were good at picking and choosing their battles as it suited them.

"I guess you're not the soft target they thought you were," Finley said.

Orion actually smiled at that. "Nothing about me is soft."

I snorted. "Some would say your cock is soft."

"Elenna would say otherwise." He looked smug. "Things were about to get interesting when we were interrupted." He was clearly trying to provoke me.

The joke was on him.

My gaze slid to her. "Sounds like the Fiorellis didn't choose their timing well."

Her face turned slightly pink. "Ten minutes later would have been much worse."

A flash of confusion crossed Orion's face, but he recovered quickly. "I last longer than ten minutes."

Finley chuckled. "Aidan, you're a shit-stirring son of a bitch."

"Don't insult my mother," I told him. "As for shit-stirring, it's hard to resist when the target is such an easy one."

I could almost see the thoughts passing through Orion's brain. His eyes narrowed, opened wider, then narrowed again.

"You have an open marriage," he stated. "That's why you don't care what she does with Fin. Or if I fucked her."

"I very much care what she does with Fin or you," I said. "You could say the relationship is open, but with boundaries."

Orion's gaze cut to Elenna.

"They both want me to have my needs met," she explained. "But I wouldn't go and sleep with just anyone. They have to agree."

For the first time since I met him, Orion was speechless. He gaped at her for a solid minute. "They agreed on me?"

"We all did," she said. "Only if it was something you wanted too though. I mean, there was no pressure or anything."

"You weren't going to get kicked off the team if you didn't fuck her," I said. That was never on the cards, but I couldn't resist another shit stir.

I continued. "He probably doesn't want her now; she's not forbidden fruit."

"Just delicious fruit," Finley said.

Orion ignored us both. "How does this work?" He directed the question to her. "If we want to fuck, how does it work? Do they have to watch?" He jerked his head towards me.

"They don't have to watch, but they have to *know*," she said. "After if not before. I won't cheat on them. I won't go behind anyone's back. If anyone is uncomfortable with this, they…" She shook her head. "They can walk away at any time. Including me."

"You don't get to walk away from me," I told her. "No matter what happens, I will never give you up. You'll *always* be mine."

"I never want to walk away from you," she told me. "Or from Fin." She glanced back over to him, then back to Orion. "I know this is a lot."

"You're not fucking kidding." He rubbed a hand over the back of his neck. "When were you going to mention any of this?" He gestured around to all of us.

"Before we went any further," she said. "If you said no, we would have gotten on with our training session."

He sat back.

"Grown-up relationships can be complicated," I said, reminding him he was half my age. Half my amount of wisdom or experience too, if he was lucky.

He flipped me off.

That was fair enough, I supposed.

Finley laughed.

"If you walk out the door right now, I'll understand," Elenna said. "Aidan is right, it is complicated. You all have to work together. I'm not asking for any kind of commitment, I just want you to understand the situation."

Orion closed his eyes for a moment. "So you'd be good with a friends with benefits situation with me while you're in a relationship with Finley and that asshole?" He opened his eyes and gestured vaguely in my direction. As if we didn't all know who he was referring to.

"If that's what you'd like, then yes," Elenna said. "But maybe don't call your head coach an asshole to his face."

"I have thick skin," I said.

"And a thick head," Finley said helpfully.

"This is still my apartment," I reminded him.

"Maybe it's time we got a house." Finley raised an eyebrow at me.

"You've been living here for three days," I said. "You're already trying to rearrange the whole situation?"

"As equipment manager, it's my job to be organised," Finley said. "And it's my job to organise other people. If that includes you, then so be it. I don't mind at all."

"Like I said, if you want to leave…" Elenna looked at us both meaningfully.

"I think she's trying to tell you not to drive Orion away," Finley said.

"If he's driven away that easily, then he doesn't deserve her," I said firmly.

Silence fell after that statement.

"I'm going to have to think about it," Orion said finally. "It's not that I don't want you, because I do. It's not even about the situation with Aidan and Fin. Sooner or later, the Fiorellis are going to come after me again and I don't want you hurt."

"I thought you had it under control," I said.

He glanced over at me. "I did. This time. They sent ten people after me. It might be twenty next time."

"You must have caused one hell of a disruption for them to go to that much effort and expense," Finley said.

Orion looked smug again. "I helped to free about two thousand women and girls. We destroyed a bunch of facilities and networks. It'll take them years to rebuild. If there's anyone left with the last name Fiorelli by then."

"I'm starting to think we should kick you out on your ass," I said. "Don't get me wrong, all that sounds incredible, but I don't want to get stuck in the middle of a war between you and the Fiorelli family."

His expression didn't change. "You're already in the middle. I was working with Ike to find the information that led to us doing what we ultimately did. Even if you weren't with Ike's sister, you work for Caleb. You can kick me out, but it's not going to make any of this go away."

"You might be needed to help keep Elenna safe," Finley said softly.

Orion turned back to her. "I think you'll find she's more capable than you give her credit for. More than she gives herself credit for. She packs a mean punch when she wants to. And then there's that eyeball shot."

She smiled. "You think I can punch?"

"You need more practice, but you got a good start tonight." His expression turned grim. "Which could have been your end."

"Lucky for everyone Fin and I weren't far away," I said. "If you got Elenna killed, having your knees broken would be the least of your trouble."

"Yeah, because if she got killed, I'd be dead too," Orion said, his eyes still on her.

"I'd resurrect you and smash your knees, then kill you again," I said. "Or better yet, resurrect you and hand you over to Ice Miller. If anyone can keep you alive for a few more days while torturing your ass, it's him."

"You talk a big talk, coach," Orion said.

"Because I can walk a big walk," I said. "Can you?"

"What are you thinking?"

I lay on my side, Aidan spooning me. He had one arm draped over my side, his fingers under my singlet, tracing circles over my stomach.

"I'm thinking about the man I killed," I said softly.

"He would have killed you," he reminded me.

"I know, I just…"

It was after midnight when Orion finally left. Aidan had requested that he and I have time alone, so Finley had disappeared into his room to sleep. Outside the apartment was quiet except for the occasional passing car. The world went on as though nothing happened.

"I know killing Oscar was hard on you." He ran a finger lightly over my ribs. "But you had no choice tonight. Either way, he would have ended up dead. If the same happened to you—"

He exhaled heavily. "I would have had to burn the

world down and everyone named Fiorelli with it. I wouldn't care if I didn't have the backing of the Brantleys, I'd do it anyway."

"I know you would." I shifted position, my ass brushing against his half-hard cock.

How many people would he kill before he was satisfied? I knew the answer to that, as many as it took until he was dead too.

"Lucky your quick reflexes prevented all that carnage," he said.

"That doesn't mean there won't be different carnage," I pointed out. "They'll come after Orion again. Sooner or later, they'll get tired of trying to figure out who killed Oscar and come after anyone who may have had a passing chance of pulling the trigger."

"I'm not letting anything happen to you," Aidan said firmly. "I haven't ruled out the possibility of wrapping you in bubble wrap, or stashing you on some tropical island where no one can find you."

"As enticing as that is," I said sarcastically, "I'm not going to hide for the rest of my life."

"Not for the rest of your life, just until we take care of the problem." He swiped his thumb across the skin under my breast.

"So, carnage," I concluded. "There's a saying that violence isn't the answer."

"That depends on the question. If the question is regarding anyone who might harm my wife, then violence isn't off the table. I don't want you to spend another night lying awake feeling guilty over killing someone who'd happily kill you first. You deserve better than that."

"Do I? At the end of the day, I'm just one of us." I'd killed two people, I was far from innocent.

He rolled me over to face him. "You absolutely deserve better. I don't know anyone in this world who deserves it more."

"You might be slightly biased." One of my hands rested lightly against his stomach, his light dusting of hair tickling my palm.

"Not even slightly." He kissed my forehead. "The world is full of assholes, but you're not one of them. I am, I should know." Before I could respond he added, "You know I am, don't try to deny it."

"You were hard on Orion," I said.

"First of all, he deserves it, second of all, he gave it right back. Cocky little brat." He slipped his hand back under my singlet and went on running his fingers over my skin.

"You don't like him?" I shivered involuntarily.

"I don't like most people," he said. "I love you. I tolerate Fin."

"I don't believe that," I said. "You and Fin are like opposite sides of the same coin."

"Don't forget I'm the head and he's the tail," he said quickly. "What does that make Orion then?"

"I think he's his own coin." Orion seemed like the kind of guy who lived by his own rules and fuck everyone else.

"That sounds about right," Aidan agreed. "He's a wildcard. He's unpredictable and a smartass. He's also one of the most talented players I've ever seen. If he can control his temper, he'll have one hell of a career."

"Why do I get the suspicion they said the same about you?" I teased.

"I should spank you for that." He slid his hand up further and pinched my nipple.

I jumped at the sudden pain and the jolt of electricity that ran all the way through me.

"Are you saying it's not true? You played right defence for five years in Canada before you became a coach. Don't tell me you didn't give your coaches hell?"

"My coaches were nicer than I am," he pinched my other nipple, "but the team wasn't losing as badly as the Demons. In fact, we were pretty fucking good."

"Have you ever considered being nice?" Concentrating on the conversation was getting more and more difficult. Every touch, every pinch made me wetter.

"I thought about it, but then I decided to give all of that to you," he said. "Maybe I'll be nice when they start winning."

"They won the other night," I reminded him.

"And I invited Orion into my home and gave him permission to fuck my wife," he said. "Is that not nice?"

"He's only one of them," I said. Before he could say any more, I added, "One is enough."

"Are you sure about that?" he asked. "You might

have a thing for arrogant pricks. In which case, Coast Riggs—"

"I'm not interested in Coast Riggs," I said. "I might introduce him to one of my friends though. Wren or Sinclair might be able to handle him."

"I don't want to talk about him anymore." Aidan gripped my wrists and rolled me onto my back before pinning me down to the mattress. "I don't want to talk about anyone else but you and me. Actually, I don't want to talk at all."

He brought his mouth down to mine and kissed me softly. He swept his tongue across my lips, before moving down to my neck and across my throat. He held my wrists with one hand while pushing up my singlet with the other.

"I love you," he whispered. He kneaded my breast and pinched my nipple again.

"I love you too." I half sat up to help him pull my singlet off the rest of the way and toss it aside. I lay back down as he slipped my wrists into the handcuffs attached to the headboard.

"What does Fin say to you?" Both hands free, he let them wander over my body, caressing everywhere, making my nipples hard and aching.

"He calls me a good girl," I said. "Please..." My clit was throbbing with heat and need.

"Please, what?" He caught my nipple between his teeth and bit down.

I shivered. "I need you to touch me. I need you to fuck me."

"Fin calls you a good girl, but you're such a dirty slut. That's why you need three men. Because you need to be fucked a lot. I might keep you tied to this bed so you can be fucked all day long. Would you like that?"

"Yes," I was almost panting now. "Yes, please."

He bit my other nipple before gripping the waistband of my sleep shorts and yanking them off. "Look at this perfect pussy. So needy. Are you wet, Elenna?" He ran his hands over my belly.

"Saturated," I told him.

"Of course you are, you're always drenched. Always ready for a cock." With bruising fingers, he bent my knees and spread my legs wide. He slammed two fingers straight into my pussy. "If you were any wetter, you'd leave an ocean on this bed. Perfect, dirty slut."

I cried out with the suddenness of his touch and with pleasure at feeling any part of him inside me. I wanted his cock, but his fingers were a good start.

"You like that?" He started to finger-fuck me, hard and relentless. Driving his fingers all the way to his knuckles before pulling out and shoving back in.

I whimpered. "Yes. More, please."

He turned his wrist so the heel of his hand was rubbing against my clit while his fingers slid in and out of me. "How close are you?"

"Close," I said breathlessly.

"Show me," he demanded. "Show me how a whore comes."

I lost control at his words, coming apart at the seams. I arched my back and cried out, while panting at the same time.

"Aidan…"

"That's my girl," he said, not slowing for a moment. "Give me everything."

My orgasm lasted for at least a minute or two, fireworks exploding behind my eyes, my release coating his hand.

Finally, I whimpered again before flopping down against the bed.

"That was perfect," he said. "Now you get my cock."

He slipped out of his boxers and curled his hand around his length. He pumped himself a couple of times before kneeling beside my head and tapping his tip against my lips.

"You can suck my cock before I fuck you."

I opened my mouth to take him all the way in. His head bumped against my throat, leaving a smear of pre-cum, which I swallowed when he pulled back slightly.

He gripped my hair and held my head still while pounding into my mouth. Every so often, I managed to swirl my tongue around his tip, and suck, but for the most part he roughly and relentlessly fucked my mouth.

When I thought he was going to come, he pulled out and moved to kneel between my thighs. He hooked his hands under my knees and placed my legs over his shoulders. He gripped my ass and slammed his cock into my pussy, all the way to his balls.

I barely caught my breath from having him in my mouth when he took it away again by thrusting so hard I thought he might break me in two.

I loved every minute of it. Every bit of pain. Every moment of feeling that he was in control of my body. Giving that up to him while I lay handcuffed to the bed. Knowing that if I told him no, he'd stop in an instant.

He'd pull out and tug off the handcuffs. He'd pour me a bath and get me a bowl of ice cream and a glass of wine. Whatever I needed, he'd make sure I had it. People called him an asshole, but he was attentive to me. He wanted nothing more than my happiness. Just as I wanted his.

"Your pussy is perfect." His eyes were on me while he thrust with firm, even strokes. "Look at you taking my cock like a little slut. You take me so well. You always have. You were made for me and my cock to own you and your pussy."

"Aidan…" I breathed. "I'm going to come again."

"Of course you are. I want to feel you. Come around my cock. Show me exactly who you belong to." He drove into me harder and harder, touching me all the way through, filling me up so full I'd miss him when he was done and out.

Tears came to my eyes and trickled down my cheeks. When I came, it felt so hard, so good I couldn't contain a sob. And another. While the whole world broke into a million tiny pieces, I wept. If I was a good girl or a dirty slut, this was why. These perfect moments when nothing existed except my orgasm and Aidan's body pushing mine, driving me to bliss.

My orgasm stole one from him. Just as I came, so did he, grunting and pumping faster before his body went still and he shattered too.

"Fuck… Elenna, fuck…" He let out a short, hard breath and slumped forward. "Fuck, you're always so…" He shook his head. "So fucking perfect." He panted for a while before lowering my legs down to the bed and sliding out of me.

"*You're* fucking perfect," I told him.

His response was a pant-snort. "I'm anything but perfect, but thank you for loving me. It can't be easy." He took the handcuffs off my wrists and rubbed them gently before lightly kissing my palms.

"Love isn't meant to be easy," I said. "Nothing worth having ever is."

He pulled me into his arms and smoothed down my hair. "That's very true. You're more than worth every moment."

CHAPTER 13

ELENNA

"Did I hear you right?" Sinclair flopped down on the couch and sat back against the cushions. "Finley is living here too? That sounds cosy."

I stepped over to the kitchen and turned on the coffee machine. "It is, but it's been…. interesting so far." In so many ways.

"You're my hero." Wren lowered herself more gracefully into a chair. "I can't even get a date and you're living with two guys."

"With another on the hook," Sinclair said. She frowned at Wren. "You can too get a date. You had one last week."

"If you can count that as a date," she said. "His breath smelled like fish, and his body odour wasn't much better. I had to excuse myself with a migraine after an hour. I need me a hot guy like Elenna has."

"Come to the game on Friday night. That'll be better

than a date." I grabbed three mugs out of the cupboard above the coffee machine and placed them on the counter.

"Only if I can talk to Tiger Pennington." Wren sighed. "Now his brother's taken, I've decided to switch my focus."

"That's a good strategy," Sinclair said. "Hockey players are slightly less temperamental than rock stars. Sort of."

Wren snorted. Her stepbrother, Braylon Ellis, played for the Demons. They butted heads harder than a pair of goats. Anyone could see they were hot for each other, except them.

I cleared my throat. "I can neither confirm nor deny. I haven't met Tiger's brother." He played the keyboard for the band Wolf Venom, but from what I could tell Beau Pennington, or Penn as he was known, wasn't close to his family. Neither was Tiger, that I knew of.

"But you've met Tiger." Wren sat forward eagerly. "Bray keeps telling me to stay away from his team, but —" She shrugged, her gaze shifting from me to Sinclair and back again. "A girl can be curious, right?"

"What can Bray do about it anyway?" I poured them both coffee and took them over their drinks. I picked up mine in one hand and a plate of chocolate chip biscuits in the other, before sitting on the couch beside Sinclair.

"How did your boxing session with Orion go?" Sinclair leaned forward to snag a biscuit.

I sighed out my nose and told them about the

attack. "You're safe here," I said quickly. "If Aidan thought for a moment we weren't, he wouldn't have left."

"I can just imagine," Wren said. "He'd probably be standing, leaning against a wall, watching us like a hawk. Maybe tossing a knife from hand to hand."

I laughed softly. "I've never seen Aidan tossing a knife from hand to hand."

"There's a first time for everything." Sinclair bit into her biscuit and moaned at the taste. "Mmm, so good. Did you make these?"

I was about to take a sip of coffee, but stopped just in time to prevent myself from choking on another laugh. "No, Fin did. He's a thousand times better in the kitchen than I am."

"Firstly, these are amazing," Sinclair said. "Secondly, how does he compare in the bedroom to Aidan and Orion?"

"You're right they are." I picked one up and nibbled on the corner. "I don't know about Orion, I haven't gone there yet. And I'm not comparing the other two to each other."

They both gave me a sceptical look.

"Come on, Elenna," Wren urged. "How are we supposed to live vicariously through you if you don't throw us a bone?"

"I'll throw you all the bones you want on Friday night," I told her. "What you do with them is up to you."

They both laughed.

"I know what I want to do with Tiger's bone," Wren said. "I want to ride that bad boy all night long."

We both slid sidelong glances to Sinclair.

She looked back at both of us. "What?"

"I think Wren is curious as to who you want to fuck," I said bluntly. "We know you have a crush on Coast, but didn't you used to date one of them?"

She sighed. "Gable Knox, one of the second line players, but that was a long time ago. Before he played for the Demons. We…" She paused for the longest time in history. "We took each other's virginity."

Wren squealed. "There you go. It might be time for a reunion. Show him all the things you've learnt over the years. I bet he's learnt quite a few things too. He's really good with his stick."

Sinclair stared at her for a few moments, blinked a couple of times then said, "That's exactly why I didn't tell you. Like I said, it was a long time ago. He probably doesn't remember."

"Bullshit," Wren said. "No one forgets Sinclair Rooney. And no guy forgets his first time. Chances are, he's been pining after you all these years, hoping to see you again. And here you are." She gestured toward Sinclair. "Ready to rock his world. If not, you never know who else might catch your eye."

"Wren is right," I said. "You might meet an ice hockey fan, or just have a fun night out with us. No pressure."

"Pressure," Wren disagreed.

"Fuck off," Sinclair told her. "I'll go, but I'm going to have a good time. Nothing else." She frowned. "How did the conversation get so far away from Elenna's sex life?"

"Because this topic is much more interesting than that?" I suggested. I loved them both to bits, but this situation was so new I was still getting my head around it. Discussing it in intimate detail was not something I was ready for just yet.

"Says you," Sinclair said. "I'd much rather talk about your sex life than have Wren hassle and pressure me." She cut Wren a look as though she was actually offended.

Sinclair wasn't offended so easily, especially by gentle teasing from us. We all teased each other, but when it came down to it, we took care of each other. Including driving down to pick up Wren from her terrible date when she was trying to make a quick exit. She'd do the same for either of us.

"I'd rather talk about what Orion did to mess with the Fiorellis." Wren's expression turned serious. "They've been trying to muscle in on both the Brantleys and the Bells for years. It's no secret they'd love to take them both down. They're as ambitious as the DiMarcos."

"That's saying something," I said. The DiMarco family fell out of favour with the Brantleys years ago. They'd been trying to claw their way back ever since.

"I think Phoenix DiMarco is happy being goalie for

the Demons. He's as ambitious as the rest of his family, but only on the hockey rink."

Being on a losing team didn't generally line up with ambition. Unless you're Aidan, determined to turn things around. If the whole team shared that mindset, they might just be unbeatable. If they could get along for long enough.

"He's hot though," Sinclair sighed. When we both turned to her, she shrugged. "What? I'm just saying, that's all. A girl is allowed to look."

"If you're lucky, you might get to touch," Wren said slyly.

Sinclair looked at me. "Please, please, hook her up with someone. If she gets laid, she might stop fixating on my potential sex life."

"Yes please to the first part," Wren said. "Not a chance to the second. Not when it's this much fun. And slightly less terrifying than being stuck in a dark gym with people shooting."

Sinclair frowned. "I'd like to think my sex life is a lot less scary than that. I don't know what you're imagining." She held up her hands in front of her, palms forward. "I don't want to know. In fact, please don't imagine me having sex."

Wren laughed. "No offence, but I'd much rather imagine *me* doing it."

I didn't want to think about either of them, but I just sipped my coffee and smiled.

"Are you okay?" Sinclair asked me suddenly. "You've

been a bit off kilter since Oscar. Shooting someone else can't have been easy for you."

"It wasn't, but it's better than the alternative," I said. "Do you ever get used to it?"

"Kind of," she said. "I can't say it ever gets easy, because I think I'd lose myself if it did. But it gets easier to sleep at night. It would have been harder if we didn't grow up the way we did. I was basically watching my father smash people's knuckles before I could walk."

Wren nodded. "I can't imagine what it would have been like to grow up normal."

"When you don't know any differently, it doesn't bother you," Sinclair said. "It's only later that you realise how fucked up it all is. But this is life. Even if we leave Dusk Bay, it'll follow us forever."

"Unless my father can find a way to stop laundering money and gems for Reuben," Wren said. "But considering that'll probably never happen, I guess you're stuck with me."

She didn't look like she minded too much. Being stuck with us, that was. She worked for her father making jewellery, which she loved, but it wasn't making her a billionaire anytime soon.

"It could have been worse," Sinclair said softly. "Your father could have sold you. It could have been trafficked to fuck knows where."

"It could always be worse," I said, equally softly. We were all close to our families, but sometimes life happened in ways you didn't expect. Sometimes people got desperate, and did terrible things.

"That would definitely have been worse," Wren said. She tucked a few strands of red hair behind her ear. "I would have clawed someone's eyes out. And then they probably would have cut my throat. On the upside, I wouldn't have gone through it for very long."

It was easy for her to say that, but the reality was, people like that were experts in breaking people like us. She would have been a shell of the woman she was now. We all knew it. None of us would bring children into the world without being sure it wouldn't happen to them. Strange that I might have the Brantley twins to thank for that.

"What else does Finley cook?" Sinclair asked to change the subject.

Relieved, I said, "So far, the best spaghetti I've ever had. Even better than Gianna's, if you can believe it. Last night, he cooked the most amazing roast chicken. If Aidan was ever thinking twice about the arrangement, he would have changed his mind last night. It was so fucking good. You'll have to come around for dinner sometime. I'm sure Fin won't mind cooking for more than three of us.

"Did I mention I'll be working as his assistant?" I asked. "I'll be taking over a lot of the administrative side. Keeping track of equipment and ordering replacements. It's only a few hours a week, but it gives me an excuse to be at the arena more often. And I have plenty of time to get my book finished."

"Elenna Christakos, Queen of Romance," Wren said. "When do we get to read this next masterpiece?"

I shrugged one shoulder. "When it's done. You wouldn't want to read it when it's the mess it is right now." I wouldn't inflict that on my friends. My first drafts were a bit like my life; hot, but messy as hell. It was all right for life, not so good for a book.

"I'm sure it'll be amazing," Sinclair said. "They always are. I bet there are people out there who don't realise how much truth there is in them."

"It's better they don't know," I said. "They'd never sleep at night if they did."

Sometimes, I wasn't sure how I managed to sleep myself. Of course, I never went into specifics. No one in my real life could say I based one of my characters after them, not for sure. That would be a very good way to end up very dead, very quickly.

CHAPTER 14

ELENNA

"You know he's going to chew her up and spit her out, right?" Finley nodded to where Wren and Tiger stood talking. Tiger should be warming up, but instead he was saying something that made her laugh. His gaze was intent on her like she was the only other person in the entire room.

Bray was sitting against a locker, lacing his skates and glaring at them both every time he glanced up.

"He'll have me and Sinclair to answer to if he does." As well as Bray, apparently. He didn't say a word, but his jaw moved with open irritation. I couldn't tell for certain, but it seemed to be directed at Wren, rather than Tiger, like he didn't trust her with his teammate.

I turned away and watched carefully as Finley inspected all of the sticks. He wouldn't send the players out on the ice if any were damaged in any way. A stick breaking could disrupt play. Same with broken skates or snapped laces. I hadn't realised how many seemingly small things he had to watch out for.

All of which could be big things if they went wrong.

Finley glanced up and grinned. "I'm sure you and Sinclair are terrifying."

"I know how to break a man's knuckles to give him the maximum amount of pain," Sinclair said dryly. "And his toes."

"Don't forget my eyeball shot," I said.

Finley chuckled. "I stand corrected. I should point out though, any person with a small measure of sense, knows not to screw with a redhead. I might look chill on the outside, but I have one hell of a temper when I get going. I bet Wren does too."

"She has her moments," Sinclair agreed. "Maybe we should be warning Tiger against her."

"I think he can handle himself," I said.

He was leaning in, saying something in Wren's ear. She actually giggled in response.

In all the time I'd known her, I'd never heard her giggle. She may ride his stick all night long, yet.

"Unless you're talking about me, then he probably does handle himself too much," Orion said. He stepped up close to me, not quite touching. The space felt smaller with him so close, like his presence swallowed up the air.

"We were talking about Tiger," Sinclair said.

"Then my remark stands." He nodded to her once.

"I'm sure you do your share of handling yourself," Finley told him, his words punctuated with a grin.

Orion turned his dark gaze to Finley. "I'd tell you to fuck off, but a hockey god provokes an equipment manager at his own risk."

"Wise lad." Finley leaned on a stick and gave Orion a brief smile. "You wouldn't want to break an ankle when your skate 'accidentally' snaps off."

"No more than you'd want to 'accidentally' be shot in the cock the next time we're in a dark gym," Orion replied, unsmiling.

Finley laughed. "Straight for the groin, hmmm? At least you don't fuck around, or mince words. I appreciate that."

"You're supposed to be warming up." Aidan stalked into the locker room. "You want to do yourself an injury?"

Who that was addressed to specifically, wasn't clear. Several of the players, including Tiger and Orion, were standing still, talking.

Tiger said something to Wren and she laughed again before he moved away. She was beaming when she joined Sinclair and me.

"He's so hot," she breathed. "He's even hotter up close. And he's so funny."

I turned to Sinclair. "She has it bad already."

Wren lightly socked me on the arm. "I do not." After a moment, she added, "I'd suck his cock though."

"He'd let you. That would save him having to use

his hand," Orion said before he walked away to warm up.

"I doubt a guy like that needs to touch himself," Wren said. "He probably has a different woman to do that for him every night." She sighed.

"Like Coast," Sinclair said. Her gaze followed the centre across the locker room. He was shirtless, his muscular body unashamedly on display. He caught her looking and winked.

A hint of colour crept up her face.

"*Now* who has it bad?" Wren teased.

"Javey," I said softly. He'd been watching Sinclair since we stepped into the room ten minutes ago, but now turned to glare at Coast.

"Interesting." Wren grinned at Sinclair, who responded by rolling her eyes.

"Why don't you go and get your seats?" Aidan slipped an arm around me and kissed my cheek. He hadn't wanted me in the locker room where naked players might lurk, but if I was going to work with Finley, I had to understand all the parts of his job.

I tried to be professional and avoid staring *too* long at any muscular hockey god who walked past without any clothes on. Except Orion. His grey track pants hadn't lied about the size of his cock. The sight made my brain misfire for almost a full minute. My pussy might have misfired too.

I wanted to lick the tattoos which covered both arms and all across his chest and back. The whole package had me tempted to drag him off into a corner and fuck his brains out.

"Go on, we're done here," Finley said when I glanced at him. "I'll give a shout if I need help with the guy's equipment during the game."

He raised an eyebrow at Wren when she choked back a laugh. "Wait until *after* the game before *you* handle their equipment."

She grinned. "I can be patient."

"Since when?" Sinclair drawled.

"Since I met Tiger," Wren said easily. "Although, there's a few others here I might wait for."

Before she was distracted with any of the other play-ers, I hooked my arm through hers and Sinclair's and led them out to seats at the side of the rink. Right behind the plexiglass, we had a good view of the entire game.

"Sunshine Coast Sunrays," Sinclair said. "They beat the Demons the last time they played."

"Who didn't?" I settled back in my seat. One win didn't mean they'd turned the season around.

I winced as Aidan shouted something at someone. I couldn't make it out, and I doubted the crowd would have heard over their own noise, but he sounded angry.

"They've got this," Lex Stone, the team's strength and conditioning coach, sat beside me. "Aidan barks a lot, but he's got them motivated." His gaze slid to Wren and he blinked a couple of times. She seemed completely oblivious.

"I know," I said, probably not entirely convincing.

"Then get ready to celebrate," Lex said lightly.

The team started to file out of the locker room and onto the ice. The crowd cheered. The arena was only three quarters full. The team's losing streak had lost them fans. Sinclair and the rest of the PR department, along with the team's GM, were working to bring them back. A team was nothing without its supporters.

Aidan followed them out. He glared daggers at Lex, until he realised the younger coach kept glancing at Wren.

She still hadn't noticed, or she wasn't interested. Lex was the quiet, introverted type. She was always attracted to brash men, like Tiger and Bray.

Lex noticed Aidan glaring and almost shot out of the seat to make way for him to sit beside me.

Aidan slipped his arm around me, which got us some stares from the crowd.

"Don't worry about what anyone else is thinking," he said in my ear.

"Are you reading my mind again?" I asked, my eyes on Orion as he skated over the ice. We were sitting right by his position, almost close enough to touch. Close enough for him to turn to me and nod.

"I didn't need to, it's obvious," Aidan said. "The whole arena is probably wondering what a beautiful woman like you is doing with a massive prick like me."

"Maybe because you have a massive prick," I said with a smile.

He grunted a laugh. "A woman like you wouldn't be satisfied with only a big cock. You need men who know how to use them. And their hands and tongues."

"And your brains," I said. "And sense of humour. It might surprise you to know, there's more to life than fucking."

"Yes, there's also hockey," he said with a faint smile.

"No one can accuse you of having a one track mind," I said. "Two tracks, maybe."

"Three," he corrected. "You, fucking and hockey. In that order. That's all I need in life." He kissed my temple.

"And the occasional steak," I reminded him.

"That too." He chuckled. "Excuse me for a moment." He rose and moved to the edge of the rink to speak to a couple of the players. His voice was low, but his tone quickly switched from pleasantly conversational when he was talking to me, to grumpy and direct.

"He's very different from Finley," Wren remarked. "If I had to say you had a type, I'd say hockey-mad. Finley is so much more laid-back. In relation to Aidan and Orion, anyway."

"Finley can be just as intense," I said. "He turned on the charm for you two."

"That tracks," Sinclair said. "Intense, overprotective… You definitely have a type."

I shrugged, my gaze followed Aidan as he walked over to speak to Orion. I didn't need to hear to understand the gist of that conversation. *Keep your fucking hands to yourself out on the ice.*

Orion smirked and nodded as though he'd think about it. For a moment, I thought Aidan would pull him straight off, but he turned and stalked away instead.

If anything developed between Orion and me, it would be interesting. Could they get along and not kill each other?

I sat back and watched the game begin. I kept half an eye on Aidan and the other on Finley, while following the play at the same time.

Aidan was always at his most intense and focused when the guys were on the ice, smashing the puck and skating around the rink like they were born on ice skates. The skill of being able to move around like that, handle a stick and have any control over the puck, was impressive. Especially at a professional level.

Sitting back here, watching, was a turn on. No wonder so many people liked to read hockey romance. Maybe I should write one someday. I crossed my legs at my knees and focused on the game.

Orion saved a goal at the last second and sent the puck spinning out of the defensive zone, to Tiger's stick. He drove it forward ahead of him, controlling the puck as if he wasn't aware of the opposition players checking ours to keep them from reaching him before theirs did.

He flicked the puck to Javey at the last moment,

right before he lost possession. When the opposing D-men took off after him, he shot it back to Tiger.

A second or two later, Tiger slid it back.

Orion passed it to Javey, who slammed the puck past the opposing goalie, to score the first point of the game.

The crowd went crazy, screaming out, "Demons! Demons! Demons!"

Sinclair, Wren and I were on our feet, cheering and clapping.

Wren put two fingers between her lips and whistled so loud it made my ears ring for a minute or two.

I glanced over to Aidan. He was clapping and actually smiling. It only lasted a moment, but long enough for me to see before his usual prickly expression returned.

CHAPTER 15

ORION

I narrowly avoided the temptation to smash my stick into the face of one of my opponents. I'd be sent off for the rest of the game, if not the season, if I had.

I wouldn't rule out smashing him in the face *off* the ice though. Prick deserved it. No one trips Orion Scully-Evans and gets away with it. I wouldn't kill him because he didn't succeed.

Lucky for him, we beat the Sunrays by two points. We should have beaten them by more, but I'd take the win. I had no fucking choice. Being better than they were wasn't good enough. We deserved to be the fucking best.

"I saw the way she was looking at you. You're getting some tail tonight," one of the guys said behind me. Coast Riggs.

"Fucking right I am, she was ready to get on her knees and suck my cock in here." Tiger chuckled.

No trophies for guessing who they were talking about. Elenna's friend, Wren. It was nothing but dumbass locker room talk, so I ignored it.

Until another guy joined them and said, "Aidan's wife can suck me off any time. Have you seen her mouth? It was made to take a dick."

The other two laughed. "If she was mine, I'd spend half my life down her throat. I hear she's—"

I turned around, identified the speaker as Spooner, one of the team's wingers and lunged at him. I grabbed him by the collar and rammed his back straight into one of the lockers.

"What did you fucking say?" I growled.

He looked at me in surprise. "What the hell, man? Get your fucking hands off me." He tried to shrug me off, but I held him hard.

"What. Did. You. Say?" I growled again.

"Just talking about the coach's woman, no big deal. Don't tell me you haven't noticed her 'fuck me' mouth? Are you gonna say no if she's on her knees in front of you?"

I saw red. My vision blurred with hot fury. "You don't talk that way about Elenna."

The prick actually laughed. "I heard she's fucking Fin too. Let me guess, the slut is spreading her legs for you as well?" He looked amused with himself until I drove my fist into his face.

Bone crunched. Blood sprayed out of his face, covering my jersey.

He cried out in pain. It wasn't quite as satisfying as silence. The inability to make a sound because I killed the motherfucker.

"Fucking hell." Hands grabbed me from behind and pulled me off him before I could smash my fist into his face again and again. I tried to fight them off, but they held me tight. Two of them. Tiger and Coast.

"You need to chill the hell down, bro," Coast said.

"I'm not your fucking *bro*," I snarled. "Get your hands off me."

One of the team's staff already hurried forward to press a towel against Spooner's face and lead him away.

"And you wonder why we're losing," Tiger snapped. "Save the fight for the opposition, dickhead."

"He deserved it." I managed to shake them both off. "They should be more respectful to Elenna."

"I didn't see you jumping in to defend her friends when we were talking about them," Tiger pointed out. "I guess Spooner was right then. You are fucking her too." He shot an amused glance in Coast's direction.

"Unless you want me to break your fucking nose too, back the fuck off," I said. I sucked in a hard breath. "For the record, if Aidan heard him talking like that, he would have ripped his nuts off. I'd be here for it."

I stalked away to pull off my jersey and wash Spooner's blood off me. If we were alone, I would have pounded the prick until there was nothing left but pulp. They would have had to use his teeth to identify him. If they weren't shattered into pieces.

I ignored the muttering behind me, got in the shower and turned the water on until it was warm enough to rinse blood and sweat from my skin and hair. I was pissed off with Spooner, but I was also pissed off with myself.

Coast was right. We shouldn't be fighting amongst ourselves. Spooner should have kept his stupid mouth shut. Locker talk about a single woman was bullshit enough. Saying shit like that about Elenna…

I resisted the urge to put my fist into the tiled wall and turned off the water. I stepped out to dry myself off.

Towel wrapped around my waist, I walked out of the cubicle to see Finley and Aidan both watching, clearly waiting.

"I'm fine." I held up my fist. "No need for any ice. I appreciate your concern." I opened my locker and started to pull out my street clothes. Jeans and a T-shirt. I was always warm, even in the middle of winter. Even when everyone else was wearing coats, scarves and gloves.

"Smartass," Aidan snapped. "Spooner claims you punched him and that it was completely unprovoked. I'm pretty sure he's full of shit, but this is your chance to tell your side of the story before you get benched for a couple of games." He crossed his arms over his chest like he was my father or something.

For the record, I knew who my father was, and it wasn't Aidan Draeger.

Finley looked equally unimpressed.

"It was provoked," I said. "He was being an asshole. Then he got in the way of my fist." I didn't want to miss any games, but we know what happens to snitches. Yeah, at times we were a step up from high school.

"Spooner is known for being an asshole," Finley said. "Most people know to ignore him."

He also wasn't my father.

I shrugged one shoulder. "He was being disrespectful about women."

Aidan narrowed his eyes. "That's nothing new. Women or one woman in particular?"

"If I answer that, Spooner gets a one-way ticket to a shallow grave." I didn't know why I gave a shit. He was replaceable, just like the rest of us.

Aidan's lips pressed together in a tight line. "What did he say about Elenna?" His voice could have frozen a fresh cup of coffee.

I shook my head. "It doesn't matter, I set him straight. He won't be talking about her again."

Finley muttered a few obscenities under his breath. "Did it have anything to do with our…arrangement?"

I pulled my T-shirt over my head. "He seemed to think that because she's with both of you, she's fair game for anyone else. Like I said, I set him straight."

Aidan growled. Literally growled.

"Fucking dirt bag," he snarled. "You're right about the shallow grave."

Finley put a hand on his shoulder. "Don't do

anything rash. How do you think she'd feel? We could have been more discreet."

"Fuck that," Aidan snapped. "What we do is our business. If I have to make an example of Spooner to remind everyone else of that, then that's what I'll do."

"He already has a broken cheekbone." Finley jerked his head towards me. "Possible broken jaw. He's going to be out for a while. That's enough of a reminder. No need to go off half cocked."

"I'd be going off *full* cocked," Aidan said. "He needs to—"

"Why don't you ask Elenna what her thoughts are on this?" Finley suggested calmly. "I don't think she'd want you to have someone killed because he said some cavemen stuff about her."

Finley was right. She'd be angrier at what they said about her friend than anything Spooner said about her. She was very protective of Wren and Sinclair. As they were protective of her. Not as protective as Aidan, Finley and me, but they looked out for each other.

Aidan looked ready to chew rocks, but after a few long moments he nodded reluctantly. "Fine. I won't have him killed, but only because people will ask questions and I don't want it getting back to her. No one talks about this to Elenna. Understood? I don't want her thinking she can't do whatever she wants to do because she's being judged by a bunch of cocky pricks."

"Understood," I said. I didn't want her to hear about it either. She didn't deserve any of it. Although, she did have a very fuckable mouth. If she was on her knees in front of me, I wouldn't say no. I'd fuck her mouth so hard she saw stars.

Fortunately, my towel covered my cock, which was quickly getting hard at the thought.

"Of course," Finley said. "We should play it low key for a while, until things simmer down."

"No," Aidan said immediately. "I won't have her feeling ashamed of any of this. If we start acting differently, she'll notice. We should be *more* transparent about our arrangement, not less. The sooner everyone realises how normal it is, the better. That includes you."

He nodded towards me. "If you're going to be part of this, I won't go hiding it. Take Elenna out. Be seen. Both of you. If anyone says anything about her again, speak to me and I'll deal with it. Don't risk damaging yourself because some narrow minded fuckwit has something to say about it." He fixed me with a glare like the shit Spooner said was my fault.

I wanted to argue that Elenna was more important than hockey, but I ground out, "Right. I'll try to avoid punching the snot out of the next prick who opens his mouth."

I wouldn't rule out using a hockey stick or a gun, but I could have broken my hand and that would have jeopardised the team, and not gone unnoticed by Elenna.

I needed my hand for finger-fucking her. I would have regretted not being able to make her come with my hand. A small part of me wanted to punch both of the men in front of me because they had touched her and fucked her, and I hadn't.

But I would.

"We should go and join the celly," Finley said. "The fact the three of us aren't there will raise eyebrows. Especially both of you. Considering how many goals you saved tonight, they'll all want to buy you drinks." He patted me hard on the shoulder.

If he was anyone else, I would have jerked away, but Finley had a way of making people comfortable. Even guys like me, who were uncomfortable around most other people. I was the intense, angry, hockey god that others sidestepped because I wasn't warm and fuzzy like other guys. Aidan and I had that in common. We commanded respect, if not friendship. Although, he was still working to get mine. For now, I'd get along with him for Elenna's sake.

"Are you two going to buy me drinks?" I rarely smiled, but I was capable of a deadpan joke.

"Aidan will," Finley offered. "If you're lucky, I might too."

One of Aidan's eyebrows twitched up. "Sounds like Finley is buying first. I wouldn't want to rob him of that privilege." Before Finley could protest, he added, "I insist. You can thank me later."

"Asshole," Finley teased.

"You're not the first person to make that observation," Aidan said flatly. "I doubt you'll be the last. You're just the most recent."

"I hate to be unoriginal," Finley complained. "I better come up with a better word for you then. How about pillock?"

Aidan turned to me. "I'm starting to rethink my decision not to have a shallow grave dug for Spooner. I could have them make it big enough to put Finley in as well." His smile was faint.

I snorted an almost-laugh. "You're the head coach. It's not my job to contradict your decisions."

"Ha! That hasn't stopped you yet," Aidan said. "Cocky prat."

"I've been called worse," I said. No doubt I'd be called worse in the future. Especially if Spooner came back. Guys like him usually didn't know when to give up.

CHAPTER 16

ELENNA

"Take care of her or you'll be talking through a mouthful of your own balls," Aidan growled.

"In case you're wondering, yes, he is always this charming." Finley smirked at him.

"I figured that." Orion didn't glance at Aidan while he handed me a helmet. He pushed one down onto his own head and helped me settle onto the back of his motorbike.

A shiver of nerves went through me, mixed with an equal dose of excitement.

"I'll have her back before she turns into…whatever vegetable it is." Orion threw his leg over and settled in in front of me.

"Pumpkin, and technically it's a fruit," Finley said.

Orion shot him a 'who gives a fuck' look and started the bike.

Finley shrugged. "Just trying to be accurate. Kids these days."

Aidan barked a laugh.

"Whatever you say, old man." Orion returned the smirk, gunned the engine and pulled the bike away from the curb.

I wrapped my arms tight around him, holding on for dear life, and because it felt good to touch him, even through his leather jacket. His body was warm, relief from the icy wind that whipped past.

"Where are we going?" I had to shout to be heard over the engine and wind.

"You'll see," he said. "Don't worry, you'll love it."

I didn't think he'd tell me, but it was worth a try. I got the impression he told Aidan and Finley while I'd finished getting ready for our date. Aidan would have insisted. If anything went wrong, he'd want to know exactly where to find us.

Or he wanted to know what to picture when he imagined us together. Assuming anything happened between Orion and me, that was. Electricity crackled between us like sparks of lightning, but whatever happened, happened. I wasn't going to force it, and neither was he.

This wasn't about Aidan, it was about Orion and me.

"Is it far?"

He stopped at a red light and glanced back at me.

"You can keep trying, but I'm not telling you anything until we get there. Do you trust me?"

"I wouldn't be on the back of a motorbike on the way to I-don't-know-where if I didn't," I said.

"Good to know," he said. "Sit back and enjoy the ride. I know I will." The corners of his mouth turned up slightly.

That was the closest thing to a smile I'd seen on his face yet. He kept his emotions so carefully guarded that when he smiled, even slightly, he meant it. No one could claim he was disingenuous.

What would it take to make him grin? Whatever it was, it would have to be pretty epic.

The light turned green. I held on tighter as we roared down the road and out of the city. We passed a handful of opulent homes perched on the side of the cliff. Brantley, Bell, Thomas, D'Antonio, Cassani, the wealthiest of Dusk Bay had homes here. Some of them were even occupied for part of the year.

We flew past iron gates designed to keep out people like us, and headed out into the country. Homes and carefully maintained lawns were replaced by farms and kilometre after kilometre of bush. The road became steeper and winding tighter as we rode into the mountains.

"Are we going hiking?" I asked.

The wind tore away his responding laugh. "Only if you want to. But I have something better in mind."

"Skiing?" I asked. We were close to the Victorian ski

fields. This was the perfect time of year for hard packed snow and snow bunnies.

"You're getting warmer," he said.

"I'm pretty sure I'm getting colder." I nestled down against his back. How was he so warm? I tucked my hands into his jacket pocket to thaw my fingers.

"I'll keep you warm." He slowed as the road became icy. The side of the highway was covered in banks of snow, thicker and higher, white so bright I was glad for my sunglasses.

"You always do," I shouted back. Between the firmness of his body and the thrum of the motorbike between my thighs, I was aroused as hell. If I let myself go, I could have an orgasm right here on the back of his bike.

"I try." He wound around a red hatchback that was travelling well under the speed limit, and accelerated again. He muttered something about slow drivers.

"You don't need to try," I told him.

"Neither do you. You're gorgeous and you don't even know it." He turned the bike down a long driveway.

I wanted to argue, but I didn't. Gorgeous was in the eye of the beholder. If he saw that in me, then he certainly saw something I didn't. I was pretty, I supposed, but not like Wren and Sinclair. They were the small, cute, outgoing redhead and the tall, stunning blonde. They stood out wherever they went.

Orion pulled the bike up outside a series of three

mountain cabins. Two sat with the curtains drawn over the window. The third looked more welcoming. Smoke curled out of the chimney and up into the sky.

He killed the engine and pulled off his helmet.

I followed suit and let him help me off the back of the bike. "This is cute." It was like something out of a fairytale. "I hope there isn't a witch in there that wants to eat us."

He looked amused. "If there is, she'll have to get in line." He took my helmet and wheeled the bike into a shed beside the cottage. He grabbed our bags off the back and led me inside.

The cottage was toasty warm. A fire danced in a wood stove in the middle of the living area. Orange flames were visible through the thick glass door.

Everywhere I looked was rustic charm. Timber tables and chairs, hand stitched cushions and rugs, handmade tapestries on the walls. The kitchen was all butcher block and shaker style cabinet doors. Pops of colour were everywhere, but nothing was overdone. It was pure, sweet comfort. Nothing I would have expected Orion to choose.

"Whose place is this?" I knew better than to think it was a rental. A place he found online wouldn't have the security he or the other guys would have insisted on. Or me, if I was honest with myself.

"It's mine," he said. "It used to belong to my aunt. She left it to me and my sister, but she doesn't get down here very often. Apparently Victoria is too cold for a

Queenslander like her. We have a neighbour we trust to maintain it and get the fire started whenever we come here. The fridge should be fully stocked."

"You're full of surprises," I told him.

"I'm often told I'm full of something, but not usually surprises." He carried our bags over to one of the bedrooms and lowered them to the floor.

I laughed. "You don't need to paint me a picture. For the record, I don't think you're full of shit."

"Give me a day or two and you might change your mind. Are you ready to see what we're doing for the next couple of hours?" He walked over to a cupboard and pulled the doors open. Inside was full of snow clothes. Thick coats, pants and boots. "There should be something that will fit you." He grabbed out a coat and a pair of pants and handed them to me.

His fingers brushed against mine as I took them. A bolt of lightning passed right through me, both from his touch and the amused expression on his face.

"You thought I brought you here just for one thing?" Before I could respond, he said, "As far as I'm concerned, this is a real date. That includes doing something fun, then having a nice dinner. Getting to know each other. I'm not Coast Riggs or one of the other guys. I don't want to stick my cock into anything that stays still for long enough. I've fucked my share of women."

He pulled a jacket out of the wardrobe for himself and started to shrug into it. "The moment I saw you, I wasn't interested in anyone else. I want to see where this'll go, but I won't rush into it. I don't want you to rush into it. I want you to know who and what I am before things go any further."

I nodded. "I respect that. My relationships with Aidan and Fin complicate things. It's definitely not something to leap into without looking to see exactly where you'll land." I laid the pants across a chair and pulled on the coat.

"Everyone comes with baggage," Orion said wryly. "You just happen to come with two old dudes who will chop my cock off if I use it wrong."

I laughed and reached for the pants to pull them on over my jeans. What would they think about being called old dudes? Neither of them were old, just older than Orion. So was I, by a year or so; what did that make me?

"So if we're not skiing, and we're definitely not lying on a beach drinking cocktails, then what *are* we doing?" I sat down and pulled on a pair of boots he handed me.

"Are you always so impatient?" he asked.

"I'm not impatient, I'm just curious," I retorted, pretending to be offended.

"Good, because you'll find out soon enough." He pulled on his own boots and led me back outside. Back to the shed where he'd put the motorbike. "Stay outside."

He disappeared into the shadows, returning a minute or two later with a huge, round toboggan. Made of red plastic, it looked like it had a lot of use, but was still strong and solid.

"I was going to take us snowboarding, but I thought this might be a more gentle introduction to snow sports."

I cocked my head at him. "You don't know how to snowboard, do you?"

"Of course I fucking do," he protested. "I can ice skate, can't I?"

"One doesn't necessarily mean you can do the other," I pointed out.

He grunted and carried the toboggan over to a nearby slope which was clear of all but a couple of trees. "I can snowboard, but it's been a long time. If you really want to know, I always preferred this. It makes me feel like a kid again."

His late aunt's cabin, a childhood favourite activity. I never expected him to be so sentimental, but I liked it. It was sweet.

"Have you ever brought anyone else here to do this?" I asked.

"Never. It felt too personal before." He held onto the toboggan and helped me to step inside and sit down.

I heard the catch in his voice and looked back to see his eyes slightly glazed. He must have a lot of amazing memories of spending time here as a child. The fact he wanted to share that with me touched me in a way I never expected. This was the man underneath the badass hockey god. He was as vulnerable as the rest of us.

Showing himself to me like this made my heart flip a couple of times. I could very easily fall hard for this guy. As hard as I had for Aidan. As hard as I was falling for Finley. Orion felt like the missing puzzle piece that was slowly working its way into place.

He climbed on behind me and wrapped one arm around me while grabbing the rope to control the toboggan with the other.

"Ready?"

I glanced back over my shoulder to see him actually smiling. There was something endearingly boyish and playful in his expression.

"Ready!"

I squealed as we started the slide down the slope.

CHAPTER 17

ELENNA

I sank deep into the water of the massive tub. The hot water and bubbles embraced my body, drawing a soft sigh from between my lips.

The stiffness in my muscles gradually eased, strained from pulling the toboggan back up the slope so many times I lost count. The more times we haired down, barely in control, the more Orion seemed to relax as well. By the end, he was almost smiling and laughing. He was, at least, enjoying himself, like the weight of the world was lifted off his shoulders and he could live for a while.

No wonder he liked tobogganing so much.

"Dinner won't be long," he called out. "The neighbour left a few things we can throw in the oven." His words were followed by a clatter of dishes and the opening and closing of the oven.

He peeked into the bathroom. "Hot enough for you?"

"It's perfect," I said. "It's a little lonely though."

His left eyebrow twitched up slightly. "Is it now? That sounds neglectful to me. How much trouble would I get in if I neglected you?"

"A lot," I said with a slow nod. "It would be grounds for…leaving lemon juice in your water bottle. Or frogs in your locker."

"Both of those would be very serious," he said. "Much worse than being kicked off the team."

"I wouldn't joke about you losing your career," I said. "But I *will* joke about frogs. Or maybe slices of pumpkin. Finley was right, you know, it is a fruit."

"Fin would know." Orion shrugged. "He seems to know all sorts of random shit. I bet he knows what a banana really is."

"I think you might be right." I sank down deeper into the bubbles, my gaze on him as he peeled off his T-shirt. No wonder he was so warm all the time, his body was smoking hot. His chest was broad and muscular, torso sculpted. Perfectly defined abs and flat stomach led down to the V of his hips.

"He'd probably say something corny like suck my banana." He undid the front of his jeans and with almost painful slowness, eased them down his legs.

I laughed, but it was choked with my sudden need to touch him. "That does sound like something he'd say."

Orion stepped out of his jeans and kicked them aside. Dark blue boxers covered his cock, but couldn't contain how hard he was getting.

I licked my lips.

He knelt down beside the bath and hooked a hand around behind the back of my neck. "Elenna," he said softly.

"Orion."

His lips were almost pressed to mine. "You're beautiful." He brushed them over the corner of my mouth.

"You're beautiful," I replied.

"Not as beautiful as you." He kissed me harder, more demanding. His stubble lightly tickled my face, but I deepened the kiss.

I swiped my tongue over his lips and slipped it inside his mouth.

He let his teeth graze over my tongue, biting gently. He slipped one hand under the water and cupped my breast.

"I feel like I've waited years to touch you," he whispered. "Lifetimes. I think we knew each other before, a thousand times. Every time, we had to find each other, and we did."

Kissing him was different to kissing Aidan and Finley, but it felt just as much like home. If past lives were a thing, we definitely knew each other. Maybe a thousand times, maybe more. Maybe a million.

We kissed while the smell of food grew stronger and stronger.

We kissed until an alarm in the kitchen dinged.

Reluctantly, he pulled back. "Sounds like dinner is ready. I'll go and fix it up while you get dry."

I sighed, but watched him stand and disappear out of the room. I climbed out of the bath, quickly rubbed a towel all over myself before pulling on a dark blue, thick dressing gown.

I stepped out of the bathroom as he finished setting up dinner on a plush rug in front of the fire. Plates of what looked like vegetable bake and two glasses of wine.

"This is very romantic." I knelt down beside him before lowering myself to my ass.

"Do me a favour and don't tell anyone." He handed me a glass of wine. "I have a reputation to maintain. Defenceman, hockey god, asshole, badass. If they knew I served up dinner in front of a roaring fire while dressed only in my boxer shorts, they might think I've gone soft."

"I don't think anyone could accuse you of going soft." I eyed his groin. Definitely not soft. "But your secret's safe with me." I poked my fork into a piece of potato and bit down on the cheese-covered goodness. It was so tasty my eyes almost rolled back in my head.

"Is that the only secret you want to keep from them?" He clearly had something specific in mind.

I swallowed and looked at him questioningly. "Probably not. Why?"

He shrugged as though it wasn't a big deal. "People

talk. I know polyamory isn't new, but some people have small minds."

"You don't want anyone to know?" I wasn't sure if that stung or not. It might depend on his response.

"I don't want anyone saying dick things about you. If you didn't want everyone to know about us..." He shrugged and bit into a piece of broccoli.

"I don't mind who knows. I have nothing to be ashamed of. If other people have a problem with it, that's their problem, not mine. Not ours." I frowned. "Unless you want to keep it a secret?"

"Nope," he said immediately. "You're right, it's their problem. They can fuck off and keep it to themselves."

"Is that why you punched Spooner?" I asked. "Fin and Aidan told me, but they wouldn't tell me why. Something about a team disagreement."

"Yeah, that's all it was." Orion wouldn't meet my gaze. There was clearly more to it, but I wouldn't push him.

"Okay," I said lightly. If he wanted me to know, he'd tell me. If I needed to know, Aidan or Finley would have told me already. Wouldn't they? Maybe they were trying to protect my feelings. Should I be annoyed by that?

I pushed the thought aside. From what Orion implied, Spooner made some remark about my relationships with the guys. If he couldn't handle it, there was no reason for me to give a shit. Without doubt, Spooner wouldn't be the last. I wasn't going to change for some player and their small-minded bullshit. Life was too short for that. I decided to change the subject.

"You used to come up here a lot?" I asked. "As a kid?"

"Every winter." He seemed relieved to talk about something else. "We used to spend hours on the toboggan, or having snowball fights. Or skiing or snowboarding. The first two, mostly, because the other two were expensive. The only reason we got to come here was because my aunt owned the place. We didn't have to pay to rent anywhere."

"Who owns the other two?" I picked up my wine and took a sip.

"One is owned by Anderson Devlin, the CEO of Devlin Air. The other is owned by Joshua Brantley. Both of them are bigger than this one. And usually empty. I think they own the places for the sake of owning the places. Some people have too much money."

"They certainly have a lot," I agreed. "All six of the Devlin brothers are at least multimillionaires. The Brantley brothers too." What would it be like to have that kind of money? I did okay, but I was no billionaire.

"Yeah, and both of them have tried to buy this place," Orion said. "Even offered double what it's worth. I refused. My sister would like to sell, but…"

"The place holds too many memories?" I guessed.

"That probably sounds fucking ridiculous." He sipped his own wine. "The memories are in my head, this place is just a place."

"It's a beautiful place," I said. "And we're making new memories here right now. They might be able to put a price on that, but I can't. I've never been anywhere like this and I've never ridden on toboggan. I've never eaten dinner in front of a fireplace, sitting on a rug."

"You're making me glad I didn't sell," he said. "In fact, if my sister wants money that much, I'll offer to buy out her half." He looked thoughtful. "I wonder what the other two would cost."

"I'm thinking a shit ton," I said. I had a fair idea how much money he made. It would be a lot even by his terms. "What would you do with the other two anyway?"

He shrugged. "Make sure we're never interrupted." He took my empty plate and glass and put them aside with his.

His hands lightly on my shoulders, he kissed me. Gently at first, then more demanding, like he couldn't get enough.

Neither could I. One taste of his mouth was addictive. I wanted, needed, so much more. His lips were warm, soft, confident. He knew what he was doing, but more than that, he knew doing it with me was right.

It was everything.

If I had any doubts about what might develop between us, they evaporated. Melted like the snow in spring.

He pressed me back to the rug and undid the belt of my robe with one tug. He peeled back one side, then the other, like he was opening the best present he ever got. Wide eyes raked up and down my body, drinking me in like I was fine wine. Or chocolate cake for his dessert.

"So bloody beautiful," he breathed. He traced the tip of his finger around one nipple as though he didn't quite believe I was real. He leaned down to replace his finger with his tongue. "You even taste good."

"It's probably the rose scented bath bomb," I said with a small laugh. Mostly, my attention was on how good it felt to have him touch me.

His laugh echoed mine. "It's definitely you." He closed his mouth around my nipple and sucked a couple of times before moving to the other one.

Slowly, he kissed his way down my body until he reached the junction between my thighs. "I bet you taste good here too." He eased my legs open and lowered his face until his nose tickled my pussy. "You smell good. If I died right now, I'd die in heaven. But I won't. Not until you come."

Barely touching me, he slid his tongue up my seam, and over my clit.

I shivered with the delicious sensation he sent coursing all the way through me.

"I was right," he said. "You *do* taste good." He started licking and sucking my clit before sliding a finger inside me.

"You *feel* good," I said.

"Do you want me to keep doing this?" He lifted his face and looked at me. "Tell me what you want."

His wasn't the demanding, dominating tone of Aidan, or Finley's sweeter, 'wanting to please me' tone. This was Orion asking me to tell him what to do. For me to be the one to dominate him. He was so in control of every other aspect of his life, he preferred to relinquish it in the bedroom. Or on the rug.

This was new to me, but I could take control.

"I want you to keep licking me," I said decisively. "I want your fingers inside me until I come."

He nodded, lowered his face again and went back to licking and sucking while adding a second finger to the first. Then a third. He worked me steadily, eyes on me for my reaction to every swipe, flick and lick.

"Orion…" I groaned. "Just like that, right there." He hit me inside and out in exactly the right places, driving me wilder and wilder. Flying down the slope faster than a red toboggan. There were no trees here, though, just bliss.

I arched my back and came hard, rocking against his face.

When he slid his fingers out of me, I moved to tug off his boxers and toss them aside.

I already knew he was big, but seeing him up this close was something else. His cock was thick, long and heavy. Red and purple with blood. The pulse under his length throbbed with rhythmic need. I wrapped my fingers around his length and pumped a couple of times.

He groaned in response, eyes half closed.

"I want to suck your cock." I lowered my mouth to him, swirled my tongue around his tip. The bead of pre-cum that leaked from his slit tasted sweet and salty. Delicious. I lightly massaged his balls with my fingers, making him harder, tenser.

He tilted his chin back and groaned. "Your mouth is so perfect." His voice was strained.

I took him all the way to the back of my throat and sucked. He thrust into my mouth slowly, his breath coming in ragged pants. I wanted to taste his cum, but I wanted to feel him inside me even more.

I slid my mouth off him. "Do you want to fuck me?" I teased his tip with the edge of my tongue.

"Do you want me to?" His eyes were dark with need, the response right there, even if he didn't say it out loud.

I didn't answer in words either. I straddled his hips and lowered myself down onto him. I took his hands in mine and pressed them to my breasts. While he palmed my nipples, I placed my hands on his chest and slid up and down his cock, nice and slow at first. Increasing in speed as he pushed his hips up, thrusting into me.

"Fuck, Elenna. You're perfect. So bloody tight."

I watched his face. The expression of bliss on his handsome face. The determination to hang on for as long as he could. He was on the edge of coming, but he held himself back until he couldn't anymore.

"I want you to come inside me," I whispered.

My words made him come completely undone. He

thrust into me several more times, grunted as he came hard, spilling himself inside my body.

The friction and sounds he was making made me come for a second time, harder than the first. The entire world disappeared, leaving nothing, but me and him, and a universe of fireworks.

I arched my back and screamed his name so loud my throat hurt. My orgasm went on for approximately an eternity before it finally abated, letting me catch my breath.

Light headed, but satisfied, I slumped down over his chest, content to lie on his warmth with his cock still buried deep inside me.

CHAPTER 18

FINLEY

I watched Aidan watching Elenna, Orion and me. She sat with a book in her hand, her legs over Orion's lap, feet on mine. I massaged her toes and tried to interpret the expression on Aidan's face.

I'd known him longer than anyone else in the room, but I couldn't always tell what he was thinking. It could be anything from pleased she was happy, to just about ready to shoot Orion and me in the eyeballs.

Wanting her to get everything she wanted was perfection in theory, but didn't stop him from being a jealous, possessive man.

She cast him a sidelong look. I figured she'd notice. She hadn't turned the page for at least five minutes.

"I think we all noticed Aidan has something to say," Orion said. "If you're about to throw Fin and I out on our asses—"

Elenna sat up straighter, her foot sliding out of my grip. "You're not—"

"I'm not throwing anyone out," Aidan snapped. "That isn't what this is about." He stalked from one side of the room to the other.

"What is it about?" I grabbed her foot and resumed rubbing the ball with the pad of my thumb.

"This is about the Fiorellis and how sooner or later they're going to stir up more shit. We need to be prepared." He rubbed a finger back and forth across his lower lip.

"We're not prepared enough?" Orion asked.

Elenna put down her book and started to wring her hands, like she did whenever the topic came up. She tried to be subtle, but I think we all noticed. I presumed it had something to do with killing Oscar, but unless she was willing to talk about it, I'd never know for sure.

"We're prepared," I said. "As prepared as we'll ever be. We take every precaution."

"You don't think it's enough?" Elenna said softly. "That no matter what we do, it might not be enough?" To her credit, her face no longer went pale when we had these conversations. She wasn't going to grab a rocket launcher and lead the charge, but she'd hold her own no matter what came at us.

"What are you proposing?" Orion said bluntly. "If you don't think three of us are enough to keep Elenna, and each other, safe, then what?"

"Is this where you suggest we put our money

together and buy one of those impenetrable mansions on the cliff?" I said, half joking. "I might have a few dollars in my piggy bank."

"It would take more than a few dollars," Aidan said. "I think we need to think bigger than that."

"A few hundred dollars?" I massaged each of Elenna's toes, one by one.

"Bigger than running away," Aidan said, his expression dark.

"Please tell me you're not suggesting going after the Fiorellis," I said. "We don't have the resources for that."

"No we don't," he agreed. "But who seems to have taken over from Dante?"

"Nicholas and Celine," Elenna said.

"Exactly," he said. "We can sit here and wait for them to come at us again or we can deal with them first."

"They didn't exactly come after us," I pointed out. "They wanted Oscar's killer. I don't think they were in a mind to start anything with us. As far as they knew, killing us wouldn't achieve much of anything. Apart from pissing off Aidan."

"Exactly," Aidan said. "They want Oscar's killer. So we give them what they want."

We all sat up higher then.

"What the fuck?" Orion snarled. "You are *not* handing over Elenna." In a short amount of time, he seemed to have grown as attached to her as Aidan and me. From the look he gave Aidan, he was about to rip his heart out with his bare hands.

"Aidan?" Elenna asked.

"No," Orion snapped. "I don't care what justification he has, I won't allow—"

"I'm not suggesting we hand over Elenna," Aidan said. "Maybe you can shut the fuck up and listen." He shot daggers at Orion with his eyes.

Orion glared, but he fell silent.

I gave Aidan an 'out with it' gesture with my hand but also said nothing.

"It's very simple," Aidan said. "We already know they want Orion dealt with. We just have to convince them he's the one who killed Oscar, on the orders of whichever the fuck Brantley you want to name. The Fiorellis aren't going to stop to ask questions."

"You're going to give me up to them," Orion concluded. He seemed undecided if he was furious or not.

"Doing that would solve about ninety-nine percent of my problems right now," Aidan said. "They won't stop coming until they've got you. If they think you killed Oscar, then Elenna is off the hook. They'll forget all about her and her relation to Ike. She can get on with her life without looking over her shoulder."

She looked stricken. "I can't ask Orion to surrender himself for me."

"I'll do it," Orion said. "Aidan is right. This will solve a bunch of problems."

Elenna stared at him. "You *can't*."

"I can and I am," he said evenly. "I should have thought of it myself."

"That's why Aidan is the brains of this outfit," I said dryly. I gave him a long, hard look. Like always, his expression gave away nothing. He was even more of a closed book than Elenna's paperback.

Aidan smirked. "That's me. Asshole and mastermind."

Elenna threw her legs off me and Orion and stood, her hands on her hips. "Do I get any say in this? Is this your way of getting rid of Orion? Do you have a plan to get rid of Fin too?"

"He better fucking not." I also stood. "You don't, do you?" If he did, I might get rid of him first.

Aidan rolled his eyes. "Of course not. Unless you've recently done something to put a target on your back with the Fiorellis or the Bells. Or the Brantleys for that matter."

"Unless you count taking care of a few henchmen in the gym," I said. "In which case, you're just as big a target as me."

Elenna looked around at all of us, horrified. "You can't be serious? I'm the one they want more than anyone else. If anyone is going to be handed over, around here—"

"It's not going to be you," Aidan told her. He took her hands in his. "Do you trust me?"

"I want to," she said slowly.

He squeezed her hands more tightly. "Do you trust me?" he repeated.

She didn't meet his gaze. Her eyes were looking at approximately the centre of his chest.

He made a sound of frustration in the back of his throat, put a hand under her chin and raised it so they were face-to-face.

"I'd never do anything to hurt you," he said.

"Then why..." She shook her head. "What if they don't have any plans to come after any of us ever again? Their resources diminished after Dante died. A lot of people won't touch them."

"A lot of people will," Aidan said. "They have enough resources to send ten people after Orion. Next time, they might send twenty. Nicholas and Celine are pissed off. That's not going to change while we sit on our hands and hope they forget we exist. People like them, they hold grudges. You know that as well as I do."

"I know but..." She sighed heavily. "You've all made up your mind, haven't you? It doesn't matter what I say, you're going to do this anyway. It doesn't matter how I feel."

"It very much matters how you feel," Aidan said. "But if I have to choose between you and Orion, I choose you."

"I choose her too," Orion said. "I choose her over myself." His expression was just as guarded as Aidan's.

"So fucking noble," I muttered.

Elenna turned to me. "Fin." She silently begged me to say something. Some reason why this was a really bad idea.

I shook my head. "I'm sorry. I tried to suggest a mansion, but apparently they think this is a better idea."

My attempt at humour fell flat. She pressed her lips together so hard her skin turned white.

"When?" Somehow she managed to keep her voice from shaking. She looked like she might use a knife or gun on one of us if she had one in her hand. When all of this sunk in, she was going to be furious. It was just as well Aidan suggested it, not me. She could be angry with him instead.

"I'll put out some feelers," Aidan said. "We'll see how long it is before they take the bait. Knowing them and how desperate they are for answers, it won't take long."

She nodded. "If you're determined to go through with this, then I can't stop you, but if you get yourself killed in the process…"

"I won't," Aidan said. "Fin and I will be fine. The Demons will be fine."

"Everyone but Orion," she said bitterly.

"I knew what I was getting into when I screwed around with the Fiorellis," Orion said. His voice was completely flat, devoid of all emotion, his expression one of acceptance.

"Sooner or later, I'd end up dead because of it. I have no regrets. Saving all those women was worth the life of one asshole hockey god." He shrugged like he'd just opened the window and let his last fuck fly away on the winter breeze.

"This is bullshit," Elenna said. "Can't we find some nice remote island somewhere and live our lives?"

She looked ready to run-off and pack a suitcase right now. Honestly, I'd be right behind her. A remote tropical island sounded pretty fucking good right now.

"They'd notice if all four of us disappear," Aidan said. "Sooner or later, they'd find us. We can spend the rest of our lives looking over our shoulders, or we can do this."

Elenna gave him a sharp look, then took Orion's hand. "I want to talk to you, alone."

He glanced at us, but let her lead him away. The door closed firmly behind them.

I patted Aidan hard on the shoulder. "Good job. I hadn't realised you were such a strategist. With hockey, yes, but not with Elenna's love life."

"What are you talking about?" he asked.

"Inviting him in and letting him get close enough to her that he'd sacrifice himself for her," I explained. "That's fucking genius. I should have thought of that myself."

He scowled at me.

"You're not denying it," I pointed out.

"It's the only choice we have," he said simply. "The only way we can protect her and ourselves."

I'd never heard his voice sound so stone-cold ruthless. Not even when Elenna ran away and he was ready to rip the world apart and kill everyone in it to get her back. This was something so dark, he gave me chills.

I stepped away from him and nodded. "All right. I guess this is what we're doing then. I'll get dinner started."

CHAPTER 19

"You're just going to go along with this?" I demanded. "You're going to let Aidan hand you over to Nicholas and Celine and that's it?"

Orion shrugged. "I'm not letting him hand you over. Just a wild guess here, you're not going to let me hand him over either."

I stopped with my mouth hanging open. It hadn't crossed my mind that was an option, but as far as I was concerned, it wasn't. Neither was this.

"That would be a no." Orion stalked over to the window and looked out, arms crossed over his chest.

"Orion…" I exhaled in frustration.

"Like Aidan said, they will keep coming after me," he said without looking back. "Even if Aidan handed himself over to them, they'd come after me. I don't know, maybe that's the answer. You and Finley can live a long and happy life together. He'd like that."

"I don't think he would," I said. "I certainly wouldn't. I don't want to lose any of you. I just found you." I couldn't believe they'd turn around and tear my heart out like this. And no one seemed bothered by it. No one but me.

He turned around. "You know what our lifestyle is like. People die all the time. Ten men came after us in the gym and none of them went home. It could easily have been us killed that night. And Aidan and Finley. Next time it might be all of us. We have to do what we have to do to prevent that from happening. It's that simple."

"It's not simple at all," I protested. "I know what they're going to do to you. They won't just kill you, not outright. They'll hand you over to someone like Ice Miller. They'll keep you alive for days." I couldn't stop the tears from trickling down my cheeks.

"Better me than you." He swept my tears away with his thumb.

"Why, because you're a big, badass hockey god? You'll feel the pain as much as I would. They'll make you scream and beg for mercy." How could he be so fucking calm? I was a nervous wreck. I wanted to grab all three of them by the back of the head and bang their heads together until they saw sense.

I was tempted to hunt down Nicholas or Celine and come clean about what happened to Oscar. They could kill me just like they killed my brother. I could make up some story about how I helped the twins screw with their human trafficking operation, and that Orion took the blame for me. Wasn't that what he was doing anyway? Why should he take the blame for me when I could take the blame for myself?

"No," he said firmly. "I know exactly what you're thinking and the answer is no. If you even consider it, I'll go back out there and tell Aidan and he'll handcuff you until all of this is over. You know he will."

"You won't do that," I said. I put out a hand when he took a step towards the door. "I could handcuff you to the bed."

The side of his mouth drew up and he looked smug. "I'd like to see you try."

I narrowed my eyes at him. "You think I can't? You might be underestimating how angry I am right now."

He scoffed slightly. "No I'm not, I just know I'm twice as big as you." He held out his hands to both sides. "But by all means, go ahead."

I placed my hands on his chest and shoved him back towards the bed. I shoved him a step before he gave up all resistance and let me push him onto his back. He grabbed my arms and pulled me down with him so I lay on top of his body.

"I'm starting to think this was your plan," I said.

"Maybe it was." He rolled me over and lay on top of me, his knees between my legs. "A guy should have one more fuck before he goes to his death, shouldn't he?"

I slapped his chest. "Don't joke about it. I still haven't decided if I'm going to let you sacrifice yourself." I rolled us back the other way, straddled his hips and tugged at the hem of his T-shirt.

He lifted his arms and let me pull it off over his head. He looked like he might argue one more time, but then he was helping me out of my Demons hoodie and long sleeved shirt.

He tugged my bra straps off my shoulders and let them slide down my arms. "So beautiful."

I reached back to unhook my bra and tossed it aside.

I wanted to tell him he was the beautiful one, but I didn't want to start another argument or another conversation. If I did, we'd only end up back on the same topic, going around in circles.

I wasn't giving up so easily, but could I sway any of them? They were stubborn and they'd made up their minds. But then, so was I.

He pinched my nipples lightly, letting them harden under his touch. At the same time, he looked at them like he'd never seen them before. Or rather, like he never expected to see them again.

I shoved that out of my mind for now and undid the front of his jeans. He lifted his hips so I could tug them down, freeing his thick, half-erect cock.

I wrapped my fingers around his length and worked him up and down until he was fully hard. It didn't take long, no more than half a dozen pumps. He was as ready as I was.

"If you want me to come in your hand..." He groaned.

"I don't," I said. "I want you to come in my mouth."

I kissed my way down his body, teasing his abs with my tongue. I dropped little kisses here and licks there until I reached his cock. I teased my way around his head, licking pre-cum from his tip. His hips twitched in response.

My eyes on his, I opened my lips and captured as much as I could of him with my mouth.

"Fuck… You have the most perfect mouth." He rolled his hips, pushing himself deeper down my throat. He tapped the back, but pulled out slightly when I gagged.

"Elenna, I—"

I took my mouth off him. "Don't hold back. Give me everything." I lowered my mouth back onto him, sucking while his eyes darkened.

My words acted like some kind of switch. Where before he was careful and gentle, now he fucked my mouth with no restraint. His breathing was more and more ragged each time he made me gag.

"How are you so perfect?" he gasped out. He reached down to take a fistful of my hair and hold me there while he pounded into me.

I smiled at him with my eyes and let my tongue run up and down the vein on the underside of his cock. He was so thick, hot and tasty. I could have sucked on him all day.

And his reaction— That was everything. Watching him become more and more undone with every suck and thrust was compelling and arousing. On the ice, he was the image of control. Here, he was anything but. Everything he felt right now was because of me. Because of my mouth, my tongue, my lips. My fingers on his balls. I was the one driving him wild. I was the one driving him closer and closer to coming.

I watched him reach the edge and tip over. His body stilled. He squirted hot cum down my throat, forcing me to swallow every drop of his release.

Even after I had, I went on sucking and licking, milking him, making his orgasm last as long as I could. I wanted him to feel it from his toes to the top of his head, like I always did. Like he did to me.

He finally stopped shuddering and flopped back, his fingers slipping from my hair. His eyes rolled back and he was all but limp.

"Fucking hell, Elenna, you're amazing. So generous and so fucking hot. I could die right now with your mouth on my cock and have no regrets."

I slowly drew my mouth off him. "No dying right now." I wanted to order him, to tell him he could never die, but that wasn't going to happen. Whether it was tomorrow or eighty years from now, we couldn't hide from the inevitable. At some point, I would lose him. I'd lose all of them. Or they'd lose me.

"Same to you." He took a moment to catch his breath before he gripped my hand and pulled me up to the pillows. Once I was comfortable against them, he scooted down the bed and parted my legs with his hands.

He slid his thumb over the entrance to my pussy. "You're so wet." He slid his thumb inside me and turned it around slowly, until it was coated with my juices. He pulled it out and replaced it with two of his fingers, before pressing his thumb into my rear hole.

"Is this okay?" he asked.

"More than okay." I reached over to the table beside the bed and pulled out a vibrator and a tube of lube. I handed them both to him. I swallowed but nodded. I was certain of what I wanted him to do to me.

He slipped his fingers out of me and coated the vibrator in lubricant. Bending my knees gently, he pried my legs open wider and pushed the tip of the vibrator into my ass.

I shivered slightly but forced myself to relax and let him put the toy in deeper. It felt strange and good at the same time. Full in the way I'd only felt a time or two before.

He slid the vibrator in deeper, while slipping two of the fingers of his other hand back inside my pussy. With a slow rhythm, he worked my ass and pussy at the same time.

"That feels incredible," I said breathlessly. It felt even more amazing when he lowered his mouth to my clit, his tongue flicking lightly while he thrust in and out of me. He set my whole body on fire.

"Orion, more. Deeper."

He obliged, pressing his fingers and the vibrator in deeper but still careful.

"I feel so full." I rocked my hips slowly, savouring every feeling, every sensation as if I could bottle it for later. If I could, I'd make enough money to buy the whole world. I didn't need the world, I just needed this, right now. Him playing my body like I was an instrument and he was an expert musician.

"Come for me, Elenna," he whispered. He licked and teased and stroked, determined to make me come. His fingers were so deep he'd feel my muscles clench around them. He must be able to feel the vibrator through the thin wall between my pussy and my ass.

I don't know if it was that thought, or a thousand sensations in my pussy and ass, but I came so hard my whole body screamed with pleasure. Every nerve ending inside me exploded with bliss. My vision went dark except for a pinwheel of fireworks that cascaded all around me.

I was vaguely aware of crying out his name somewhere in the middle of my orgasm. I wanted to stay in this place forever. Too soon, I was coming down, floating back to earth. Flopping back as he slid the vibrator and his fingers out of me.

"I fucking love when you come," he said. "Knowing what I do to you. Me, not Aidan or Finley."

"You," I whispered. "You make me feel amazing." Right then, I was breathless and boneless. Utterly satisfied. For the time being.

I dropped my head back to the pillow and sighed. There had to be a way that he didn't have to make the sacrifice for me. I couldn't lose him so soon. I *wouldn't*. I didn't know how, but I was going to stop the Fiorellis from killing him. Even if I had to kill again to do it.

CHAPTER 20

ELENNA

"Phoenix needs new shin guards," Finley said in a rush. "No, not those ones, the other ones." He waved vaguely.

I put aside the first set I picked up, and grabbed another. "These?" I was yet to work out exactly what the difference was, but Finley always seemed to know. Not just their size, but their preference for one brand over another, or one fit over another. Whatever it was, he knew what every player needed, even the newer ones.

He flashed me a grin. "Yep. Don't worry, you'll learn them all, in time." He grabbed the guards and hurried over to where Phoenix was getting ready.

I watched the goaltender pull on the shin guards without really seeing what he was doing. Instead of paying attention, I was wondering if Phoenix could pull any strings with his brother, Ric, to ask the Brantleys to deal with the Fiorelli family once and for all.

I sighed. Aidan had more clout with Caleb than

Phoenix or his brother did. If Aidan couldn't get them to help, then there would be no point in involving Phoenix. Realistically though, Phoenix wouldn't have involved himself. His priority was the man he saw when he looked at himself in the mirror. The team was his second love.

Phoenix must have felt me watching, he looked up. Our gazes met for a second or two before his slid away like I was too far beneath him to pay any attention to.

Yeah, he was definitely not getting involved.

"Don't waste your time with him." Coast stepped up to me, his helmet dangling from his fingers. "His head is too far up his ass to have time for anyone else."

I didn't think Phoenix heard until he flipped Coast off.

Coast chuckled. He pressed a hand to the wall behind me and leaned in. "I was thinking, can you ask Aidan if I can switch numbers? I like seven, but I much prefer sixty-nine." He gave me a wink.

"If you want a tongue to do sixty-nine with, you should back the fuck off before Aidan hears you," I said sweetly.

"Feisty," he said, his smile not diminished in the slightest. "I like that in a woman. If you ever get tired of Aidan, Fin, or Orion, or want to squeeze in another guy, you know where to find me."

"I'll bear that in mind," I said. "I like a man who knows when no means no."

"Ouch," he laughed. "She shoots, she scores. Direct

shot, right through my heart." He pressed a fist to his chest.

I smiled in spite of myself. "I have a feeling you'll get over it. Right around the next time you see a woman."

He pouted playfully. "I'm not that easy. It'll take at least a good five or six minutes to recover."

"That's the spirit." I placed the tips of my fingers on his chest and pushed past him. "It's healthy to be resilient."

"I hope you do better on the ice today than that." Tiger scowled at him.

"Yeah, we want to score out there," Javey teased.

"Hey, I can score on and off the ice," Coast said.

"Says you," Tiger said.

"Yeah, says me." Coast smiled at me again before stepping away to finish getting ready.

"Nice job," Finley told me. I hadn't noticed him watching, he must have seen the whole thing. "It's easy for me or one of the other guys to tell him to fuck off, but he won't listen until he's been shot down face-to-face by a woman."

"And by telling him to fuck off, you mean threaten to break his legs," I said.

"Something like that," he agreed easily. "He'll respect you more now."

I shrugged. "Good. And maybe you and the others will learn I can stick up for myself."

"Never doubted it." He knelt down to scoop up a pile of towels. "The beauty of an away game, someone else gets to do the laundry." He tossed the pile into a hamper.

"It's the little things," I teased. It was different being here, in Opal Springs, as a member of staff, not just as Aidan's wife.

In the early days, before Ike was murdered, I'd stay back in Dusk Bay when the team played away. Now, there was no chance of the guys leaving me at home alone. I didn't even try to ask. They'd ignore me if I insisted. They'd tie me up and stash me on the plane if they had to.

Now, no one would question my presence. They could, and did leer and flirt in the absence of my guys, but mostly they treated me like they treated anyone else that worked for the team.

"Wait until you get a day when you do five or six loads," he said. "Then you get fucking sick of doing laundry." In spite of his words, he didn't seem too bothered. He had the perfect job for a guy who was obsessed with hockey, but never had the level of skill needed to be professional. He got to live the life, and kept all of his teeth.

"Point taken." It wouldn't bother me, it kept me close to my guys. All the better to find an opportunity to change their minds about throwing Orion to the wolves.

"Looks like we're ready," Finley said. "It's going to be a tough game. The Ghouls are as hungry as the Demons."

"But not as awesome," Coast called out from a few metres away.

"No one is as fucking awesome as us," Bray agreed.

"Stop talking about it and get out there and kick some Ghoul ass," Aidan said from the doorway. He caught my eye and smiled briefly.

I smiled back and stood aside to watch the team make their way out to the ice. Orion was the last one out. He stopped to give me a hug.

"We've got this," he said. "We're going to spill some Ghoul blood out there." His tone was deliciously vicious.

"Make sure it's theirs and not yours." I kissed him. Like a lot of the team, he preferred his helmet without the visor in front of his eyes.

"If I don't leave some blood behind, am I really playing hard enough?" He twitched an eyebrow, but didn't smile. His expression was one of ninety-nine percent concentration on the game, one percent on our conversation.

"Exactly," Aidan told him. "Get out there." He followed the rest of the team, leaving the locker room to Finley and me.

"We have something else we need to do while we're here," Finley said, speaking softly in my ear. "And if you think I'm thinking what I think you are, I'm not talking about fucking. Unfortunately." He jerked his head over toward the side of the room where a pile of equipment bags lay.

"Grab that one and that one," he pointed. "Don't think about it too much and don't ask too many questions. You know what goes down."

"Yeah, I do." I grabbed the handles of the two bags he indicated and pulled them up my arm. They weren't heavy. If I had to guess, they contained diamonds or something similar. Whatever was in there didn't feel like guns, or slabs of any particular drug.

Admittedly, I didn't have any experience handling drugs, but I preferred to assume it wasn't that.

I followed Finley out of the locker room and down the corridor of Opal Springs arena. He seemed to know his way around, because he didn't slow as he led us through a doorway and down another corridor that led out of the arena.

A man in a uniform that indicated he worked for the Opal Springs Ghouls greeted us outside the door. Once a small, mining town in New South Wales, Opal Springs was now one of the biggest and fastest growing cities. Approximately the size of Dusk Bay, they had a team in the AIHL for about as long. And, apparently, a shady underbelly too.

The man nodded to me and Finley, took the bags and loaded them into the back of a red SUV. In return, he slipped Finley an envelope which he folded and stuck into his pocket.

He nodded to me and we headed back into the arena.

"That was easy." I glanced back to see the SUV pull away before the door closed behind us.

"Everything is planned well in advance," he said. "The minute the roster of games is released, the organisation of shit like this starts." He frowned. "That may go the other way around. I stay out of that side of things. Aidan would know more, if you want to know. When it comes to this sort of shit, I'm just the grunt. I recommend you to do the same. The less we know, the better for us."

"Ignorance is bliss," I quoted.

"In this case, ignorance is less likely to get you dead." He slipped his hand into mine and we stepped out in time to see Javey smash the puck into the goal. The score was already 1-0. His goal evened the score.

Orion skated back toward his place behind the blue line. A metre or two before he got there, the right winger for the Ghouls slammed hard into him on the way to his own position. Obviously purposeful.

For a moment, I thought he was going to punch the other player. Instead, he glanced in Aidan's direction before skating on and stopping exactly where he was supposed to.

That winger looked surprised, but shrugged and got into his position. Evidently he was hoping to provoke Orion and mess with his focus.

Judging by the way the puck slid past him a minute later, he'd only screwed with his own. Orion seized control of the puck and drove it back before slamming it off to Tiger.

The winger mouthed, "Fuck," and made it his job to crowd Orion every chance he got.

Whatever he did, Orion ignored him except to elbow him out of the way, although it got more forceful each time. He was clearly becoming irritated.

Aidan ordered him off the ice, leaving another player to slip into position while Orion cooled off. A couple of minutes later, he was back on, composed again.

The Ghouls scoring twice more before the end of the first period diminished that. Not helped by a different winger who also crowded Orion and checked him into the boards whenever he got the chance. Both he and the opposing wingers were on and off the ice several times all period, switching out but never letting up.

By the time the alarm sounded, Orion and Aidan both looked ready to break bones.

"If I wouldn't get a penalty, I'd break their fucking knees," Orion growled as he stepped off the ice and tugged off his helmet.

"It's part of the game, get over it," Aidan snapped.

Orion shot him a look, but didn't say anything. He stomped over to grab a water bottle and take a drink.

"At least he didn't punch any of them," I said.

Aidan snorted. "Not yet. Give it time." He narrowed his eyes at Orion, in case he was listening and took that as permission to drive his fist into his opponent's face.

"He's doing well to keep his feelings in check," Finley said. "Sometimes I miss the grand old days when it was okay to punch the shit out of the opponent. In those days, there was more fighting than there was playing." He sighed wistfully.

"Now we play smart," Aidan said.

"Some of us do anyway." Coast grinned. "In case anyone was wondering, yes, I am speaking for myself."

"You and your ego," Tiger said.

"There's nothing wrong with having an ego," Coast told him. "Maybe you should try it sometime." As if Tiger's ego wasn't just as big.

Tiger flipped him off, which, considering the size of his glove, made me laugh. He reminded me of one of those big foam hands.

"All right," Aidan said. "Save it for the opposition. Get out there and win."

CHAPTER 21

AIDAN

"Are you ready?" I looked Elenna up and down, drinking her in with my eyes.

As long as I lived, I may never truly believe she belonged to me. She was so fucking gorgeous she made my breath catch in my throat. I wanted to rip her clothes off and fuck her harder than I've ever fucked her before. There would be time for that later.

If she didn't keep looking at me like I had a gun to Orion's head.

"You still haven't told me what we're doing." She pulled her hair up in a ponytail and tied it back with a black hair band.

"It's a surprise," I said. "Can I not have a date with my wife? I thought you'd enjoy seeing more of Opal Springs."

"Have any of your contacts heard back from Nicholas or Celine?" she asked. Blunt as ever.

"No," I said. "As far as I know, the message hasn't got to them yet."

"Or it has and they're going to step through the door and kill him the moment we leave the hotel." Her mouth was set in an unhappy line.

"They won't," I said. "Not in a hotel full of Demons, each of whom knows how to use a gun." They didn't know exactly what might come, but they were always ready for something. Some of them came from backgrounds more violent than mine. Phoenix, in particular. If anyone was ready to deal with an attack, it was Phoenix DiMarco. Not to mention Finley.

"We won't be going far," I added. "It's just across the road."

"I might have to explain the meaning of sightseeing," she said dryly. "The hockey arena is across the road. We saw that already."

"Part of it." I held out my hand. For a moment, I didn't think she'd take it. She was pissed at me about Orion, with good reason. Things could very easily go sideways. I'd make sure they didn't. This was going to go exactly how I planned. When I was done, Nicholas and Celine would be off our backs. Permanently. Elenna could breathe easy after that. That was the only thing I cared about. The only thing in this world that mattered.

Finally, she slipped her hand into mine and we stepped out of the hotel room. Finley and Orion were with the rest of the team, drinking and commiserating.

Tomorrow, we'd watch the game over and over again and figure out exactly where things went wrong.

By that, I mean the way they plays we'd practised a thousand times before didn't come off the way they should. The opposition had our measure from puck drop to the end, anticipating our moves better than we anticipated theirs. We'd have to work on different plays for the next time we played the Ghouls. Not to mention working on better understanding theirs and being more flexible. We'd tweak and practice and next time we'd win.

I led Elenna across the road, to a door on the side of the arena. One of the staff let us in, nodded and waved us past before closing and locking the door behind us.

"If you're planning a fuck in the locker room—" she started.

"I thought that might come later." Her hands still in mine, I led her across a reception space and through a set of glass doors.

We pushed into the rink where we'd just been beaten by the Ghouls. Only some of the lights were on, illuminating the ice. Soft music drifted from speakers in the ceiling.

"This is so nice, but if you think I'm going to forget—"

I pulled her to me and kissed her mouth. "For an hour or two," I said finally. "We're not going to think about anyone but you and me." Sharing her with two other men was worth it if she was happy, but this time was for us only. I didn't want anyone else in her head, or her body, but me. I would dominate her thoughts until I took her back to our hotel.

She sighed. "Fine. You and me and that's it. But just for now."

I gripped her chin hard enough to leave a bruise. "Do I need to remind you who you belong to? Me. You will put them out of your mind." I kissed her again, then led her over to chairs where skates already waited for us to put on.

"You know I've only skated once or twice, right?" she asked.

"I was with you both of those times," I said. "Did I let you fall? I won't let you fall now." I'd sooner rip off my own eyelids with a pair of pliers than let her get hurt.

She let me draw her to her feet and help her over to the ice. I wrapped my arms around her and pulled her to my body. Holding her like that, I began to skate slowly.

"Isn't this nice?" I nestled my face into her hair.

"It is," she admitted. "I just—"

I tightened my hold on her. "Later." I wasn't above punishing her if she didn't let it go for a while. We'd both enjoy it. I'd make sure there was no one near to hear or see us. The rink was outside, but protected by walls on all four sides. If I exposed her ass to the cold air, she'd think again about disobeying me.

My cock was now half hard and pressed against her hip.

She finally relaxed into me. "Do you miss this? Skating. Playing. Shoving other players out of the way?"

"I can still do all of those things," I said. "Not as much as I used to. I miss it, but I like what I'm doing. The Demons are improving. Before long, they'll be dominating."

"What then?" she asked. "What do you do when you reach the top? Where will you go from there?"

"I stay on top." I cupped one of her breasts. "What other choice is there? There's only one way I'm going down." I let my other hand drift to the front of her jeans.

"You wouldn't consider coaching a different team?" Her body trembled lightly under my touch. "One that isn't playing at their best, that you can work with?"

"I'd consider it," I admitted. "There are a lot of factors to consider. Pulling you out of your life in Dusk Bay, for one thing."

It wasn't a matter of whether she wanted to go or not. If I decided to move us, then she'd move with me. Even if I had to tie her up and carry her there myself. Nothing would make me leave her behind. Not that she'd consider staying when I was leaving. She belonged to me. Wherever I went, she went. She'd promised me that. I'd hold her to it until the day one of us was dead.

"Yeah," she said softly. I suspected Finley and Orion crossed her mind, but she had the sense not to mention them now. Shame, I was looking forward to baring her ass to the cold.

"That's a long way off," I said. "I intend to make champions out of the Demons and keep them there. Every player in the country, in the world, will want to come and play for us. We'll be fighting them off."

"Literally," she said with a faint laugh. "Things could get ugly."

I kissed her hair. "Things are always ugly. It's what we choose to do with them that matters."

"That's true," she said. "Or we can put on romantic music and pretend nothing is wrong."

I turned her around and pushed her back against the boards so quickly she barely had time to blink.

She gasped out a breath. The sound went straight to my cock.

I gripped a handful of hair and tugged her head back. "I didn't say nothing was wrong," I growled. "I wanted time alone with you. That's not a fucking crime."

"You're going to let them kill Orion for what I did," she said. "For what we did. You want me to pretend that's not going to happen? I can't." Her eyes glistened.

I wanted to wrap my hands around his throat and strangle him for being inside her head right now. Instead, I wrapped my hand around hers.

"I thought you trusted me," I said, my voice dangerously low. "I thought we understood each other. You know everything I do is for you. Don't you?" I squeezed a little tighter. "Don't you?"

"This isn't about me," she said. "This is about taking responsibility for something that had nothing to do with him."

"Do you think he would have hesitated to pull the trigger if he was there?" I asked. "He would have killed Oscar for you. *I* would have." I fucking should have. She thought I didn't notice how often she washed her hands. How she flinched at the sight of raw meat. I should have killed the little prick to save her from the anxiety.

"He wasn't there, and he didn't," she argued. "I did. If anyone's to blame, it's—"

"Me," I finished for her. "It's me and I'm going to fix this." I let her go and skated back a few steps. "I promise you that. I will fix this." I ran a hand over my hair and glanced around. "I'll fix this and none of us will die."

She frowned at me. "But you said…"

"I said I'll make sure the Fiorellis blame Orion," I said evenly. "I never said I'd let them kill him. You really think I'm that much of an asshole? That I wouldn't have some kind of plan to make this work in our favour?" I saw from the expression on her face that she did think exactly that.

"Aidan…" She put out a hand.

I shook my head. "You think I'm some kind of monster?" I regarded her evenly.

"Of course I don't," she said.

I skated back and pressed my body against hers, pushing her hard against the side of the rink.

"You should," I said softly. "Because I am. But you, you're my whole world and I'll fucking destroy anyone who tries to take anything away from you. Including myself."

I leaned forward and inhaled the scent of her. I buried my face in her hair and took a moment to regain my composure.

"I love you," I said, my voice low, choked with emotion. Love wasn't something I was used to experiencing. Not as intense and all-encompassing as this. There was nothing in this world I wouldn't do for her, no line I wouldn't cross. I'd rip apart everyone on the face of the planet if she needed me to. With my bare hands, if necessary.

"I love you too," she whispered. "But I'm very tempted to kick you in the nuts for letting me assume you were planning to let Orion go to his death."

"I'm used to telling people what to do and having them do it," I said. "Answering to someone else is new to me. I don't intend to start doing it for anyone but you."

"Does he know?" she asked. "Does Fin?" She worked her arms out from between us and snaked them around my neck.

She didn't even try to strangle me. I wouldn't have blamed her if she had.

"Fin knows me well enough to know I have something planned," I said. "Orion... He doesn't seem like the sort to sacrifice himself. He probably has a Plan B, just in case I don't. But if he did sacrifice himself, it would only be for you."

"You don't think he cares about you enough?"

Was she actually teasing? I leaned back and looked at her. The barest of smiles brushed the corners of her mouth.

"He'll learn," I said, deadpan but joking. "How can anyone *not* love me?" I could think of at least a billion reasons. And not a single one of why Elenna loved me. The fact she still did after everything was a fucking miracle.

"It's probably your preference for banana flavoured ice cream," she said.

"I should be offended by your attack on banana ice cream," I said lightly. "I think I'll let it slide just this once." I brushed my lips over hers.

"Oh, you will?" she teased.

"You don't want me to?" It seemed she wanted me to punish her after all. I hooked my hand in the front of her jeans and worked the buttons loose. I spun her around and tugged them halfway down her thighs. Her black G string left her ass cheeks bare and pink.

I grabbed her hands and placed them on the sides of the rink so she could hang on while I bent her forward. I slapped my hand down on her ass.

She jumped slightly from the sudden strike and the pain, but didn't make any attempt to move away.

I slapped her again until her cheek was bright pink, then switched to the other cheek.

"Have you learned your lesson?" I asked.

"Banana ice cream is still yucky," she said over her shoulder. Cheeky minx.

I snorted a laugh and leaned down to bite her ass cheek.

She let out a soft squeal.

I slid my hands between her legs, pushing her panties aside to press my fingers into her drenched pussy.

Sometimes, I truly didn't understand how a woman like her was with a man like me. The second I saw her, she instantly dominated my thoughts. Body, heart and soul, I wanted and needed her. She was more important to me than oxygen.

Her muscles around my fingers as I pressed them deeper made breathing more difficult. Knowing I was going to make her come made my cock harder than a steel rod.

Anticipation was almost as good as watching her writhe and hearing her scream.

I rubbed my fingers over and around her clit, slipping inside to caress her G spot.

"Tell me," I said, my voice rough.

"Tell you why banana ice cream is disgusting?" she teased.

I slapped my other hand down on her ass. "No. Tell me who you belong to and how you feel."

"I love you and I belong to you," she said breathlessly. "Aidan… Fuck me. Right here."

I turned her back around and shoved her jeans down as far as they'd go, then worked one leg off over her skate. I pushed her back against the boards, grabbed her ass and picked her up while I undid my jeans and pushed them out of the way.

I wrapped her legs around my waist, pulled her panties aside and slammed my cock all the way into her pussy. I let out a grunt of exertion and stood enjoying her before I started to thrust, hard and fast.

The air was cold on my bare ass. I barely felt anything but the tightness of her wet channel and the way her muscles squeezed my cock, forcing me closer and closer to coming.

"Aidan…" She clung on to me, brown eyes on mine as I slid in and out of her gorgeous body. "I'm going to come."

"Of course you are. You're my slut. Your body was made for fucking. Made for coming. You feel the most alive when I'm pounding into you, don't you. *Don't you?*"

"Yes, yes, yes," she panted out. "I'm living my best life when I have a cock inside me. I'm a slut. I'm *your* slut."

"Yes, you are," I agreed. "Come for me like the slut you are."

She threw back her head and cried out as she came, her muscles tightening around me like a vice.

I couldn't stop myself from coming if I tried. I came hard, pounding into her and spilling my cum into her body, just like she was made for me to do. She existed to take every drop. One day, when all of this was over, I'd put a baby in her with my body. For now, I'd have to be satisfied with filling her this way, with my cock and my release.

We both sagged against the boards, me holding her to keep her from falling onto the cold ice.

"That was…" She was still trying to catch her breath.

"Yes it was," I agreed. I would have liked to fuck her while the stands were full, but this would have to do for now. It was enough to imagine several hundred people watching us screw. Imagine them hearing her scream as I brought her to orgasm. She'd make every last one of them come with her. "We should do this on our own rink when we get home. After I lick banana ice cream off your body."

I lowered her down and helped her to put her clothes back in place before I fixed my own. I offered her my hand.

"It's time to eat." I led her off the ice and over to a picnic I'd set up in the stands. We'd eat dinner, then I'd eat her.

CHAPTER 22

"I should be mad at you too." I flopped down beside Orion and searched around for my seatbelt.

"You know, some people think it's bad luck to sit in a different seat on flights," he said.

"Because I might accidentally-on purpose spill hot coffee in your lap?" I asked sweetly.

He looked back at me steadily. "It's not bad luck if you do it deliberately." He clicked his seatbelt together and adjusted it over his lap.

"A lot of athletes have weird superstitions. Like, they think if they sit in seat 6A instead of 9B, they might play badly."

I knew that about hockey players. Aidan always insisted on sitting in row five. Even when the Demons were losing. Apparently that didn't extend to where I sat, as long as I was seated and my seatbelt fastened.

"What do you think?" I asked.

He shrugged. "I don't give a shit what seat I sit in. It never makes a difference in whether I suck or not."

There was definitely something he wasn't saying.

I finally found my seatbelt and fastened it. "So, what is your superstition? Don't tell me, you have to dance naked under the moonlight before every game?" A girl could hope.

He snorted softly and tightened his seatbelt. "No, I do that for fun."

I laughed and pushed my bag further under the seat in front of me with my toe. "Maybe it gives you luck and you haven't realised it yet."

"Not enough luck. Next time, you can dance naked with me and we'll cream the Knights." He reclined the seat as far back as it would go.

Cream would *definitely* be involved.

"Let's put that on the maybe list," I said. "Seriously, what is your superstition? Lucky socks? A lucky cup? Avoiding black jellybeans?"

"I avoid black jellybeans because they're disgusting." He grimaced.

What was I thinking with these guys? First Aidan liked banana ice cream, now Orion doesn't like black jellybeans? What next? Maybe Finley liked Brussels sprouts. Ewww.

We stopped talking for a couple of minutes to watch the safety demonstration.

I thought, as I always did, that if there was ever an actual emergency, I'd completely forget every detail the flight attendant mentioned, but I listened anyway. Maybe it would sink in if I heard it often enough.

The plane started to taxi towards the runway.

"So, you were telling me about your superstition." I smiled over at him.

"Was I?" He looked back at me, his dark eyes hinting at humour.

"I mean, you don't have to tell me," I conceded. "Your superstition might be that if you tell me, it won't work."

"We could go with that, but the fact is if I tell you, you might laugh." He shrugged slightly.

"Try me," I said.

He placed a hand on my thigh, his fingers slipping between my legs.

Men. Give them a millimetre and they'll take them all and run.

"The fasten seatbelt is still on, because we haven't taken off yet," I pointed out.

"I like to live on the wild side," he said. He crept his fingers up until they grazed over the front of my jeans.

I shivered. "Superstition first. I promise I won't laugh. It's not like you dip your stick into the toilet."

"I know it's big—" he started.

"I mean your hockey stick." I elbowed him. "Don't tell me it's not a thing, because I know it is."

"It's not a thing for me," he said. "I keep all of my sticks as far away from the toilet bowl as possible." He paused for a moment. "I eat a Vegemite sandwich before each game."

"That's not weird," I said. Okay, it was to some people, especially those who weren't Australian, but it wasn't especially strange to me. I preferred it on toast, personally, but each to their own. For the record, just a swipe of it, it's not Nutella.

"With cheese," Orion added. He rubbed his fingers up and down the front of my jeans.

"Still not weird." He was making it more difficult to concentrate. If he said Nutella and cheese, I might be grossed out. Nutella went better with bacon than it did with cheese, as far as I knew. Excuse me if I didn't try to find out. That sounded like a waste of both ingredients.

"And pickles," he said. His expression was completely bland. Unlike the object of his superstition. That sounded anything *but* bland. Repulsive was a better adjective.

"I feel like that should be illegal." I made a face in disgust.

"Do you think that would stop me from eating it if it was?" He rubbed up and down more firmly.

"Probably not," I agreed. "That sounds foul. Anything with pickles is bleh." I stuck out my tongue.

"You know what they say, the perfect relationship is between someone who hates pickles and someone who will eat them for them. You can eat all my black jellybeans."

That sounded like a perfect compromise. He was

more than welcome to eat every pickle in the world if he wanted to.

"If you keep talking about black jellybeans, you're going to make me hungry." He was going to make me come too at this rate. The fact he was clearly aware of, and seemingly determined to make happen sooner rather than later.

The plane reached the end of the runway and lifted off, leaving my stomach behind for a few seconds. It caught up just as we reached the clouds. They were heavy today, hanging low, threatening rain. From the look of the forecast, they'd follow us all the way to Dusk Bay.

"You should try Vegemite, cheese and pickles," he said. He moved his hand back up to my thigh as the flight attendant walked past. She must have heard his comment, because she stopped and gave him a funny look before moving on.

I waited until she was a safe enough distance away so she wouldn't think I was laughing at her. Rather, I was in full agreement with the expression on her face. I presumed she wasn't going to suggest that to the in-flight caterer anytime soon.

"You don't know what you're missing." He squeezed my leg.

"Yes I do." I wasn't talking about sandwiches any more.

I glanced over to the seats beside us. The players seated there weren't paying us any attention, as far as I could tell. That would change quickly if Orion put his hand down the front of my jeans. Or if we got naked and fucked, here and now.

He unfastened his seatbelt when the light turned off and pushed himself up to look back through the plane.

"Devlin Air's toilets are bigger than the average plane," he remarked as he lowered himself back down.

"I've noticed that," I said. "But we should really talk about this whole thing with the—"

"Later," he said.

I fixed him with a look.

He gave me the same look back, with additional extra stubborn hockey god, and a sprinkle of smoulder.

"You realise how unfair that is?" I asked.

He leaned over and let his breath brush my neck. "I want to get you off. If that's a crime, I don't give a shit."

"It's not a crime," I said. "Pickles are a crime." They weren't, they should be. Seriously, I didn't care if people ate them, as long as they left me alone with my pineapple pizza.

He chuckled and pulled the buckle of my seatbelt to unfasten it.

"People will notice," I said.

"Do you care?" he asked.

"Not really," I said after a few moments thought. "No one should be ashamed of orgasms."

"No they shouldn't," he agreed. "As long as they don't see. You coming is for my, Aidan and Finley's eyes and no one else. I'd hate to have to throw my team-mates off the plane."

"That would end badly for everyone," I said.

I slipped out of my seat and walked up the aisle, not meeting anyone's eyes. Orion was right behind me. Aidan and Finley were sitting together at the front of the plane. Knowing them, they were fully aware of what was going on. Were they hard? Did their balls ache at the idea of Orion and I fucking? My clit throbbed thinking about it.

I slipped into the vacant toilet, which was still a tight fit. There was barely room to turn around, much less fuck around. Somehow, Orion squeezed in too and locked the door.

He pressed me against the wall beside the sink and popped the button of my jeans through the buttonhole. He grabbed the waistband of my jeans and black panties and slid both down my hips far enough for him to get his hand in between my thighs.

He teased my pussy with his fingertips, rubbing over my already wet entrance and up to my clit.

At the same time, I pulled down the front of his track pants and wrapped my fingers around his hot, engorged cock.

He groaned and rolled his hips, sliding himself in and out of my grip. "Fuck, Elenna."

"Please," I said breathlessly. It was a tight space, but I wanted him, needed him. My pussy was wet and ready. So fucking ready.

There was barely room, but he managed to pick me up and place me on the side of the sink. He manoeuvred until he was standing between my legs, and wrapped them around his waist, pulling me onto his cock.

I closed my eyes and moaned softly. "I love the way your cock feels inside me."

"I want to make you see stars," he said.

I half opened my eyes. "I can see a whole fucking constellation right now."

He chuckled. "That's me. Orion the hunter."

I closed my eyes again. "You caught me." Literally and figuratively. I couldn't have run away if I wanted to, I was jammed too tightly into the corner.

"You're the one who caught me," he said. "Elenna means sun; I'm stuck in your orbit."

A constellation was a bunch of suns, but I didn't bother to contradict him. Instead, I enjoyed the way he felt inside me as he started to move. Slow thrusts at first, but gradually becoming faster and more frantic. Neither of us wanted to rush, but our bodies couldn't seem to stop. We drove each other harder and harder, bucking and grinding until we reached the edge and hurtled over at the same time.

I gripped on to his shirt, clinging as a dozen constellations burst in front of my eyes. The hunter, the bear, the Southern Cross. They all blurred together like the death of one universe and the birth of another.

We sagged together, puffing and panting, holding on like neither wanted to let go.

Finally, when we caught our breath, he slid out of me and tugged his track pants back into place. He took a step back as best he could and helped me fix my jeans.

"I feel like I'm supposed to say something corny like welcome to the mile high club," he said, a smile threatening to appear on his lips.

I laughed silently. "That would be corny, but I think the gracious thing for me to do would be to say thank you, you too." I did up my button and smoothed my shirt and jumper, just in case.

He cupped my cheeks and leaned in to kiss me. He looked as though he was going to say something, but he didn't.

"We should get out of here before someone needs to use the toilet," he said. "And before we miss lunch."

"We wouldn't want to miss lunch." I straightened his shirt and unlocked the door.

"Definitely not." He followed me back down the plane to our seats, both of us ignoring any glances we got all the way back.

CHAPTER 23

ELENNA

"I give you credit for not punching Aidan in the cock," Wren said. "You must have been tempted."

"A little bit," I admitted. "But we sorted it out, and he knows to keep me in the loop from now on."

"In the loop," Sinclair echoed. "You *are* the loop. Sure Aidan and Fin were friends before you came along, but their relationship with each other and Orion is different because of you. They're going to have to learn to communicate with each other and you. Otherwise…" She toyed with the handle of her coffee mug.

"I know," I said. "We're going to implode. Or explode. Or whatever." I stirred the froth into my coffee. "Aidan likes to think he has everything under control and that everything will fall into place because he says so."

"Daddy Aidan," Wren remarked.

I hummed my agreement and sucked on the bowl of

my spoon. "He's used to telling everyone what to do. The team listens to him. Even when they pretend they aren't. They've seen the changes he's made is impacting their performance. He's not the kind of guy who will ever let go."

"We noticed that about him," Sinclair said. "If you hadn't fallen for him, he probably would have stalked you until you gave in."

I snorted, my lips pressed closed around my spoon. "That sounds accurate."

"Regrets?" Wren asked.

"At being with him? No." I hesitated.

"But?" Wren prompted.

"But if I wasn't, no one would be trying to point the finger at Orion for Oscar's death," I concluded. I picked up my coffee and held it in my hands.

Occasionally, I glanced around the almost empty coffee shop for indications anyone was listening. If they were, they gave no sign. Of course they wouldn't. We kept our voices down low anyway.

"Unless he did it instead," Wren said. "It's no secret his days were numbered either way. Oscar, I mean. If it wasn't you or Orion, any number of people would have ended him. The Brantley twins, Mannix Cassani and his people, one of the Bell sisters, the list goes on."

"I wish they had. If one of them did it, it would have been their problem," I said. "It wouldn't have been mine or any of my guys'."

I was starting to think I should have tried to stay

away from Aidan. It was a pointless thought, because I hadn't and he would have had me sooner or later. He would always have handed Oscar over to me to deal with.

That was Aidan's idea of a grand, romantic gesture. Much more so than a picnic in the stands, and skating. If he could, he'd offer me the heads of my enemies on a silver platter, on a daily basis.

Hopefully I didn't have so many that he could actually do that. To be honest, I didn't want human heads as a gift, touching as that was.

"Do you think Aidan is in over his head?" Sinclair asked. "That was why he didn't tell you what was going on?"

I thought about that for a while. "No," I said slowly. "I think it's the opposite. He's so cocky, he figured everything would work out. But he listened when I told him what I was feeling and next time…" I scrunched up my face. "I don't want there to be a next time."

"I hate to say it, but there's always a next time," Wren said regretfully. "There's always someone wanting to stir up trouble. If everyone with the name Fiorelli died tomorrow, someone would take their place. Someone would want their power. It's like that game where you whack those things and another one pops up."

"Teenage acne?" Sinclair joked.

Wren laughed. "More like whack a mole than whack a zit."

"You're right," I said reluctantly. "About the Fiorellis, not the pimples. Thank you for the traumatic flashback though."

They both grinned.

"I wouldn't be a teenager again for anything," Sinclair said. "Way too much angst."

"Way too much pressure to lose your virginity," Wren said.

"Pressure from yourself," Sinclair teased.

"Of course," Wren said lightly. "I was desperate to know what the big deal was. Turns out the first time was a pretty small deal." She made a face. "Just goes to show, just because a guy is a star football player, doesn't mean he has a big cock or knows what to do with it."

"That's why I went for someone who did know what to do," Sinclair said. "My father wasn't impressed with me fucking his best friend, but it was worth it."

They both turned to look at me.

I shrugged. "There's not much to talk about." I sipped my coffee.

"That makes me think there really is something to talk about," Wren said. "Come on, we shared."

"You realise that in no way obligates me to do the same," I said dryly. I was never a big fan of peer pressure.

Sinclair reached over and put a hand on mine. "Of course you're not. If you don't want to talk about it, we understand. Right, Wren?" She cut our friend a look.

"Right," Wren agreed. "But if you want to, we're here to listen."

I glanced down at the table. "It's really no big deal. Just one of my father's business associates. We went out a couple of times, fucked and then that was it. We saw each other around here and there but never owed each other anything. Before you ask, I'm not naming names." It was almost a decade ago, barely a blip in my memory. Probably not even that in his.

Wren looked disappointed. "I was hoping it would be a prince or something."

I laughed. "I don't even know any princes. And if I did, they wouldn't be interested in me."

"They should be," Sinclair said. "You're gorgeous. Your eyes are beautiful and your hair is so thick and luscious. And you have breasts." She glanced down at hers, slightly smaller than mine.

"You have breasts," I told her. "You could have been a model. Both of you."

"I'm too short," Wren said. She didn't look especially bothered by the fact. Maybe because she had breasts bigger than both of us. And a perfectly shaped ass.

"They're so heightist," Sinclair said.

"I don't think that's a word," I said.

"It is now," she said with a laugh. "I'm not wrong though. Height shouldn't be a restriction to doing things, especially when you're as gorgeous as Wren."

"I'm more pissed off about not being able to reach the upper cabinets in my kitchen," Wren said. "That's why I always go for tall guys. So they can get stuff out for me."

Sinclair snapped her fingers. "I knew there was a use for guys. Other than to give us orgasms. Which, when you think about it, is pretty useful."

"Speaking of orgasms," Wren said. "I'm going out with Tiger on Thursday night. He is taking me to dinner. I hope it ends with lots and lots of orgasms. He seems like the kind of guy who can deliver."

He seemed to me like the kind of guy whose ego wouldn't let him do otherwise, but if that worked in her favour, I was all for it. And if he hurt her, I wouldn't hesitate to punch him in the cock. Or dip his stick into the toilet. His hockey stick, that was. Although, if he hurt her badly, dipping his other stick wasn't off the table.

Sinclair leaned forward eagerly. "You'll give us details, right? I am feeling very celibate right now. If I don't get laid soon, my pussy is going to grow over."

"Tiger has plenty of friends," Wren pointed out.

"I know, I'm acquainted with all of them," Sinclair said. "I spend my waking hours trying to keep their reputations intact. A lot of my sleeping hours too. You wouldn't believe how many spot fires I have to put out. One is still smoking when another one ignites. If it's not jealous fans on social media making trouble, it's the players living up to their own reputations. Don't ask about the winger and the five puck bunnies." She rubbed her temples with her thumb and two of her fingers.

Her job must be exhausting at times, trying to save people from themselves. Or at least, covering their asses when they put them in the wrong place. Their reputations were in her hands.

"Now I want to ask about exactly that," Wren said.

"If it wasn't for the NDA, I'd give you all the details. It's as salacious as fuck." Judging by the expression on Sinclair's face, she barely believed half of it herself.

"Well if you say it's salacious, then it must be good," Wren said. "I guess you can't name any names."

Sinclair mimed zipping her lips and dropping the key down the front of her bra. "Not if I want to keep my job. Unless it meant saving one of you from heartbreak. Sisters before… NDAs. Or something like that." It didn't precisely roll off the tongue.

"Not Tiger then," Wren concluded. "If you hadn't said winger, I would have guessed it was Coast Riggs. If anyone would get caught fucking around with five puck bunnies, it would be him."

"Probably." Sinclair shifted in her chair uncomfortably. "We shouldn't be talking about this. Elenna might put it in one of her books."

"Anything that salacious deserves to go in a book," Wren said. She actually licked her lips eagerly. If a book wasn't at least eighty percent sex, she didn't want it. She even had a T-shirt that read Smut Slut. She wore it as proudly as the one with 'Tell me to STFUAGMTD-LAGB' on it.

As far as I knew, the acronym never worked. Maybe because most guys didn't know that she was asking them to give her their dick. If they would, a lot of them would be only too happy to comply.

"I wouldn't if there was a risk of Sinclair getting into trouble for it," I said. "Besides, I'd rather write about a puck bunny and five players. Or three."

"Now that's a book I'd read," Wren said. "Although, anything you write, I'll read and enjoy."

That was sweet of her, but she'd read everything I'd shown her, to date. Sinclair too. They were both supportive of my work, often making suggestions that improved each book before I released them. I was lucky to have them as my friends.

"I need to find more time to actually write," I said. "Assisting Fin and travelling with the team, not to mention worrying about Orion, takes up more time than I thought it would."

I'd barely had a chance to open my laptop, much less put down any words. I'd have to make some time. Hopefully, whenever Aidan's plan to deal with Nicholas and Celine was done with, I could get back to normal. In the meantime, writing romance was the last thing on my mind. Especially dark romance. Why write it when you can live it?

"Yes you do," Wren said. "But your two most loyal

readers will be here when you're ready." She waved a finger between her and Sinclair.

"In the meantime, we'll have to get our fix of smut by hearing about Wren's date with Tiger," Sinclair said slyly.

"Or better yet, we can hook you up with someone," Wren said to her. "Then we can all be having lots and lots of orgasms." She nodded, satisfied with that conclusion.

Sinclair raised her coffee cup. "I can drink to that. Orgasms for everyone."

Wren and I raised our mugs too and laughed.

My guys and I needed to work on our communication, but our orgasm-giving skills weren't lacking. They all seemed to have made it their life's work to make sure I came as often as possible. I wanted the same for them. You know what they say, happy cock, happy…

I'd have to work on that one.

CHAPTER 24

"Do you understand the difficult position this has put me in?"

I sat on the couch between Finley and Orion, while Aidan was addressed by Reuben Brantley himself. As the head of the Brantley family, he usually left things like this to his younger brother, Caleb, or one of his henchmen.

For him to come here personally, this was a big deal. Especially given that Reuben was very obviously pissed. His piercing blue eyes bored holes in each of us in turn, lingering on me, and Finley's arm around my shoulders. He was around the same age as Aidan, in his early forties, with the same anger, burning right beneath the surface.

"It wasn't my intention to create trouble," Aidan said evenly. If he was intimidated by Reuben, he showed no sign. "My goal is to protect my wife and those we care about. The Fiorelli family has been a thorn in all of our sides since—"

"I'm well aware of the trouble they've caused." Reuben's voice was low, but cut straight through Aidan's. He was used to having people do exactly what he said, without question. Leaping to obey, to avoid his wrath. He didn't need to raise his voice to be heard. When he spoke, everyone listened.

I thought Aidan might snap back, but he didn't. He knew when the puck was already in the goal and there wasn't any point chasing it down. Not to mention that Reuben could have us all killed, with nothing more than a couple of words. Watching Aidan keep his anger in check was fascinating. He was going to lose it later and I couldn't wait.

"They haven't been as big a problem since Dante's death," Reuben continued. "Until now. I've managed to keep them more or less contained, with close eyes on everything they do."

"Like my brother," I said without thinking.

Reuben's gaze turned to me. He was even more of a closed book than Aidan. He made an indeterminate sound in the back of his throat and turned away.

Finley squeezed my shoulder, to reassure me, or perhaps to stop me from getting up and punching Reuben in the face for putting my brother in a situation that got him killed.

Doing that would only achieve exactly nothing but

getting me and my guys killed, so I wasn't even tempted.

Besides that, as much as I hated to admit it, Ike knew what he was getting into. He would have jumped in with both feet and enjoyed the ride. Until it ended abruptly and painfully.

"Geneva Fiorelli contacted me, demanding I hand over the person who killed her stepson." Reuben toyed with a button on his perfectly tailored suit. He carried an air of danger and violence, but enough of his dealings were above board to convince some people he was legitimate. Nothing more dangerous than a successful businessman. Everything was perfectly legal.

For those of us who knew better, he was one of the most powerful men in Australian organised crime. The Australian mafia, or near enough. He'd order a bullet in someone's brain and not even blink.

"Cute that she'd pretend to give a shit about any of her stepchildren," Finley remarked. "I'm guessing this is less about Oscar and more about her trying to flex muscles."

"That's exactly what it is," Reuben said without looking away from Aidan. "I don't need her flexing muscles."

"You need her to stay in her cage, theoretically speaking," Aidan said.

If I wasn't watching closely, I would have missed it, but I could have sworn Reuben flinched. It was the most minute movement, little more than a twitch of the side of his face. Half a second later, I thought I must have imagined it. Men like him didn't flinch.

"Theoretically speaking, yes," he said evenly. "All of this has stirred up trouble and I don't like trouble."

"I have the situation under control," Aidan assured him. "I appreciate you coming all this way to pass on Geneva's message. We can sort it out from here."

Reuben's expression didn't change, but the sense of annoyance increased. "You claim Orion was the one who killed Oscar." He wasn't asking.

"Yes, it was me." Orion sat back on the couch, his legs crossed at his knees, looking every bit the cool, calm, arrogant hockey god. "You're welcome." He smirked when Reuben turned to him.

"You also helped my youngest brothers in their crusade against human trafficking." Again, Reuben wasn't asking.

Orion's body stiffened, his thigh pressed against mine. "Yep. And I'd do it again."

Finley muttered something that sounded like, "Cocky little fuck." He sounded approving.

I squeezed his leg. He turned and smiled.

Reuben toyed with a ring on his right hand. It looked expensive. Like everything else about him.

"You can assure me that handing Orion over to the Fiorellis will settle the matter." Reuben looked back at Aidan.

"You have my word," Aidan said. "We're taking responsibility for that situation. It was a miscalculation on my part and I'm fixing it." He looked pained to say words like those. Especially when none of it was that simple.

"If any of this comes back to bite me on the ass," Reuben said, "I will hold you personally responsible. I don't need to tell you what the repercussions of that would be."

"Not at all," Aidan agreed. "We fully understand the situation and the consequences if I fail. But I won't fail. The wheels I've set in motion will get the job done to the satisfaction of all of us."

"Except Orion." Reuben glanced my way, clearly trying to gauge my response. "The Fiorellis won't go easy on him." He didn't seem too concerned. I couldn't rule out the possibility he thought they'd deal with one of his problems, saving him from having to bother. Why though, I didn't know. Unless helping Hunter and Parker was something he disapproved of. There didn't seem to be much love lost between him and them these days. I didn't know why and I didn't much care. That was their problem, not mine.

"I can take it," Orion said. "I've dealt with worse than them before." He glanced at Aidan, who snorted.

"You have no idea." Aidan rubbed his hand over the back of his neck. "I'm curious what Caleb thinks about us surrendering the team's best defenceman. I've started to turn the Demons around."

"Caleb wants the Fiorellis to go away more than he wants the team to succeed," Reuben said coolly. "However, I'm certain you can achieve success without one player."

For some reason, that sounded like another threat.

"I'm certain I can too," Aidan agreed. "I appreciate you confirming where his priorities are." We all knew he was trying to goad Reuben, but the oldest of the Brantleys didn't give him much to come back with. Not without saying Caleb didn't give a shit about the team. He probably didn't, but the team doing badly reflected on him. He had to put up *some* pretence.

"We all want the Fiorellis to go away," I said. Me in particular. They created trouble for Reuben, but they hadn't murdered any of his brothers. From what I gather, they tried, but so far they hadn't succeeded. What would Reuben do if they had? I had a feeling he wasn't the type to leave blood on the street, even in retaliation for the death of one of his own. Not his brothers anyway. Fuck only knew if he cared about anyone else. That was his business.

"If we could achieve that without unnecessary expense and bloodshed, we would," Reuben said.

In that order, no doubt.

"Just necessary bloodshed," Orion said lightly. "You're welcome." His dark gaze watched Reuben like a lion waiting to pounce on a mouse.

Reuben was far from a mouse. The consequences for attacking him would be worse than death. I didn't want to think what he'd have done to any of us. Okay, all of us. Any retaliation would have repercussions beyond Orion's actions.

I put a hand on Orion's. "No one wants this to happen. Least of all me."

"Like I said, necessary blood," Orion said. He shrugged like it was no big deal at all.

"I'll send you the details outlining where the transaction will take place," Reuben said. "A location insisted upon by Geneva."

"Of course," Aidan agreed. "We're only too happy to give her exactly what she wants."

"I'm sure you are," Reuben said. "I don't want to hear about any of this again until it's dealt with."

"Leave it to me," Aidan said. "Everything will go as smoothly as I planned." His confidence was almost contagious. If I didn't think this could all go horribly wrong so easily, I'd be as calm about this as he seemed to be.

"Of course it will," Reuben said. He looked as though he was about to once again remind Aidan of what would happen if it didn't, but he decided he made his point already.

He wasn't the kind of man to waste time or words. As long as I'd known him, he never had been.

If I was honest with myself, I'd say that was part of the attraction. I wasn't immune to the lure of a powerful, good-looking man. It was one of the things that drew me to Aidan in the first place. I hated the bloodshed, but I loved the power and danger these men carried with them. It was an addiction I'd never tried too hard to break. If I was honest with myself, I wanted more of it. Not with Reuben now I had my three guys, but there was a time when I would have gone there.

"Can I offer you a drink?" Aidan asked. "I have a bottle of Macallan waiting for just the right opportunity."

"No, I have another meeting," Reuben said. "Don't fuck up." He nodded to his henchman Damon. Without a backward glance, they left the apartment. Their presence lingered long after they were gone, like a dark cloud.

Aidan closed and locked the door behind them. "Good, I didn't want to give them my best whiskey anyway."

Finley chuckled. "Yeah, that would have been quite the waste. However, I'll have a glass, neat. Thanks for the offer."

Aidan smirked. "Not a chance. That can wait until after we pull this off."

"If we do." Orion turned his hand and laced his fingers in mine.

"We will," Finley said. "We're staking your life on it."

"I noticed," Orion said, giving him a particularly dry look. "Nothing important."

"You're very important," I told him. "To me and to Aidan and Finley. And the team."

"Then we really better not fuck this up," Orion said. "Like Aidan said, I'm the best defence the team has.

Lose me and the Demons go back to losing." He looked smug.

"You really are a cocky fuck, aren't you?" Finley grinned.

"A cocky hockey fuck," Orion agreed.

"How about that, you know how to rhyme," Aidan said, his tone flat. "You should have joined a rock band or taken up poetry."

"I can play a mean set of drums," Orion said.

"Shame this place is too small for one of those." Aidan stepped over to the kitchen and poured himself a drink of cola.

"Time to get a bigger space then." Orion ran his thumb back and forth across the back of my hand.

"Not if it means having drums in the house." Finley grimaced.

"We can agree on that." Aidan toasted Finley.

"If the house was big enough, you'd never hear it," I pointed out.

"Whose side are you on?" Finley asked, pretending to be offended.

"I'm on the side of everyone getting what makes them happy," I said. "If drums make Orion happy, then I don't see the harm." He was the one taking the biggest risk all too soon. Why shouldn't he get something in return for that?

"That's a problem, you don't see the harm," Finley said. "You hear it. Thud, thud, bang, bang, and all that bullshit."

"That sounds like the music you listen to," Orion told him.

Finley looked affronted. "You clearly don't know good music when you hear it. There's nothing wrong with what I like."

"If you say so." Orion shrugged.

"I do say so." Finley nodded.

I glanced up to see Aidan regarding us all thoughtfully. I cocked my head at him questioningly.

"I was just thinking about everyone getting what they want," he said slowly, but with darkening eyes.

CHAPTER 25

ELENNA

"I like the sound of where this is heading," Finley said. "Assuming I'm right about where I think this is heading." He ran his knuckles down the side of my cheek.

"It's heading in whatever direction you want it to head," Aidan said. He crossed his arms over his chest and lifted his chin.

"We can take it and run, or…" Finley kissed the side of my neck.

"Or you can tell us where you want us to go," Orion did the same on the other side. "If that's what Elenna wants?"

Two of my guys at once, while Aidan watched? Hell, yes please. If he wanted to take part too, I was here for that, but the idea of him orchestrating slammed blood into my pussy faster than a puck sliding into the goal.

"It is," I whispered. "Please."

Aidan nodded. "Show me her breasts."

"Yes, Coach." Orion grabbed the hem of my jumper on one side and Finley on the other. Together, they pulled it up and over my head.

Finley grinned at my Demons shirt on underneath. "Are you wearing Orion's number?"

I twisted around to show him the back. "Of course." If two of them were players, things might get tricky. Lucky for me, only one was and Aidan didn't insist on me wearing his old number unless it was on a jersey from his former team.

"Nice, but you're overdressed." Orion pulled off my T-shirt and Finley unhooked my bra.

Orion grabbed the straps and slid it the rest of the way off.

I sat back around so Aidan could see me. He looked approving, his cock hard as hell, straining the front of his pants.

"Touch her," he told them both.

They did as he asked, Orion with his hand and Finley with his mouth.

My head dropped back as need flooded through me, not far enough that I couldn't watch them both kneading, rolling, sucking and licking.

"You like that?" Aidan asked me.

"Very much," I said. "You like seeing them do this to me?"

He swallowed, his Adam's apple bobbing up and down. "Even more than I thought I would."

I got the impression he'd imagined this many times.

I loved that it already exceeded all of his expectations. It certainly exceeded mine, and we'd barely begun.

"I need to see her pussy," Aidan said.

"Funny, me too," Finley said around a mouthful of nipple.

Aidan shot him a look. Finley responded by raising a hand in surrender and helping Orion pull off my jeans and panties.

"Show me," Aidan demanded.

Orion and Finley both took one of my legs in their hands and spread them wide, opening me out for all of them to see.

"How wet is she?" Aidan asked.

It was Finley who reached over and ran a finger up my seam from my rear hole to my pussy.

"She's wet," he reported. "But there's room for her to be wetter."

"Make her wetter," Aidan said. "Taste her."

Finley moved over to kneel on the floor in front of me and ran his tongue up and down the way he had with his finger.

Aidan took a few steps over so he could watch over Finley's shoulder. "Good. She loves being eaten."

That was very true, but no one pointed that out. They didn't need to.

"Don't neglect her nipples," Aidan told Orion.

"Yes, Coach." Orion started licking and sucking my nipples like they were the most delicious treat he ever tasted.

Between both of them, and Aidan's gaze, I felt like I was on a fast train, hurtling towards the cliff, unable to stop myself from flying over into the abyss.

I came hard against Finley's mouth, while his tongue was barely touching me. I gripped the back of Orion's shirt and dug my nails into the fabric and his skin under that.

I kept my eyes open, focused on Aidan's face as I came apart for the longest time, before coming back together again.

"That's my slut," Aidan almost purred. "You like his tongue very much."

"I love his tongue," I said in a whimper. I shivered as Finley went on licking and teasing, while my pussy was hypersensitive.

"Let her taste herself." Aidan waved to Finley, who rose just high enough to press his lips to mine.

His mouth tasted sweet and salty with my release. I traced all the way around his lips with the tip of my tongue.

"Can I taste?" Orion asked. He looked at both of us, then at Aidan.

Aidan paused, thoughtful and speculative before he nodded. "Taste her from Fin's mouth."

I blinked in surprise, then swallowed.

The two guys stared at each other.

All four of us knew they didn't have to do anything they didn't want to. Even Aidan wouldn't be angry if they backed up and said no. He'd move us on to something else.

The moment drew out.

Something silent passed between Finley and Orion. Some kind of understanding. The beginning of an invisible bond between them.

They both moved together slowly, until their mouths brushed against each other. That was all it was. Barely more than a touch.

They moved apart for a few moments before they crashed back together, deeper this time. The kiss they shared was a gentle, experimental one. Testing to see how they felt about it. To see if the other would pull away.

Neither did.

They kissed lightly for maybe a minute before drawing apart.

"She tastes good on you," Orion whispered.

"You don't taste so bad yourself," Finley whispered back.

Holy shit, that was hot.

Aidan cleared his throat. "Orion, I want you to fuck Elenna."

Orion nodded before pushing his track pants down his hips to free his erection. He grabbed my hips and pulled me to the edge of the couch.

Finley placed his hands on my shoulders and drew me back against him. The way I lay, Aidan could clearly see Orion slide his cock into my slick heat.

"She takes your cock so well," Aidan said. "Fuck her harder. I want to hear my slut scream."

Orion obliged, gripping my hips and driving himself into me before pulling all the way out and slamming back in.

"Such a good girl." Finley ran his hands up and down my breasts, palming my nipples and making them harder and harder.

"Let her taste your cock," Aidan said to Finley.

Finley didn't hesitate to slip out from under me, replacing his body with several cushions. He undid the front of his jeans and pressed the glistening tip of his cock to my lips.

I licked his head and around to his base before teasing up and down the seam under his length.

"Open your mouth for him," Aidan said. "I want to see him fuck your mouth."

I opened wide and let Finley slide his cock inside. I closed my lips over him and sucked.

Aidan groaned. "That's it. My perfect whore. Look at you fucking two men at once. You're loving this so much aren't you?"

I could only make a sound in the back of my throat in response. I was enjoying every moment of it.

Orion pounded into me so hard I cried out around Finley's cock. Fuck, everything felt so good.

Aidan undid his own pants and pushed them down far enough to wrap his fingers around his own cock.

I wanted to touch him too, but this was about him

watching and not touching me. Instead, I gripped Orion's bicep with one hand and Finley's balls with the other and sucked in rhythm to Orion's thrusts.

It felt so easy, so right. We fell into a rhythm like we'd done this a hundred times before. Maybe we had in a hundred past lifetimes. It seemed like we already knew each other inside and out. We fit together like a puzzle with all of its intricate, perfect pieces that slotted together to make something incredible. Something beyond special.

"Come inside her," Aidan said breathlessly.

I wasn't sure who he was referring to, maybe both of them. Either way, they both fucked me harder and faster, while Finley's hand found my clit and added that to the rhythm.

My breath was coming in careful pants now, in and out of my nose, while I sucked.

"I want to see her gag," Aidan said. He leaned around to better see Finley's cock sliding in and out of my mouth. His hazel eyes were so dark, so laced with desire. So aroused from the show we were putting on for him. We were the chess pieces for him to move how he wanted us and we were loving every second of it.

Finley obliged by thrusting in deeper, his cock tapping the back of my throat and triggering my gag reflex.

"Good girl," Finley soothed. He did that a couple more times, watching my face as I retched and tears leaked down my cheeks. My mascara must be running something terrible right now. I knew Aidan would love that, he always did. The messier I looked, the happier he was.

"You're going to come down her throat, and she's going to swallow it all like our perfect slut that she is," Aidan said.

Finley groaned and came at the same time as I came again. Gasping and panting, I almost choked on the mouthful of salty cum he squirted into my mouth.

Right before I did, I managed to swallow.

I coughed and gagged a couple of times before catching my breath.

"Come inside her pussy," Aidan said. His voice was strained with the effort to keep control of himself and us.

"Yes, Coach," Orion said. He grunted a couple of times before his body tensed and he orgasmed, filling my body to the brim with his cum.

A moment later, Aidan came, coating his hand with his release.

I watched it squirt out of his tip like a fountain with painful pressure behind it. He grunted hard, milking himself for every drop of release, both the sensation and the juices.

Fuck, that was as hot as anything the other two did to me.

All four of us panted for a while, catching our breath and coming down from the biggest rush I ever had.

Having two guys inside me at once while a third

watched was the hottest thing I ever experienced in my life. Considering how well all three guys spoiled me separately, that was saying a lot.

This moment, these guys, were everything.

I would have fought for them before, but I felt as if this experience flipped a switch. We went from being me and three partners, to a family. Like…somehow we formed a bond that was stronger than anything.

Okay, it might just be the orgasms talking, but I hoped not. I'd never felt so complete before. So wanted and needed and loved. Surrounded by so much heady testosterone and cum.

Then there was Finley and Orion kissing. There were many conversations we still needed to have, and things to work out. And we would. We'd make the time to understand each other. Nothing, and no one was going to break us apart now.

I'd personally make sure of that.

"Holy shit," Orion said. "That was awesome."

"Well, I don't want to brag," Finley said with a grin.

Orion reached over and punched him on the arm. "Not just that part, dickhead." His cock was still happily nestled deep inside me, ready to get hard again at a moment's notice.

Finley laughed, and looked completely unapologetic. "At least you're including that part, dickhead."

"You're welcome," Aidan said with a grunt. He stepped over to the kitchen to wash his hands and fix his pants.

"We don't have to call you Daddy now do we?" Finley teased. He tucked his own cock back into his pants.

Aidan rolled his eyes but didn't answer.

I suspected he would have been open to coach, daddy or even sir, as long as we did what he told us to. If—when—we had more sessions like this, I was one hundred percent ready to obey him. I never wanted to hold anything back ever again.

"You wanna talk about it?" Orion sat on a seat in front of me, putting on his skates.

"Nope," he said without looking up. "We have enough shit to deal with."

His shoulders heaved as he sighed. Now he looked up, but didn't quite meet my eyes.

"It wasn't shit, okay? I should be focusing on the game and Aidan's plan." Not quite an apology, but I got it.

I sat down on the edge of the chair beside his. "Yeah, me too. Just wanted to clear the air, you know? We have a lot riding on the next couple of days and I don't want things to be awkward. You still have to trust me with your equipment. No pun intended."

It was a long time since I thought about another guy's equipment. Aidan and I didn't have that kind of relationship. Ever since I met Elenna, her and everything about her, was stuck in my brain.

My life was about her and hockey and that was about it. That kiss the other day reminded me other people existed. Orion existed. Not as a replacement for her, but...

Hell, I didn't know. It might be nothing more than another complication none of us needed. Not right now. But my brain was all about precision and being methodical. If an issue came up, I dealt with it, rather than dwelling on it.

The situation with Elenna was different because of Aidan, but this... This was different because the timing was all sorts of fucked up. We might die tomorrow.

On the other hand, if we did, shouldn't we live today as best we could?

"I trust you with my...equipment." Orion looked more awkward than I'd ever seen him. He was cocky and confident, arrogant and self-assured.

Or so he came across.

He wouldn't be the first person with false bravado. Not the last either. Elenna had started to peel back his layers, but now I was curious to see what was underneath for myself.

"Of course you do." I patted him hard on the shoulder. "You're an excellent judge of character."

"I don't know about that." He smirked and leaned over to fix his laces.

I sensed he had something to say, so I waited and gave him time to put together the words.

Finally, he said, "Do you have a lot of experience with other guys' equipment?"

Any other time, I would have teased him for his choice of words. Instead, I decided on direct honesty.

"A little. Not in a few years." Then, as usual, I went for a bit of levity. "Mostly I've been celibate on account of my ugly face."

He responded with a short, half a laugh in the back of his throat. "Not everyone can be as hot as me."

"Or as modest." I crossed my knees and looked out over the locker room.

Most of the guys were almost ready, some fixing helmets into place or pulling on gloves.

For the most part, they didn't say much, their minds occupied with mental preparation.

Coast and Tiger teased each other quietly in the corner. Something about Tiger being infatuated with someone. Fuck only knew how long it would last. Guys like them had attention spans about as long as the average regulation period.

"Why waste time being modest when you're this awesome?" Orion looked amused, but didn't quite smile. He didn't even do that when we won a game. What would it take to make him grin?

"I'm sure you're rolling in endorsement proposals," I said. "Let me guess, underwear and your own brand of perfume. I can see you in an ad campaign right now."

I held my hands in the air in front of me and sketched out the shape of a big screen.

"Standing in front of the Eiffel Tower, looking off into the distance, white underwear full of about five socks." I dropped my hands and ducked to the side as he went to punch my arm.

"I don't need socks in the front of my underwear," he said smugly. "Five is a very specific number though. Is that how many you use?"

"Nah," I said lightly. "I need six. Between that and my ugly mug, it's a wonder Elenna is interested in me. It must be my personality and ability to make a fucking good chocolate cake. The way to a woman's heart, and all that." I grinned at him, but my gaze dropped to his mouth. He had the plushest lips I ever saw on another guy.

I swallowed and looked away.

"I should get you to teach me how to cook after all this is over," he said. "Then I could keep being her favourite."

My gaze swung back to him. "Who says you're her favourite?" I pretended to be offended.

"Who is whose favourite?" Elenna asked. She held a skate in one hand and new laces in the other. She started to push the laces through the eyelets.

"Orion was just saying he's jealous of me because I'm your favourite," I said. I closed out that statement with a firm nod.

"Fin is delusional," Orion told her. "I'd never say that, because it's not true."

"You're right," she said. She paused to concentrate for a moment.

"See?" I said triumphantly.

She stopped and glanced at me. "I don't have a favourite. I care about all of you equally."

"But if you did, it might be Aidan, because he's the one whose ring you wear," Orion said softly.

I exchanged looks with him. Something passed between us and I nodded slightly before looking back at our gorgeous woman.

"Like I said, I don't have any favourites." She gathered the ends of the laces and held them up to see if they were even, before tugging the shorter end.

"Not amongst them." Coast must have overheard at least part of the conversation.. "Everyone knows I'm really her favourite. And if I'm not, I should be." He winked at her.

"You'll play really well with two broken arms," Orion told him.

Coast grinned. "Even with two broken arms, I'd play better than you."

Elenna stepped in front of Orion. I grabbed him to keep him from jumping up and doing anything rash.

"You're fucking delusional," Tiger said to Coast. "Stop trying to stir up shit."

Coast shrugged and jammed his helmet down onto his head. "Just trying to lighten the mood, bro. You know what Aidan said about us needing to get along better as a team."

"Teammates don't hit on other guys' women," Orion snarled.

I held him harder until he managed to relax. "He's just fucking around."

"If he keeps fucking around, he's going to find out." Orion shook me off.

"Ignore him," Elenna said. "I'm not bothered by his bullshit and I'm not interested in him. Save it for the ice."

"What she said." I glanced at her. "Coast isn't your favourite, right?"

She laughed. "He's my favourite first line Demons centre who's usually in the starting lineup, and not a guy I want to date or fuck. He's not your competition."

"I knew that," I said as if I hadn't asked. Even a guy like me gets insecure now and again. Only a little bit though. Sort of.

I mean, Coast was a good looking guy and if Elenna wanted him too, I'd support her, but three of us seemed to be enough for her.

She slid me a look and a warm, reassuring smile. Fuck, she made my heart flip every time. Not to mention making my cock and balls both harder. I knew exactly how I felt about her, but now was not the time to express it. Not in a locker room full of smelly hockey players and testosterone.

"Who's ready to kick some Echidna ass?" Aidan shouted out.

"Us, as long as they're not literally echidnas," Coast called back. "I prefer my prick in my pants, not my foot."

"You should have been called the Clowns, not the Demons," Aidan told him. "All right, get out there and puck them up!"

***

"Are you and Orion all right?" Elenna sat beside me, her eyes on the game.

"I think so," I said. "What do you think about what happened?" We'd skirted around the issue until now. Personally, I was still getting my head around Aidan telling us what to do and how fucking hot that was. It took me a while to admit to myself kissing Orion wasn't just me getting caught up in the moment. Once I was honest with myself, I could be honest with them.

"I liked it," she said. "What do you think about it?" She looked over at me. "How are you feeling?"

"Fine and dandy," I said lightly. "You know me, I go with the flow."

She gave me a, 'really, you're going to play it that way' look. "What way do you want the flow to take you?"

She put a hand on my thigh. "You don't have to tell me if you're not ready. It's a big deal. Or maybe it isn't and that's okay too. Whatever you guys do, you know I'll support you."

"You're the best," I told her. "I'll be honest and say I dunno what might happen. For one thing, we may be dead and gone this time next week."

She flinched. "We won't be. We'll all be fine. I trust Aidan to get us through this. I know you do too."

In spite of the strength of her words, there was unease behind them. The plan to have Ike spy on the Fiorellis should have been ironclad too, and it turned badly so quickly no one had time to get him out.

Or… they had, but the Brantleys turned their backs and pretended they weren't involved. Either way, he was equally dead.

"Yeah." I looked back at the ice as Orion ducked and wove around an opposition player.

He moved effortlessly, like he was born on the ice. I wouldn't have been surprised if he could skate before he could walk. Every movement was natural, fluid. So was his stick work. Hockey stick that was, although watching him fuck Elenna was already a cherished memory.

Picturing the way his cock slid in out of her made mine stand up and pay attention.

As casually as I could, I rested my hand over my groin, palm up, while at the same time trying to convince my cock to go down. The whole arena didn't need to see me getting a boner.

"He's really that good isn't he?" she said just loud

enough to be heard over the roar of the crowd.

"He's at least as good as he says he is," I said with a grin. "Maybe better, but don't tell him that. His head is big enough."

"Yes, it is," she said slyly.

There I was, thinking about his cock again. And her pussy. Would anyone notice if we stuck away for a quickie in a corner somewhere? Shit, they would, or that was exactly what I'd do. I promised my cock I'd have time with her later. He'd have to be content with that for now.

"If you're not careful, you're going to corrupt my innocence," I joked.

She laughed. "I'll apologise in advance if that happens, but I'm not sure who's doing the corrupting around here."

I leaned over and whispered in her ear. "You never need to apologise for leading me astray. Although, I think you're right, I don't think you can. I have a map on my phone that tells me exactly where to find the road there."

She laughed again. "That wouldn't surprise me one bit. I think I have that app too."

She leaned against me. I draped my arm across her shoulders. I didn't care who might look and pass judgement on us. If they were jealous or condemning, that was their problem.

I was living my best life with the best three people I knew.

"If you're not careful, Coach, we're gonna get used to winning." Coast playfully rammed his shoulder into Aidan's upper arm.

Aidan shoved him off and smirked. "It's about time you got used to winning. I was starting to think you guys didn't know any different." He levelled a finger at Coast's nose. "I knew you had it in you."

"You believed in us." Coast wobbled on his legs and crossed his eyes while he regained his balance. "Thank fuck you did cause the asshole before you didn't."

He actually threw his arms around Aidan and gave him a hug before staggering away.

I laughed and shook my head at the very drunk centre. Truthfully, most of the guys were drunk and I was halfway there. Even Aidan indulged more than he usually did.

At the same time, he was on guard, watching the

exits whenever people walked in and out. That after assuring me that Hazards, the popular pub, was one of the safest places in the area. Almost as safe as our apartment. Considered neutral territory at the very least, the place was full of folks employed by the Brantley family.

Daisy Lasalle sat in the corner with one of her boyfriends, Ric DiMarco. They shared a table with his brother Phoenix. Her other boyfriends were nearby, along with Mannix Cassani, Ares Turner and Ice Miller, with their girlfriend Kennedy Knight.

Anyone who tried to screw with that seven would find themselves regretting it, much less everyone else in here.

"I think he likes you," I teased.

Aidan actually laughed. Not just a restrained chuckle, but a genuine, relaxed laugh. "He's a good guy when he has a rein on his arrogance. And a fucking good centre."

Evidently neither Orion nor Finley told him what Coast said in the locker room, because Aidan wouldn't be so full of praise for him if he knew. He'd haul him aside and threaten him with who knows what.

"And completely oblivious to the crush Sinclair has on him." I nodded to my friend who stood nearby with Wren, her eyes on Coast.

"That sounds like Coast," Aidan said. "He always knows where the puck is on the ice, but he doesn't have a clue about shit like that. Just as well it's not the other way round. If they're meant to be, they'll figure it out."

"It might be too late by then." I noticed Javey watching Sinclair, drink near his lips. He hadn't taken a sip for at least the last ten minutes. Nor had he taken his eyes off her.

"You know what?" Aidan turned and slipped his arms around my neck. "That sounds like a problem for them, not us. I have no interest in getting involved in the love lives of anyone else." He kissed me slowly.

I wrapped my arms around his neck and kissed him back. When we came up for air a couple of minutes later I asked, "What about Fin and Orion's love life? You wouldn't have suggested they kiss each other if you didn't see something there."

He looked smug. "I wasn't wrong. I know Finley has dabbled with other men in the past. Orion, he's figuring things out. They needed a little nudge. Maybe nothing will come of it, but I gave them a start. You know they wouldn't have kissed if they didn't both want to. They're as stubborn and hardheaded as each other."

"Hello pot, I hear you talking about the kettle," I teased. "In this case, kettles."

"That's what you love about us," Aidan said. "We don't give up or give in easily. Not when it comes to things that really matter. Love and hockey."

"You're right, that is what I love about you," I said. "Although, you could add chocolate to that list." Whatever the list was, chocolate should probably be on it somewhere.

"Forget chocolate, I should have added fucking." He

nestled his face in my hair. "Don't ask me what order they go in."

I laughed and rested my head against his shoulder. "I wouldn't dare, just in case you decided hockey came first. Then we might have a problem."

"No problem, you come way before hockey," he said. "Just don't tell the team I said that. Coast and Tiger will pout at me."

"Shit," I said with such an alarmed tone, he drew back and looked at me, eyes wide. "Heaven forbid they pout at you."

He smacked my ass so hard it stung. "Don't be a brat. I thought something was genuinely wrong."

I pouted at him.

He smacked me again. "I think I should take you home, tie you up and spank you until your ass is bright red."

"They'd notice if we snuck out early," I pointed out. They wouldn't really, everyone was too drunk to care. Those who weren't were having too good a time to pay attention to us.

"I don't care." Aidan glanced around. "I don't want to leave Fin and Orion here tonight." He was confident the Fiorellis would wait and meet at the appointed time and place. Honour amongst thieves and all that. But trusting them could easily end badly for everyone.

I spotted Orion and Finley to one side of the room, playing pool with Lex and Bray. Judging by the expressions on their faces, Finley was winning. He probably convinced them he didn't have a clue how to play and encouraged them to bet big against him. He was sweet on the outside, but on the inside he was as devious as anyone else here. And just as happy to take their money.

Aidan took my hand and led me over to the table.

"Just in time to see me whip their arses," Finley said cheerfully. "For once, I'm having a good night."

"For once, my ass," Bray growled, but he was grinning. "I know a fucking shark when I see one."

Finley made a show of looking around. "You see an AGL player? Oh, right, I see Storm Ryan over there with Andre."

Bray grinned and shook his head. "Not that kind of shark, dickhead. The kind who pretends he can't play pool and then takes everyone's money. Orion, why didn't you warn us about him?"

Orion shrugged and took a sip from his bottle of beer. "If you can't spot a scam a mile away, that's your problem."

"You didn't know, did you?" Bray asked.

"In case you didn't notice, he's taken my fucking money too," Orion said.

Finley grinned. "Hell yeah, I have. That'll come in very useful, thanks guys. You up for another game? Double or nothing."

Something I've noticed about professional athletes, they were all as competitive as hell. Even when they knew someone was better at something than they were, they couldn't seem to resist the challenge.

"You're on." Bray placed the triangle on the table and started to carefully position the balls.

Orion nodded and grabbed a piece of chalk to rub over the tip of his cue.

"I'm out," Lex said. "This is too rich for my blood." He crossed his arms over his burly chest and stood back to watch, and sip on the drink in his hand.

"Aidan?" Finley raised an eyebrow at him questioningly, then turned the expression on me. "Elenna?"

I raised my hands. "I have no idea how to play pool."

Finley grinned. "We'll teach you, won't we Aidan?"

"Sure." Aidan picked up a cue for himself and handed me one.

I frowned at it. "Which end is which?" I caught Bray in the corner of my eye, grinning.

Finley chuckled and turned the cue the right way. "You hold it like this."

He showed me how to lean over the table and rest the cue on my hand, with the other at the end of the stick to push it forward. "Aim for the balls, and hit as hard as you can. Try to only hit the ones on the table." He grinned and covered his groin with both hands.

"Okay, I guess I can try," I said with as much uncertainty as I could manage. I drew the cue back and drove the tip into exactly the right point on exactly the right ball that I'd intended.

It hit with a thud and split the triangle of balls in every direction. Two of them went straight into pockets, one on the side, the other on the end.

I straightened up. "Did I do all right?" I asked sweetly.

Bray laughed. "I told you I knew a shark when I saw one. She has that vibe."

I grinned at him. "I couldn't resist. How much was that bet for again?"

"We didn't make one," Finley said. "If you beat me, I'll eat you out."

"And if you win?" I asked. I had a feeling I knew the answer, but I decided to humour him.

"I get to eat you out." He grinned bigger. "It's your turn again."

Who could argue with a bet like that? If I lost, I got orgasms and if I won I got orgasms. That was my idea of a perfect win-win situation.

"I'll make you the same bet," Aidan said to me.

"Me too, but with sucking my cock," Orion said. His gaze was firm on mine, like he was resisting the urge to glance towards Finley. After a few moments he frowned and turned to Bray, the message obvious. 'Don't make any dickhead remarks about my girlfriend.'

Bray raised his hands, beer in one, cue in the other. "A hundred bucks is plenty for me. I don't want to end up having the shit beaten out of me by three guys with pool cues. Or a woman who actually knows how to use one." He jerked his head towards me. He didn't actually look worried, but it was just as well he was sensible and respectful. The night didn't need to end in violence. Especially not amongst teammates.

"Good answer." Finley patted him on the shoulder. He waved for me to have my next turn.

I leaned over the table and proceeded to show no mercy on any of their asses.

"Where did you learn how to play?" Lex asked, clearly impressed with my ability to hit balls with a stick.

"I used to work here," I said. "Behind the bar. When the place was closed, the staff would stick around for a drink and a few games. The guys thought I couldn't beat them, so I made it my mission to learn how to do just that. Taking their money was sweet."

He smiled and nodded. Unlike the quiet, angry types like Orion, or Aidan, he was the shy silent guy who was taller than most of the players, and wider too.

He was a goalie before he had to retire due to injury. He seemed to have devoted his life to making sure no other players got injured like he had. While injury was inevitable, he could at least help to reduce the severity and the amount of time the guys spent off the ice.

"I'm here for any woman who can shut up a guy with a big mouth," he said.

"Me too," I agreed. I idly wondered if he would get along with Wren. She was a 'take no shit' kind of woman and he seemed the sort to appreciate that.

I'd introduce them if I got the chance. Although, he might have to fend off Tiger if he was interested.

I should probably focus on my own love life before I worried about anyone else's, but I wanted my friends to be happy and the guys on the team were quickly becoming friends, even family.

If I helped them to live happily ever after, then there was no harm in it.

Right?

CHAPTER 28

"So, about that spanking." I slowly ran my fingernail down the side of Aidan's cheek, down his chin and throat to the top of his chest.

He regarded me, his head turned to the side in interest. "What about it?"

"You threatened me with one," I reminded him. "If you can call it a *threat*. I think of it more as…I don't know, an enticing suggestion." Very enticing. Arousing too. As deterrents went, it wasn't particularly effective. Which was the point. If he wanted to stop me from doing something, he would, but not like that.

"Really?" he drawled. "I need to work harder on my threats, if my own wife doesn't take them seriously." He wrapped his hand around my wrist and pressed his thumb into my pulse point.

"I take them very seriously," I said. "So seriously, I'm wet thinking about it."

"How wet?" He raised his eyebrows in question, but slowly, like he had all the time in the world.

"Very wet," I replied. "Practically ready to drip down my leg."

"If that's the case, I need to threaten you more often." He pulled me in for a kiss.

"Who is threatening whom?" Finley stepped out of the kitchen with a cup of coffee in his hands.

"Aidan said he'd spank me, but I'm still waiting." I didn't take my eyes off Aidan.

"Ah. I always thought you could do with a good spanking." Finley sipped his coffee and leaned against the island as though this was his new favourite spectator sport.

"She could, couldn't she?" Aidan grabbed my other wrist and held them both together. "I know just the men to administer it."

He pulled me over towards our bedroom, grip firm to the point of pain.

I resisted, tugging back against him and dragging my feet.

"Playing it that way, hmmm?" His voice was deep and rough. Just how I liked it.

"Who's playing?" I retorted. "If you want to spank me, you have to work for it." My pussy was throbbing in anticipation.

He squeezed my wrists tighter. "Then that's what I'll do. Remember our safe word."

For some reason, our safe word was watermelon. I'd

never used it, not yet.

He hauled me over to the bed. I wriggled and squirmed while both of them pushed me down onto my stomach, my hands above my head.

Finley grabbed the handcuffs. Between them, they clicked them around my wrists.

"We need to get these jeans off her," Aidan said.

Finley rolled me onto my side and held me while I struggled, leg kicking, to make it more difficult for Aidan to undo my jeans and slide them down my hips. I narrowly missed kicking him in the face. He ducked away at the last moment before he hooked his hands into the waistband and pulled.

I swivelled my hips and groaned. I loved this wild side of Aidan. The forceful side. He took what he wanted from me, no hesitation, no regrets. In return, I gave him everything. But he'd have to work for it.

He got my jeans halfway down my thighs.

"Turn her over, on her stomach," Aidan ordered.

They both turned me. Aidan tugged my jeans the rest of the way off, then my panties. A rush of cold air hit my wet pussy, arousing me like a touch.

Finley shoved up the back of my shirt and unhooked my bra. He ran his hands over my back, his skin rough against mine.

"She feels so perfect," he said, almost reverent.

"Shame she's such a bad slut," Aidan growled. "She needs to learn I don't make threats. If I say I'm going to do something, I follow through." He brought his hand down on my ass hard enough to make me squeal.

"She makes the best sounds," Finley said. His praise was a fascinating counterpoint to Aidan's degradation. Both made the pulse in my clit work harder.

"Yes, she does."

I glanced sideways.

Orion stood in the doorway. He was dressed in only a towel, his hair damp from a shower.

"Join us," Aidan ordered. "I'll teach Elenna a lesson while Finley teaches you."

Silence drew out for almost a full minute. I thought Orion might turn and leave.

Finally, he stepped into the room and sat down on the bed beside me.

"On your stomach, towel off," Aidan snapped at him. "Finley, there's another set of handcuffs in the drawer beside you."

Orion slipped out of his towel and lay down, his face turned towards me.

"You don't have to do anything you don't want to do," I said. "No one will mind."

"I know," he said. A moment of vulnerability crossed his features. The man underneath the hockey god exterior. I'd bet anything he didn't show that often. He was usually too guarded. Too composed. I loved seeing this side of him.

"I want this." His mask was back, but not as rigid as

before. A course or two of his brick wall was down, if not the whole thing.

"We need a safe word," Finley said. "How about hippopotamus?"

Orion snorted. "Fine." He looked like he wished Finley would get on with it. Eager to feel, but not to show that side of himself too much. Conflicted, but committed at the same time.

"Too easy then." Finley fastened the handcuffs around Orion's wrists and clicked them into place. "Good boy."

Orion's eyes went darker. Evidently he liked praise as much as me. I didn't know why that surprised me, but it did. I guess because he never seemed to need anyone's approval but his own. Maybe mine. I suspected the extent of his feelings for Finley went deeper than I'd suspected. Deeper than any of us knew, including Orion.

Finley slapped his hand against Orion's ass cheek, hard enough to make a loud crack.

Orion twitched and rolled over a little to face me, so he wasn't lying on his growing erection.

"Good boy, you liked that didn't you?" Finley soothed.

Orion grunted his agreement.

Finley spanked his ass a couple more times while Aidan spanked mine. He smacked me hard enough to hurt just the right way. After a few, my ass was stinging and as red as Orion's.

"That's enough," Aidan ordered. "Take the handcuffs off them."

Finley hurried to comply.

I sat up and pulled off my shirt, before releasing my breasts from my bra, which was hanging off at the back.

"Did I tell you to take those off?" Aidan growled.

"I can put them back on if you like," I said smartly.

He gripped my throat and pushed me back down onto the bed on my back. "What happens to bad little sluts?"

"We get punished." I bent my knees and curled up as if I didn't want him to touch me everywhere.

"That's right. I've already punished your ass. It seems like I need to teach your mouth a lesson." He held me in place with one hand and pushed down his pants with the other.

Fingers tangled around a handful of my hair, he pulled me over to the edge of the bed. His eyes dark, expression enraged and aroused, he shoved my mouth onto his thick, hard cock. He rammed himself between my lips so hard and deep I gagged.

"That's it, gag on my cock like the whore you are," he said. He pounded in again and again until tears poured from my eyes. Every single time, he thrust until I gagged, then pulled almost all the way out.

His relentless thrusting and ragged breathing was almost enough to make me come without a touch. He pulled out of my mouth before he came himself.

"Next time, you might think about what comes out of your mouth," he growled.

I definitely would. I'd say the exact same thing if it got me his cock like that.

He let go of my hair and stepped back while I caught my breath.

I glanced over to Orion and Finley. They sat watching. Orion's cock was rock hard in his lap. Finley's was trying to break the seams of his jeans.

"Do you want to see them touch each other?" Aidan asked.

"Only if they want to," I said.

Kissing was a big step. Spanking was an even bigger one. Touching each other more than that? That was huge.

"Elenna," Aidan barked. "I asked you what *you* want. Do. You. Want. Them. To. Touch. Each. Other?"

I was both aroused and ready to whimper at his tone. He was so forceful he could scare and turn me on at the same time. Knowing the things he was capable of, I should be terrified.

When I hesitated, the look he gave me filled me with chills and heat. Aidan in control was a hell of a sight. I couldn't have kept from being honest if I wanted to.

"Yes, I do," I said in a hurried whisper.

Aidan nodded and turned to the other guys. "You heard her." He stopped short of telling them *how* to touch each other. He understood there were limits even he couldn't push.

For now.

Finley and Orion turned to each other.

Slowly, slowly, Finley pressed his lips to Orion's. While they kissed, feather light, his fingers grazed over the length of Orion's cock.

I thought Orion might pull away, but he leaned into the kiss and the touch.

Finley wrapped his fingers around Orion's cock and pumped him a few times.

Orion moaned.

Apparently feeling overdressed compared to the rest of us, Finley drew back from Orion and shed his jeans.

"You're welcome to touch me, if you want to," he said. His cock was as erect as Orion's. Pre-cum leaked off the tip. It was here Orion touched him, brushing the pad of his thumb over Finley's head to wipe that drop clear.

He turned and pressed his thumb between my lips, letting me suck Finley's juices from him. He smiled and turned back to tentatively run the tips of his fingers over Finley's cock.

"Good boy," Finley said. He wrapped his fingers back around Orion's length, pumped him a couple more times before lowering his mouth and licking the head.

Orion grunted in pleasure.

Aidan rolled me onto my side so I could keep watching them. He parted my legs and lay down behind me. He gripped my hips and pulled me onto his cock.

It was my turn to moan. His harder length sliding into my slick heat was pure heaven. That and watching Finley's lips close over Orion's cock. He moved slowly, his eyes on the defenceman's. If Orion made any move to pull away, or showed any sign he didn't like what Finley was doing, he'd stop in a heartbeat. Finley was all about praise and his partner's pleasure.

I didn't think he had much to worry about, because Orion looked as blissed out as I felt.

"You like that?" Aidan whispered in my ear. "Watching them?"

"I like it very much," I said. I didn't know what was hotter, the sight in front of me or Aidan's thrusts. In the end, I decided it was a tie.

"Good, but you need more. Orion." Aidan slowed his strokes. His fingers dug into my hips, sure to leave bruises later.

Eyes half closed, Orion reached out to run his thumb over my nipple and down my stomach to my clit. I quivered the moment his fingers brushed over my most sensitive place. I was ready to come from just that touch.

"Give her more," Aidan ordered.

Orion ran his fingers around my clit in rhythm with Finley's sucks and Aidan's thrusts.

I rolled my hips in rhythm with all of them, driving myself harder on to Aidan's cock, while riding Orion's fingers. I pictured them brushing against each other while they fucked me.

"I'm going to come," I said, my breath ragged.

"So am I." Orion's voice was shaky.

I glanced over to Finley, certain he heard. If not, Orion's breathing would have given him away. He didn't take his mouth off the other guy's cock. If anything, he seemed to be sucking faster and harder. Like he wanted Orion to blow his load down his throat.

I cried out as I came. I wanted to close my eyes and let the wave of bliss wash over me. I forced myself to keep them open so I could watch as Orion also came.

His hips rolling, thrusting him in and out of Finley's mouth. A hundred universes of bliss and heat and cries of pleasure exploded around me, washing over like an exploding constellation.

I came down as Finley slid off Orion and scooted over to me.

He smiled before pressing his lips to mine and trickling Orion's cum into my mouth. My eyes widened in surprise, but I smiled back, waited until they were all watching, and swallowed.

"Holy shit," Aidan grunted and came, losing his own load inside my body. "Such a… Good… Fucking… Slut." He thrust in a handful more times before slumping against me and holding me tight.

"That was something," Finley said softly. He looked pained until Aidan slid out of me and draped my leg over Finley's, letting the equipment manager's erection take his place.

Aidan and Orion sat up to watch while Finley

fucked me, his cock sliding in and out of my pussy, which was drenched with my release and Aidan's.

"You feel divine," he told me. He rammed into me a few times before he too came, filling me to overflowing with his cum.

"I'll never get tired of watching other people fuck you," Aidan told me. "It's almost as good as doing it myself."

"I'll never get tired of anything any of you do," I said, suddenly sleepy.

I snuggled into Finley and started to drift off while he was still deep inside me. I might just lie like this forever. Me and my guys.

CHAPTER 29

"Are you sure this is a good idea?" I asked.

The question was rhetorical. Aidan wouldn't be doing it if he didn't think it was. I'd never met anyone who was as stubborn and single-minded as he was. Which was saying something. Especially in comparison to Finley and Orion.

Aidan glanced at me. "Your ass needs more spanking?" He didn't even attempt to keep his voice down. Or the smile from tugging at the corners of his mouth, in spite of the gravity of the situation.

"If this goes wrong, your ass is going to be the one spanked," I said tartly. "I also don't make threats."

"Because you wouldn't dare." He slipped his gun into the back of his pants and shot me a look.

I returned it, unflinching. He wasn't scaring me now. Most of my fear was directed outside our apartment. Precisely in the direction of anyone named Fiorelli.

"Are you sure Elenna shouldn't stay behind?" Finley asked. "I don't like the idea of taking her into the lion's den."

"I don't either," Aidan said. "But I don't want to leave her behind. Or you."

"There's also the little matter of me not being willing to stay behind," I said. "If you try to leave without me, I'll follow you. And you know you can't tie me up to stop me from doing that, because if anything happens to you, I'll be fucked."

Aidan rubbed the back of his neck. "I could ask Wren and Sinclair to watch over you."

"You don't want anyone else involved in this," I pointed out. "The more people who know, the bigger the chance of this going wrong. I don't want my friends involved anyway."

They were more than capable of taking care of themselves, but this was our shit. It didn't need to be theirs too.

"We should put Elenna on the first plane to somewhere else," Orion said, his tone as dark as his expression. He hadn't said much since Finley sucked him off, but didn't seem to have any regrets. Right now, he was focused on getting this done.

"I'm pretty sure people would notice if you put me on a plane at gunpoint," I said dryly. "Which is what you'd have to do to get me on one."

There was no way in hell I was leaving Dusk Bay while all of this was going on. I'd rather be scared and know what was happening than safe and oblivious. And worried. Not to mention the fact the Fiorellis would wonder why I suddenly left. If I had nothing to hide, why run? Raising their suspicions could be a death warrant.

"I could arrange a private helicopter," Aidan said. He looked at me like he was planning to do just that.

"Or we could get this over with," I said. "We don't have the time it would take to get a helicopter here."

"Don't count on it," Finley said. "You'd be surprised how quickly Aidan and I can get something like that sorted. We have skills and contacts. Between us, we could get one here in," he glanced at his watch, "ten minutes."

"I'm still not getting on it," I said. "Besides, if you really wanted me gone, you would have either got me drunk or spiked my drinks and put me on an aircraft last night."

"Fuck," Aidan said softly. "But that's the only flaw in my plan." He tangled his fingers in my hair and leaned over to kiss me. "Seriously, I thought about it, but you would have shot me in the dick when you woke up and returned."

"Exactly, I would have," I said. I wouldn't, but I would have been pissed off.

If I was that drunk, or unconscious, I'd be vulnerable, and there was no way in hell Aidan would have put me in that situation. He had enemies only too happy to hurt me to get to him. Some wouldn't hesitate to use me in any way they could. And record every second to taunt him and drive him to do something rash.

"If Aidan has no dick, then there's more pussy for Orion and me," Finley said with a grin.

"Don't make me shoot you in the balls," Aidan told him. "I'd hate to waste a bullet."

"Sure you would." Finley grinned broader. "The truth is, you like me too much to do that. Besides, Elenna would miss my balls. Orion too." He glanced towards him, but not with pressure to agree. He simply seemed curious about Orion's response.

Orion might have agreed on the inside, but on the outside his expression gave away nothing. Not agreement, not disagreement. Little more than a passing interest in the conversation. He was as focused now as he was on the ice, his body tense and ready.

"I'd miss your balls," I told him, as much to soothe his ego as to take his attention from Orion before the situation became awkward. "They're some of my favourite balls."

"Along with pool balls," Finley said jokingly. "I owe you a rematch sometimes."

"You owe my pussy some orgasms," I retorted.

"I'm happy to deliver as many as you can take the moment we're done here." He nudged Aidan over with his shoulder, then kissed me.

"I'll take all of them." I kissed him back, then pulled away from both of them to walk over to Orion. I placed a hand on his muscular bicep, which was threatening to break the seams of his black T-shirt. His skin was so warm he was almost hot to the touch. No wonder he wore a T-shirt while the rest of us were dressed in a couple of heavier layers.

"From you as well. Are you okay?" I looked up at him. He was so panty meltingly hot, he still took my breath away every time I looked at him. Sometimes I wondered if he was actually real. How could anyone as good-looking as him actually exist? Not only exist, but be into me?

"Hunky-dory," he said. "I eat Fiorellis for breakfast and spit out their bones." His words were light, but his expression and tone were as dark as his eyes.

"If anyone could spit out bones, it's you three," I said.

"I prefer to eat the bones," Finley said. "It's good for the digestive system." He patted his flat stomach.

I would have made a joke about eating bones, or sucking them, but it might fall flat right now. Not to mention remembering him with his mouth around Orion's cock, then sharing his cum with me would make me hot and wet.

Too late.

All of us together like that, it was intense and wonderful. We let go of most of our inhibitions and embraced each other and our intimate desires. We trusted each other enough that we could start to let go. We could touch and be touched, watch and be watched. No one was excluded. Everyone was respected and cared for. Everyone's needs were met. Everyone was free to explore and learn about themselves and each other. There was something incredibly special about every moment of it. Something just for all of us.

"The sooner we go, the sooner Finley can be shitting out Fiorellis," Aidan said.

"Hell yeah." Finley offered his fist to Aidan to bump. "Let's hope they don't give me indigestion first."

"Take some antacid with us." Aidan checked his gun was still in place. "Better yet, a gun."

"I have one of those." Finley tapped a hand where his was hidden under his Demons hoodie. He was making no effort to hide who he was. As if anyone would mistake the gorgeous redhead for anyone else. There weren't many red haired Irishmen associated with the Dusk Bay Demons hockey team. Or any other of the teams, for that matter. Just one and he was mine. Ours.

Aidan glanced over at Orion, who nodded.

"I'm ready." He waved a hand vaguely towards his gun. "But I'd like a minute or two alone with Elenna first." Before they could argue, he grabbed me just above the elbow and drew me into his room.

"If you're going to fuck, make it quick," Finley said. He sounded like he was laughing as he said it.

Orion rolled his eyes and didn't bother to close the door behind us. "I wish that was what I brought you in here for." He glanced down at the floor.

"Me too." I spoke lightly, but frowned at the same

time. "Why do I get the feeling this is much more serious?"

Like so often, I couldn't tell what he was thinking. He seemed slightly more wound up and on edge than usual. Not surprising, under the circumstances, but this was Orion. He was always in control of himself. Almost always.

He looked back up. "Because it is. If I don't make it through the rest of today—"

"You will," I said firmly. "If you don't, I'll haunt you. It won't matter if you're dead and I'm alive, I'll find a way. I'll have your remains put into a puck so everyone can smack the shit out of you until the end of time. I'll even make sure they all put their sticks into the toilet first. One that hasn't been flushed."

That was literally the most disgusting thing I could think of. Not the part about the puck. Knowing humanity, that was a thing already. Something hockey obsessed people opted to do after they died. Whatever, I wasn't going to judge.

He surprised me by smiling. "Except for the toilet bit, that sounds pretty sick to me. I'd spend forever on the ice."

I grimaced at him. "Leave it to a guy to see an upside to a threat like that. Don't tell me, you want people to beat the shit out of you."

He shrugged. "Nothing I wouldn't deserve."

I placed my hands on his firm chest. "You *don't* deserve that. I don't believe that for a minute. But still, don't die, because I might be tempted to do it to piss you off."

He closed his hands around my forearms. "I'm leaving you my cabin," he said. "If anything happens to me, I wanted you to know, it's all yours."

I blinked. "You don't have to—"

"I want to," he interrupted. "That night up there with you was one of the best nights I've ever had. *The best.* You reminded me life doesn't have to be a non-stop shit show. It can be fun sometimes. I intend to come back here when all of this is over and take you up there again for longer. But if I can't, it's yours and I want you to go up there and enjoy it. If you want to take those two degenerates, it's up to you, but have fun there."

"Orion—"

He placed a finger against my lips.

"Promise me. If anything happens to me, you'll go up there and toboggan your cute little ass off. And laugh. Toast marshmallows over the fire, fuck on the rug, whatever. Promise?"

After he lowered his finger, I exhaled. "Okay, I promise. But you have to promise to try really, really hard not to die."

He smiled again. Twice in as many minutes. That must be some kind of record.

"I will try as hard as I can not to die. I have other plans that include me, you and lots of orgasms."

"Funny, I have the same plan." I stood on my toes and kissed him slowly, deeply. My heart ached at the idea of going to his cabin without him. However sweet the gesture was, I'd much rather have him in my life than knowing I own a piece of property. Even one that came with a cool, red toboggan.

When this was over, I wanted all of us to go up there and have fun. Could we all fit in the toboggan? I didn't know, but we'd have a shit ton of fun trying.

CHAPTER 30

ELENNA

"This is the place." Aidan parked his black SUV behind the long warehouse.

According to the sign across the side, the warehouse housed appliances. Another one across the back said not to trespass. The building itself was in a good state of repair, suggesting it wasn't abandoned, just out of the way at the end of the industrial complex. Nothing about it suggested any shifty activities took place here. Naturally, this was the perfect location for it.

We didn't say anything as we climbed out of the SUV. All of our senses were on alert for anything out of place. Any sign the Fiorellis changed the plans in some way, or decided against showing up. Given how adamant they were about finding Oscar's killer, the latter seemed unlikely.

The former, on the other hand, was a much bigger

possibility. We trusted them as far as we could actually spit their bones.

The guys arrayed around me, Aidan led us to the back door. He tapped on it three times, then three more.

A minute or two passed before the door opened.

Nicholas stood just inside the door, Celine a few metres behind him. Neither had a gun in their hand, but they'd both have them, ready to use in a heartbeat.

"You're late," Nicholas said.

Aidan shrugged. "So what? We're here."

Evidently Nicholas had no answer for that. He stepped back and waved us inside. His gaze lingered on me for a few seconds longer than necessary. Longer than he looked at my guys.

I gazed back at him as if I wasn't intimidated as hell. I was sure he could see right through me. That he knew I was the one who pulled the trigger, blowing his brother's brains out. Did I have guilt written all over my face? Aidan was right, I should have stayed back at the apartment. I was going to give everything away.

Nicholas turned away and stepped over to Celine.

"We appreciate you coming here to surrender our brother's killer," Celine started.

"That's not what we're here for," Aidan said coolly. He stared them both down.

Neither flinched. The only indication of Nicholas' annoyance was the tick of a muscle in his cheek. Celine's hand hovered near her hip, presumably where her gun was.

"What are you here for then?" Celine asked. Her voice was colder than the ice on the hockey rink. It could have frozen a candle flame. She reminded me of Oscar. Would she cry the same way he had when he was bound, duct tape over his mouth?

Was it wrong that I wanted to find out?

"He's stalling," Nicholas snapped.

"Not at all," Aidan said easily. "Condolences for your brother's death, but you have higher priorities and I believe it's something we have in common."

"I don't want to discuss—" Nicholas started.

Celine cut him off. "What are you talking about?" She turned a narrow-eyed glare to Aidan, before looking at the rest of us, one by one. Appraising us as though discerning each of our weaknesses, learning them, so she could exploit them.

"First of all." Aidan strolled around the inside of the warehouse, glancing at boxes that may or may not contain fridges or washing machines. "Getting revenge for Oscar will only continue the cycle of retribution and death. If you kill one of mine, I'll have no choice but to kill one of yours. And so on. The continued cycle doesn't help anyone. I'm sure you'll agree with that." He turned back to face them.

"It doesn't have to continue," Nicholas snapped. "It can end here, with Oscar's killer."

It could have ended with Ike's killer, but Aidan and I both wanted justice. Hell, it could have ended before Ike died. I wanted to yell at them, to ask what killing him actually achieved. They could have exposed him as a spy and kicked him out. They didn't have to tie him down, put a gun to his head and pull the trigger.

I bit my lip to keep from speaking out. From crying out. He was my baby brother, nothing would convince me he deserved to die like that.

"I'm not going to let you get the justice you think you need," Aidan said. "If you do, I'll kill one of you, or one of your siblings. That will significantly weaken your family and your position in it."

"What are you talking about?" Nicholas snarled.

"He's talking about our stepmother," Celine said softly. Apparently she was the brains between the pair of them. That made her more dangerous.

Aidan didn't say anything for a few moments; he let Celine's words sink into Nicholas' mind.

Nicholas turned to stare at her, but realisation wasn't long in sinking in. A range of emotions flashed through his eyes and on his face. Finally, he settled on wary.

"What are you proposing?"

"We've all seen Geneva's power rising," Aidan said. "How many times has she undermined you and operations Dante put in place? I'm well aware Orion here tried to disrupt your human trafficking operation, but she was already making inroads there. Wasn't she?"

Orion grunted. "She made it easier for us to do what we did."

Nicholas looked ready to pull out his gun and shoot

someone. I didn't think he knew exactly who, either. Maybe Aidan or Orion, or maybe Geneva. One thing was very clear, he didn't like having his weaknesses exposed like this. Who did?

"We suspected she's been working against us for a while," Celine said. "Or at least, working to further herself and her biological children. Ever since Dad died, the family has become more and more fractured. Some of our biological siblings have taken her side."

"Like Oscar did." Finley spoke for the first time.

Heavy silence fell.

Nicholas glared at Finley with undisguised resentment. Obviously Oscar's allegiance was a sore spot, and Finley poked right into it.

"Ike exposed that fact, and that was what got him killed," Finley said. "Because Oscar was betraying you. That would piss anyone off."

"But Oscar isn't the only one," Aidan said. "You're both still more powerful than Geneva, for now. Oscar's killer did you a favour. Wanting revenge for his death is to save face, I understand that. But losing your legacy to Geneva and your other siblings would be much worse. Wouldn't it?"

Nicholas and Celine exchanged glances.

"What are you proposing?" Celine asked again. Her dark blue eyes were full of scepticism, but she wasn't walking away. Not yet.

"First of all, stop wanting Oscar's killer dead." Aidan

counted the points off on his fingers. "Second of all, I propose an alliance between us, to prevent Geneva from becoming more powerful."

"What's in it for you?" Nicholas asked.

"You know where our loyalties lie," Finley said. "Reuben doesn't want Geneva to take Dante's place. Or surpass him. That would be bad for business. He'd rather deal with one of you two."

Reuben would rather deal with neither of them, but Aidan and Finley had a point.

Dealing with Geneva before she became a problem would be better than waiting and letting her become a bigger, more destructive and disruptive force.

"I vote for letting them all fight it out between themselves," Orion said. He stood with his arms crossed, looking unimpressed. "Why should we bother to help them?" His dark eyes took in everyone, while giving away nothing. Only the press of his lips together suggested he'd rather kill Fiorellis than work with them.

"Because chances are they won't do us all a favour and self-destruct." Aidan glanced at him quickly. "I'd rather work with these two so we can bring down Geneva than take the risk. Then comes the added bonus that both the Fiorellis and the Brantleys will owe us some big favours."

Now I understood the full extent of Aidan's plan. He was right, he was never going to hand Orion over to these two. He wasn't going to let the henchmen dotted around the warehouse kill any of us. The offer to help Nicholas and Celine was the perfect opportunity for all of us.

The idea of working with them wasn't quite so terrible now I knew Oscar was working for Geneva, not them. That knowledge assured my agreement too. Not that Aidan needed it. If I disagreed vehemently with this whole plan, he'd push on with it anyway. I might pretend to disagree later, if it got me another spanking. At the end of the day, this was the right thing for all of us.

If Nicholas and Celine agreed.

Nicholas grabbed Celine by the arm and pulled her aside. They talked in low, harsh whispers for a few minutes. Every so often, he'd gesture with his hands, chopping the air and indicating his frustration or annoyance. Gradually, the gestures reduced and he crossed his arms over his chest instead. His whole body looked tense, tighter than a guitar string.

Hers was only slightly less so. Her temper was much more in check than his. Whatever she was saying was based on rational thought, not emotion. I wasn't sure if that would work in our favour or not. She could just as easily have been reasoning out why they should kill us now and stuff our decomposing corpses in one of the boxes to ship off somewhere else.

"You think they'll go for it?" I asked Finley, keeping my own voice low.

He shook his head. "I dunno. If they know what's

good for them, they will. What choice do they have? Geneva will be the one to chew them up and spit out their bones. She's becoming influential enough to get noticed and that draws in all sorts of people. People who want their slice of the pie and can't get it from the Fiorellis. Plenty will turn to the Mancinis, especially if some of the Fiorelli kids can convince them."

I wasn't sure Orion was wrong in his suggestion that we should step back and let them implode. If Aidan thought for a moment that was possible, that's exactly what he'd do.

When it came down to it, he understood the way these people worked better than I did.

Nicholas and Celine stepped apart. She walked back to us while he stood and scowled.

"We accept your help," she said. "Only in dealing with Geneva and our siblings. That's the extent of the deal between us. We owe you nothing more."

"We want a promise," Aidan said. "We'll help you if you don't come after any of the four of us. In turn, we won't come after either of you two." He didn't add 'unless we're forced to.' That was a given.

They weren't trustworthy people, but they, like us, would keep their word when they gave it, up to a point. Promises were never given lightly and only broken when they had to be. If they agreed to this, Orion and I could sleep safely at night. For now.

Celine glanced back at Nicholas, who nodded reluctantly.

"You have a deal," she promised. "Like you said, Oscar betrayed us anyway. We'll put the word out that we've dealt with his killer and the matter is done with." That way, they'd save face and Geneva wouldn't come after us, believing Oscar hadn't been avenged.

"Whatever you have to do," Aidan said. "It looks like we have some talking to do and plans to make. Let's deal with Geneva before she realises what's going on under her nose."

"As long as you realise who is in charge here," Nicholas said.

"I'm absolutely confident I know who's in charge here," Aidan said, his tone clearly saying it was him. "I've been doing this a lot longer than anyone else here. If anyone knows how to get to Geneva, it's me. I am, however, open to suggestions." He spread his hands like this was their chance to have some input into what happened.

Nicholas growled, but Celine waved at him to back down.

"We're happy to hear what you have to say," she said smoothly. "I suggest fighting amongst ourselves would be counterproductive." She arched a perfectly shaped eyebrow at Aidan as though he was the one causing the tension.

"I agree completely," Aidan said. "Let's sit down and have a civil conversation." He turned that same look on Nicholas.

"Well, it's going to be interesting," Finley said under his breath.

I snorted softly. It was definitely going to be that. A few egos might need to be put aside for a while.

CHAPTER 31

"This is bullshit," I said.

Aidan crossed his arms over his chest like the smug bastard he was. "You're welcome. In case you've forgotten already, this agreement saved your ass."

"This…agreement means working with some of the biggest assholes anywhere in the country." Not to be unappreciative, but he'd made a deal with the devil.

"You didn't seem to mind us when I was sucking your cock," Finley said with a grin.

I fought to contain the heat that threatened to surge onto my face and my dick. The memory of his mouth on me was seared into my brain. Elenna's mouth and his. At the moment, it was a distraction I didn't need.

"I'm not talking about you." I snapped, but not as harshly as I would have a couple of weeks ago. I was losing my edge because of these guys and Elenna. The jury was out as to whether it was a good thing or a bad one.

"I was referring to Nicholas and Celine," I said, as if they didn't know that and weren't being smart asses. "I appreciate you stopping them from coming after me, but let's not pretend it wasn't Elenna you were looking out for. You would have thrown me under the bus to save her."

"Of course I would," Aidan said. "You'd do the same to me. Or to yourself. Any one of us would sacrifice ourselves for her. But when it comes down to it, this arrangement works for both of you. So, you're welcome."

"And now we're stuck working with those toads." I glanced out the restaurant window and across the street to where Elenna was having lunch in a small coffee shop with her friends. We were close enough to reach her if something happened, but far enough away to give her some independence. Or some pretence of it anyway. I would have preferred to sit at the table with her, or the one next to her. This compromise made my skin itch. She belonged to us, did she really need to be away from us, even this far?

She laughed at something one of her friends said. My heart flipped in response. She was so fucking gorgeous. More than I deserved. More than any of us deserved.

"If it's any consolation, they probably said the same about us," Finley said. "Although, Aidan has the closest resemblance to *actual* toad." He grinned while Aidan flipped him off.

"That sounds like the voice of jealousy to me." The head coach sipped his beer. None of us would drink enough to get drunk, not while Elenna was all the way across the road, but one or two wouldn't hurt. If we didn't have drinks or food in front of us, the restaurant would kick us out.

"Of course I'm jealous," Finley said. "I've seen myself in the mirror. I'm no Prince Charming."

"You're not so bad," I told him. He looked a bit like Ed Sheeran and Chris Hemsworth had a love child, with Hemsworth's muscles and Ed's hair colour. Unfortunately, he sang like a rubber chicken getting strangled.

"That's what my mum always says, but she might be a tad biased." Finley held up a hand with two fingers spread slightly apart.

"Orion might be a tad biased too," Aidan pointed out. "It's hard not to see someone in a positive light when they've sucked your cock."

Heat threatened my face again. "I'm not biased. I already thought that." I shook my head. "Stop changing the subject. We were talking about Nicholas and Celine."

"No we weren't, because there's nothing to discuss." Aidan took a long pull on his beer. "This is what's happening. You have to agree, nothing I said was wrong. Geneva will make trouble for us and I trust her even less than I trust them. She's a lot more ambitious and a shit load more ruthless. I would have had her removed myself, but this works more to our advantage. If Nicholas and Celine come to trust us, then we're in a good position. We can negotiate between them, and Caleb or Reuben."

I frowned. "And by that you mean absorb the Fiorellis into the Brantleys the way the Bells are being absorbed?"

"I doubt the Bells see it that way," Aidan said. "But yes. Everyone is becoming more and more Brantley every day. Why not Nicholas and Celine?"

"That would make Reuben very powerful," Finley remarked. "Maybe he'd be encouraged to throw more money at the Demons."

"Potentially," Aidan said, looking cagey like he did when he had something in mind and wasn't going to share. I already knew better than to ask. He was nothing if not a stubborn fucker.

"Either way, we're going to be right in the thick of it," Finley said. "What could go wrong?"

"I can think of a few things," I said darkly. "Most of them revolve around us ending up dead." I glanced back towards Elenna. She was talking about something her friends seemed to find hilarious. Was she blushing? I wished I could lip read so I knew what she was saying. I also wished I could take her away from all this and keep her safe.

In the back of my mind, I pictured her lying dead, a

bullet through the centre of her forehead. Maybe one in her heart. Her skin pale, cold as ice. The life gone from her beautiful body. So fucking still.

There was nothing I wouldn't do or give to stop that from becoming reality.

"Whatever you're thinking, it's not going to happen," Finley said softly. "None of us will allow it. We'll do everything possible to make this turn out okay. And if we can't, we'll find a deserted island and hide there for a decade or five. We can live on fish, coconuts and orgasms."

"We could go there first," I said. I turned back to them, knowing there was no way they'd run away now. The moment Aidan threw in with Nicholas and Celine, we had to follow through. If we didn't, they'd find a way to break their promise. They could go to Geneva or even to Reuben and tell them fuck knows what. Reuben wouldn't care if we ended up dead, as long as we didn't cause him any inconvenience.

"I didn't pick you for a quitter," Aidan said.

"I'm not," I said brusquely. He was baiting me, but I couldn't resist taking it. "I've never quit anything in my life. I don't want any shit to happen to Elenna. If we have to walk away to do that, then..." I shrugged one shoulder.

"We're not walking away," Aidan said. "Not from the Fiorellis, or the Brantleys, or the Demons, for that matter."

"Especially the Demons," Finley said. "Now we're

finally winning, now would be a really bad time to go anywhere."

Anger flared inside my chest. "Your priorities are—" I placed my hand, palm down on the table and started to push myself to my feet.

Before I could blink, Finley picked up a fork and jabbed it into the table, right between my pinky and ring fingers. He missed stabbing my skin by a hair.

"My priorities are just fine," he said calmly. "I also care what happens to Elenna. You know as well as I do that she wouldn't run away either. She trusts us to keep her safe, and that's what we'll do. While at the same time, keeping a problem contained which could make life worse for a lot of other people." He took his hand off the handle of the fork and sat back.

I lowered myself into my seat and pulled my hand away. The fork remained embedded in the timber tabletop.

"You're right," I said finally. "She wouldn't run away. Even when she should."

I couldn't stop my gaze from drifting to Aidan. This was his plan. If shit went sideways, it would be his fault. Something none of us would hesitate to remind him of every chance we got. Assuming he didn't get us killed. That was one hell of an assumption right now.

"She has no reason to run away," Aidan said. He too glanced over to where she sat.

For a man who was frequently angry and always arrogant, he had a surprisingly soft expression in his eyes when he looked at her. If anyone doubted his feelings for her, they had only to see that to understand. He loved her completely.

So did I.

"Hard to run when one of us is with her every moment of every day," Finley said.

"Exactly," Aidan said. "That won't change any time soon. If I could, I'd handcuff her to me. Unfortunately, if I did that, she'd be pissed off." He seemed as though he was still considering the idea. Debating whether her safety was more important than her feelings for him.

"Yeah, she would. Her friends would probably try to get her free," Finley said.

"I'd like to see them try," Aidan growled. He didn't disagree that they *would* try though. Wren and Sinclair seemed to adore her as much as we did. And she adored them.

"In mud," Finley said. "Clothing optional."

That melted Aidan's scowl. He chuckled. "The only woman I want to mud wrestle naked is Elenna. With or without handcuffs."

"I bet you would," Finley said. "Because you know who would end up doing the laundry when you spread mud everywhere."

"I'm having a hard time seeing a downside to this." Aidan looked thoughtful, but the corners of his mouth hinted at a smile.

"Of course you would." Finley rolled his eyes. "You'd be the one having fun while I clean up after you."

"Doesn't sound like fun to me," I said. "Unless you're into having mud up your ass."

"There are other things I prefer to have up my ass," Finley said. He gave me a meaningful, heated look that made my balls hurt.

I cleared my throat. "Anything would be better than mud." Kissing him and having him suck me off were big enough steps without thinking about fucking his ass. Of course, now I was thinking about fucking his ass. I hadn't even fucked Elenna's yet. I wanted to. My cock was itching to get between her two perfect cheeks. How tight would she feel? My guess was perfectly tight and sweet. As sweet as her pussy, and her mouth.

"I bet you're not thinking about scoring a goal right now," Finley teased.

I almost let myself smile. "Yes I am."

Aidan snorted. "Not on the ice."

"Ice was definitely not in my brain," I said. "Don't either of you pretend you're any better. If we could, we'd all spend the rest of our lives in bed with her."

"Yes we would," Finley agreed. "And with each other. While Aidan watches and tells us what to do. I don't hate that idea." He turned to Aidan. "Can we do that?"

"As you pointed out a couple of minutes ago, the Demons have started winning," Aidan said. "That wouldn't happen without the three of us. When they realise they're losing, they'll come and bang on our door. That would be slightly disruptive."

"A deserted island is sounding better and better," Finley said. "We wouldn't even need doors. Just a roof and somewhere to call a bed."

"And sand up your ass," I said.

Finley waved his hand dismissively. "It would be totally worth it."

"Until you run out of sunscreen and burn red as a lobster," Aidan said.

"Fuck," Finley growled. "I knew there had to be a flaw in the plan. Why did I have to be a redhead?" He ran a hand over his hair like somehow the colour might rub off.

"Nature telling you you're not destined to live on a desert island," Aidan said. "We're all much better suited to the ice hockey rink."

And creeping around the shadows.

My gaze returned to Elenna.

For her, I'd creep around in every shadow.

CHAPTER 32

"I hope Aidan knows what he's doing," Wren said around a mouthful of strawberry cheesecake. "As far as I can tell, nothing good ever came from interacting with people like Nicholas and Celine. Or Geneva, for that matter."

"If you keep adding to it, the list will be long," Sinclair pointed out. "And probably includes us too."

Wren swallowed her mouthful so quickly she almost choked. When she was done coughing and washing her cake down with gulps of coffee she managed to say, "Speak for yourself."

"Oh, I am," Sinclair said with a smile. "I'm a very dubious person. I work in PR for a hockey team owned by other very dubious people. To anyone on the outside, that makes me suspicious as fuck."

"You're not suspicious," I told her. "Working for

suspicious people doesn't automatically make you suspicious. I work in the same place, remember?"

She grinned.

I socked her lightly on the arm. "Just because you're right doesn't mean I'm not offended," I said jokingly. I'd killed two people. That certainly didn't make me a perfect angel. No matter what the circumstances were.

She rubbed her arm. "I think you just helped to make my point. So violent."

"Quick question," Wren said. "Do your guys think we don't know they're there?" She jerked her head towards the window.

"They know we know," I said. "And if they didn't, they do now." I considered giving them a little wave, but decided against it. They were trying to be discreet. Ish.

"I can't decide if you're lucky or not." Sinclair said slowly. "On one hand, they're all gorgeous. On the other, that's a lot of testosterone, even without everything that's going on. And then there's the relationships with each other. Aidan and Finley are friends and Aidan is Orion's coach. How do they get along, especially when it comes to sharing you?"

I toyed with the handle of my fork, occasionally poking it into my custard tart. "They get along okay, most of the time. Aidan and Orion seem to leave their problems at work. Mostly, they want to make me happy, and that includes getting along. In and outside the bedroom."

"I think I've decided you're lucky," Wren said. "Because that sounds pretty amazing. They obviously care about you a lot. If anyone took a wrong step towards you, they'd be over here like a shot. That's kinda hot."

"You better be careful taking steps towards me," I said laughingly. "Wouldn't want to end up in a headlock."

She laughed. "Maybe I would. Not with one of them though." She cocked her head. "I wonder if Tiger is the sharing type?"

"He might be," I said. "His brother is." I couldn't imagine Tiger getting along with anyone well enough to share, but stranger things had happened.

"Good point," Wren said as she poked her fork into a strawberry. "Maybe he could be convinced."

"Who would you want to have him share you with?" Sinclair asked.

"Is the rest of the team too much to ask?" Wren laughed. "Imagine all those cocks." She sighed wistfully.

"Imagine never being able to walk again," Sinclair said.

"You say that like it's a bad thing." Wren popped the strawberry into her mouth.

"She has a point," I said to Sinclair. "She could get them to carry her everywhere."

"This is sounding better and better." Wren chewed thoughtfully and swallowed. "Is there a signup sheet for this? Because my name will be right at the top. I bet Sinclair would be second."

"Not for a whole hockey team," Sinclair said. "I wouldn't say no to a couple of them." She stabbed her carrot cake like it was someone's face.

"Let me guess, Coast Riggs." Wren raised a red eyebrow at her in sympathy.

"Of course not," Sinclair said weakly. "A guy like him would never be interested in a woman like me. He doesn't even know I exist."

"Then he's not worth your time," Wren said. "There are plenty of other fish in the sea."

"I don't want a fish." Sinclair grimaced.

"There's plenty more *men*," I said. "I've seen the way they look at you. You could have your pick." If she stopped mooning over Coast. But the heart and clit wanted what they wanted. Sometimes, they even agreed with each other.

She sighed. "I suppose I should put myself out there more."

"No 'suppose' about it," I said. "I want both of you to be happy. If that's with one other person or ten, or none, you have my full support."

"Maybe I'll get a dog," Sinclair mused. "They love you no matter what. For all my other needs, there's a multitude of vibrators on the market."

"I've never met a vibrator that was as good as having an orgasm given by someone else," Wren said. "But if that's your best life, then I'm happy for you too."

"If that's my best life, I might as well go straight to having fifteen cats," Sinclair's shoulders slumped.

I couldn't help laughing. I couldn't imagine Sinclair with that many cats. She was way too young to be a crazy, old cat lady anyway.

"Definitely not," Wren said. "At least get sixteen cats to make it even."

She grinned as Sinclair flicked carrot cake in her direction. She ducked to the side, narrowly missing being hit by a piece covered in icing. "Elenna is right. I've seen guys staring at you too. If you give one of them a chance, you never know what might happen. You might forget all about Coast Riggs and live a long and happy life with some hot guy and sixteen cats."

"I don't think I want to share a guy with that many pussies," Sinclair said.

We all laughed. Sitting here with them let me forget everything else for a while. Especially the part where we were about to make an enemy out of Geneva Mancini, her biological children and whichever of her stepchildren were on her side. The prospect was daunting and might end up with me as dead as if they handed me over to the Fiorellis for Oscar's death. This was a risky game Aidan was playing with all of our lives. One wrong step, one miscalculation and we'd be fucked. Not in the good way.

"You look like you're contemplating your life choices," Wren said to me. "How many cats will your boyfriends let you get?"

Boyfriends. It was strange to hear that out loud. I could hardly get my head around having three partners, especially being legally married to one of them. How did I ensure that Finley and Orion never felt second to Aidan? Or ensure that Aidan never held our vows over the other guy's heads.

I'd like to think he wouldn't throw his weight around, but this was Aidan we were talking about. He was the very definition of alpha male. He liked things done his way, end of story. Whatever it took to get there, he'd do it. Even if it meant putting a wedge between him and the other two. If he felt the need to do it, he'd do it. It was that simple.

"None, I'm allergic to cats," I said. "I wasn't thinking about that."

"I know," Wren said. "I know what you're thinking. Do you want Sinclair and I along with you when things go down? Safety in numbers and all that."

"It might be safer for you to stay as far away from it as possible," I said. The last thing I wanted was to drag them into my shit and get them killed.

"Sounds like you need us," Wren said. "We're here for you if you do, right Sinclair?"

"Absolutely," Sinclair agreed. "Whatever it takes. I don't want to look back in ten years, when Geneva is too powerful for anyone to deal with, and wish I'd done something. I've always thought she was a snake. Even more so than Dante was."

"That's saying something," Wren said. "He was a major asshole."

"That's my point," Sinclair said. "I could get behind an ambitious woman, but she'd stab someone in the back without thinking about it. Without flinching. Even if they were members of her own family. If I were her children, I wouldn't turn my back on her."

I could say the same about most of the people I knew. Reuben Brantley. Samuel Bell. They'd all do what they had to to cling onto it. Hadn't I just had the same thought about Aidan?

He was different though. Aidan caused friction, but he'd never kill Finley or Orion to get his way. He was as loyal as he was ambitious.

"Neither would I," I said. "The sooner she's dealt with, the better for all of us."

Wren leaned forward and rested her elbows on the table. "Can we be sure none of the Demons are working for her? For all we know, Coast is a trusted minion."

"He is not," Sinclair snapped.

"How do you know?" Wren turned her face to regard her.

Sinclair shifted in her seat. "I just know, okay? The same way I'm sure you know Tiger isn't."

"Do I know that?" Wren asked.

"If you don't know, then you might want to reconsider going out with him," I said. "At least until all of this blows over and we know for sure."

She swiped her tongue over her lips. "Yeah, you're right," she said slowly. "It's only for a little while. Then after that..." Her eyes widened. "I guess it won't matter, because if he's in tight with her, he probably won't survive."

I reached over to put a hand on her shoulder. "I'm sure things will turn out fine."

Honestly, I didn't think for a moment Tiger Pennington was involved with Geneva, but if it kept Wren safe, it was better to assume everyone was suspect.

"Which brings us back to hoping Aidan knows what he's doing," Sinclair said.

I hoped the same thing.

"Of course he does," I said. If I didn't have faith in him, I couldn't ask them to. "In a couple of days, this will be over and we can laugh about it. Or...be relieved."

People were going to die, laughing was unlikely.

My hands were coated with a thick layer of blood and brains again. Oscar's life was warm as it splattered on to me. It cooled while his body cooled. It hardened, caked under my nails. Layers and layers that wouldn't come off no matter how hard I scrubbed.

"Elenna? Elenna?"

I blinked and realised Wren was shaking me lightly. I was wringing my hands so hard they hurt. Hands which were clean of blood, bones or brain. Oscar was long gone, cremated, according to Aidan. If only I could put my guilt on a fire and incinerate it too.

I lowered my hands to the table in front of me. "I'm okay. Every so often, I remember what…what I did. It comes back to me like that."

"Have you seen anyone?" Sinclair's face was scrunched with concern.

"I'm seeing you two," I said. "I don't need professional help. What would I say anyway? What could I say that wouldn't get me locked up?"

"Reuben really needs to invest in more therapists," Wren said. "Ones who won't judge, or turn any of us in to the cops. You know, I was going to go into psychology, but I didn't get the grades at school. Lucky I love what I do, because I wouldn't have been good at much else."

"Yes, you would," I told her. "You would have been an amazing therapist. I would totally have gone to you for help." She was smarter than she gave herself credit for. Not everyone was academically inclined. Not to mention the sad fact that academics wasn't tailored for every person. Someone would always fall through the proverbial cracks, even someone as amazing as Wren.

Wren dipped her chin, but smiled. "I appreciate the vote of confidence, but I don't think I'll go back to school to find out. Making jewellery is more my calling."

"You're amazing at it," Sinclair said. "But dangerous to my bank balance."

Wren grinned. "Sorry, not sorry."

"I thought you might not be," Sinclair said dryly. She glanced towards the window and frowned. "Uh-oh. Looks like shit is about to hit the fan."

I stepped out into the street with my friends close behind me as Aidan led the guys out of the restaurant on the other side. He glanced at me and headed over at a trot, reaching me as the car door opened.

Reuben stepped out, his two closest minions behind him, Damon and Gianni.

"It seems we need to have another conversation," Reuben addressed Aidan, ignoring the rest of us. "Your apartment." He gave absolutely no room for argument, even if Aidan was inclined to try.

Aidan nodded and gestured toward the front of the building, fifty metres or so down the block. "It must be important if you've come all this way."

"Of course it is," Gianni said. "Reuben is a very busy man, but when it comes to things like this—"

Both Reuben and Damon cut him a look; Reuben's glance telling him to be quiet, Damon's almost as unreadable as Orion. His bright blue eyes seemed to take in everything while giving nothing back. Compared to him, Orion was an open book.

Gianni mimed zipping his lips, but smiled at me and even gave me a wink.

I gave him a faint one back. If I knew anything, it was never to underestimate Gianni. He was an expert in getting people to talk, whether it was with charm or torture. Men like him knew how to inflict the maximum amount of pain with the minimum amount of effort. From what I understood, his methods were a lot more subtle than Ice Miller's, but just as effective.

I wouldn't envy anyone who ended up in their hands.

Finley and Orion walked on either side of me, Orion carefully putting himself between me and Gianni.

Damon gave Wren and Sinclair a deliberate glance when we stepped through the front of the building and headed to the elevators.

"They're involved now," Reuben said, giving neither of them an opportunity to leave before the conversation became intense. Or even deadly, judging by the expression on Reuben's face. Would he come here personally if he was going to kill us?

Yeah, I honestly preferred not to find out.

We squeezed into the elevator and rode up in silence. I caught Sinclair looking at Damon and Gianni, but quickly dismissing them as potential 'other fish.' Just as well given how dangerous they were. She could take care of herself, but these were not men to toy with. All three of them made me nervous as hell.

We exchanged the tight space of the elevator for the more comfortable one of our apartment, but with Reuben and his men, it felt tiny. Suffocating.

"Coffee?" Finley asked cheerfully. Without waiting for an answer, he stepped over to the kitchen and started the coffee machine.

"I see you got my message," Aidan said. Appearing unconcerned, he crossed his arms over his chest and leaned back against a wall.

"Damon is in the habit of passing them on," Reuben said as though he didn't appreciate the subtle accusation. "I preferred to hear it straight from your mouth. You're proposing to work with Nicholas and Celine Fiorelli." It wasn't a question.

"It's less about working with them than it is about working *against* Geneva Mancini," Aidan said without flinching. "I'm sure you appreciate my initiative, in planning to take down a potential enemy before she becomes a major problem. I know Dante was a thorn in your family's side for quite some time. Geneva seems hellbent on picking up where he left off. Including attempting to recruit people who work for you. I sent Damon a list of those I know of."

I glanced at Aidan, trying to keep the surprise from my face. This was the first I'd heard of a list. Were any of the Demons on it? If they were, did Finley or Orion know? I was going to be pissed off if they all kept that from me.

"I passed those on too," Damon said bluntly. The only hint of annoyance was a slight narrowing of his eyes. "Reuben wants them all eliminated."

"Not all," Gianni corrected. "Anyone who might tell us about others should be kept alive until I can talk to them."

Reuben nodded to indicate his agreement with both of them. "I would like Geneva and anyone working with her to be neutralised. As long as you understand the promises you made to the Fiorellis who are working against her are not promises from me. Even with Geneva out of the way, the rest of them are a problem. One I've spent enough time and resources on. Once Geneva is gone, I want the rest of them dealt with."

"Understood," Aidan said. "Will you be extending any further resources—"

"I think you have enough," Reuben interrupted. "Every single member of the Dusk Bay Demons can be put to use."

"I'd rather not risk their hockey careers." Aidan scowled.

"Then deal with it yourself," Reuben snapped. "I don't care how you get it done, just get it done. Otherwise the Demons will be looking for a new head coach."

Aidan visibly bristled. If this was anyone but Reuben and his men, he'd probably punch them in the face or pull out his gun. Threatening him was a sure way to piss him off.

"Here you go." Finley hurried over with a cup of steaming coffee for Reuben.

It wouldn't take a genius to guess what Aidan was thinking. If that coffee was poisoned, his heart wouldn't break. Six of us could overpower Damon and Gianni, surely?

We could, but Reuben's brothers would bring down hell on all of us. No remote, deserted island would be far enough to save us.

With full knowledge of that, Reuben sipped his coffee, gracious enough at least, to nod his thanks to Finley.

"Who really killed Oscar?" Gianni asked.

I barely managed to keep from letting my mouth drop open, and gaping at him.

"I did," Orion said.

Gianni laughed. "Pull the other one, it plays 'Jingle Bells'. Who was it really?"

Sinclair and Wren looked at me speculatively. I should have insisted they stay inside the coffee shop. They wouldn't be involved now if they had.

"What makes you think Orion didn't do it?" Finley asked. He handed Damon and Gianni each a cup of coffee.

"Because Orion was with Reuben's youngest brothers when Oscar was killed," Gianni said. "Don't worry, it's a little-known fact, only everyone in this room and the twins are aware of it. There's no need for the Fiorellis to find out."

I glanced at Aidan. I had a feeling Gianni knew exactly who was responsible and this was some kind of test. If we didn't tell them, we'd fail. I saw the same thing on Aidan's face.

I swallowed and stepped forward. "It was me," I said softly.

"With my help." Aidan moved to stand beside me, his arm around my shoulders.

"You." Reuben regarded me for several long, painful moments. Finally, he gave me a curt nod. "He tortured your brother. Retribution for that is understandable."

"Ike wasn't the only one," I said. "If it wasn't me, it would have been someone else."

"It would," he agreed. "I had people looking for him to take care of him."

"Hunter and Parker were disappointed it wasn't them," Gianni said with a grin. "They enjoy killing assholes like Oscar as much as I do." He stepped over closer to me. "Did you enjoy it?"

I resisted the urge to step away. "No. No I didn't. He can't hurt anyone else. That's the only thing that makes it worthwhile." But hundreds of others were ready to take his place. People like Gianni and the Brantley twins. At the end of the day, they were no better than Oscar.

"That, in my humble opinion, is a very good reason to kill someone," Gianni said. "Oscar was a sadistic asshole. I'm a sadistic asshole, but I'm a discerning, sadistic asshole, in that I only kill people who deserve it. Especially people who do things to animals, children and women." His gaze went to Reuben, whose expression was grim.

I had a feeling there was a story there, but this wasn't story time. Not even if they wanted to share with us. Being curious about men like this was a dangerous pastime I didn't indulge in. Fuck knew I had enough on my plate as it was.

"That's admirable," Finley said to Gianni. He seemed genuinely impressed. Then again, it was Finley, so of course he was. He wasn't a man who'd go around killing innocent people for shits and giggles. He wouldn't admire anyone who was.

Gianni grinned. His smile was almost as terrifying as Reuben's scowl. "Isn't it though? I might not be pretty, like Reuben and Damon, but my heart is in the right place."

I wasn't sure if it was, but I kept that thought to myself. He was a criminal like his boss. Like Finley smuggling Caleb's goods. Like me helping him. Like everyone standing in this apartment.

"I trust your knowledge of Elenna killing Oscar won't leave this room," Aidan said to all of us. His tone clearly said he'd personally kill anyone who spoke about it.

"I see no reason for anyone to discover that information," Reuben said. "At this point, it serves no purpose."

He seemed disinterested in the topic. That was fortunate. He could have been angry I took the privilege away from his brothers, or whomever else he sent after Oscar.

I mentally translated that as meaning that if at some point it served a purpose, he'd share it. Until then, there was no need. If there were no Fiorellis left, it wouldn't matter anyway.

"In case you need a reminder," Reuben added, "Amity Fiorelli is off-limits. My brother Lucas has her well in hand."

"She's knocked up again," Gianni said gleefully. "For the third time." For some reason, he seemed to find that hilarious.

I wondered if Reuben sent Lucas to seduce Amity and get her pregnant in the first place. Honestly, it wouldn't surprise me for a moment. He'd likely do that with the rest of the Fiorellis if it would get them off his back. And onto theirs. Thinking about him seducing Geneva was a thought I didn't need in my brain. Or any other woman, for that matter. That was firmly in the 'it's his business' basket.

"Noted," Aidan said. "If she stays out of our way, we'll stay out of hers." Which would change the moment she became a problem. Hopefully she wouldn't. Leaving three children without a mother would be terrible, no matter what her crimes.

"Do that." Reuben nodded. "Make good use of the resources you have. Keep me informed. The minute

Geneva is gone, I want to know. And anyone else who is working with her."

"Consider yourself informed," Aidan said. He was obviously running out of patience for this whole conversation. Having to answer to Reuben clashed with his need to be in control.

In another lifetime, it would be Aidan calling all the shots. Imagining him with all that power at his finger-tips shouldn't have been hot as hell, but it was. I loved it when he took charge, whether it was of me, Finley and Orion, or the Demons. I had no doubt we'd pull off what Reuben wanted us to pull off. And then some. Aidan was too ambitious, too precise not to.

Without another word, Reuben downed the rest of his coffee, handed the cup back to Finley and left, his minions in tow. Only Damon glanced back as a silent reminder of what was at stake.

CHAPTER 34

FINLEY

"Well, that was interesting." I placed Reuben's empty cup in the dishwasher and closed the door.

Aidan and Orion were scowling, which was nothing new.

Elenna looked as troubled as she always did when any conversation turned to Oscar or anyone in his family. Her friends, Sinclair and Wren, sat to either side of her on the couch, talking softly to her and each other.

"That's one word to describe it." Aidan lowered himself into the chair opposite Elenna and massaged his temples with his fingers.

"It's bullshit," Orion declared. "He wants us to do his work for him." He glared in Aidan's direction. "We agreed to help take care of Geneva. I don't remember signing up to deal with the rest of them."

Aidan exhaled loudly. "I didn't either, but it is what

it is. One thing at a time. We accomplish one and we'll address the other. Let's not get ahead of ourselves."

"We don't need to get ahead of ourselves, we have Reuben to do that for us," I said. "Wouldn't it be nice if he just dropped in for a friendly chat and some donuts?"

"I don't think Reuben is capable of a friendly chat," Sinclair said. She frowned, and a moment later added, "I'm not sure I can imagine him eating donuts either."

"That's when you know someone is dubious," Wren said. "When you can imagine them eating the hearts of their enemies, not donuts."

"For what it's worth, I can imagine all of you eating donuts," I said. I made a mental note to bake some later. They were fiddly, but totally worth it.

"I can't help thinking that's a euphemism for something else." Sinclair smiled.

I chuckled. "Maybe it is."

Aidan gave me a funny look and I raised my hands in surrender. "You're a 'heart of his enemies' kind of guy too."

He grunted. "What's really important here is that we keep our priorities straight. That's the Demons and Geneva, in that order. Whatever Reuben wants will have to wait. We have a home game tomorrow night and our plan to deal with Geneva right after that. Anything beyond that…" He shook his head.

"What do you need us to do?" Sinclair sat forward, her hand still on Elenna's arm.

"I said you don't need to get involved." Elenna frowned at Sinclair, then at Wren.

"We already are." Wren gestured around the room. "We're in this together. And anyway, do you think we'd turn our backs on you that easily? You know we're stubborn bitches. It's one of the things you love about us."

Elenna turned to Aidan, silently pleading with him to say something, anything, to agree with her.

He massaged his temples harder. "They're right, they are already involved. Since Reuben isn't going to give us any more help, then we need to take it where we can."

"That's a backhanded compliment," Wren observed. "Sinclair and I both know how to handle a gun, and ourselves. We'll be an asset, just tell us where you need us and what you need us to do."

Elenna closed her eyes and looked pained. She knew when she couldn't win an argument. She opened them again and pinned Aidan with a glare. "If you get my friends killed—"

"If they're dead, it means the rest of us are too," Aidan said. "I won't put them in harm's way. No more than necessary."

Elenna didn't look placated, but she nodded anyway. Knowing Sinclair and Wren, they'd probably follow us, or somehow figure out exactly what we're up to and jump in with both feet. Both were as ballsy as Elenna.

"Don't worry," Wren said, leaning over to give Elenna a squeeze. "We've got this. Promise."

Elenna squeezed her back. "You better," she growled. She was adorable when she was as aggressive as Aidan or Orion. She was a lioness, protecting her pride. There was nothing she wouldn't do for the people she loved.

"We'll be fine." Sinclair took her turn in hugging Elenna before both she and Wren stood. "We should get out of here. I have a meeting at work that I'm late for."

"Who is it this time?" Wren grinned.

Sinclair grimaced and they both stepped out the door, closing it behind them. No doubt I'd find out later who the player behaving badly this week was. It was always *someone*. Managing equipment was a lot easier than managing hockey players and their egos. I didn't envy Sinclair her job.

Aidan sat back. "I know you don't like involving them, but we can use their help. Someone needs to watch Geneva and make sure she's exactly where we need her. They shouldn't be at risk, for the most part."

"It's the smaller part I'm worried about," Elenna said. "Geneva didn't get where she was by being stupid. Sooner or later, she's going to suspect something is going on. When she does…"

"She won't suspect we have anything to do with it," I said. "We have the element of surprise. That's going to make all the difference."

Aidan moved to sit beside Elenna. "I don't mind admitting Fin is right. No one is going to expect us to work with Nicholas and Celine. Including them, if I'm honest. They're probably waiting for us to stab them in the back."

"Which we will if Reuben has his way," Orion pointed out.

"Like I said, let's deal with one problem at a time," Aidan said. He cupped Elenna's cheek and leaned in to kiss her mouth.

Watching them together was always exciting, but this felt different somehow. Like Aidan was kissing her while he could. Like he'd decided that no matter what, if anyone was thrown to the lions, it would be him.

There was zero chance I was letting him go there alone.

I caught Orion's eye. He nodded. He got the same vibe. Clearly agreeing that Aidan was not going to do this by himself. If he didn't get out of this alive, none of us would.

I walked around the kitchen island, placed a hand on Orion's muscular bicep and looked him right in the eyes. He had every chance to step away before I brushed my lips over his.

The next thing I knew, his hand was on the back of my neck and he was kissing me back. I grabbed Elenna's arm and drew us all into the biggest bedroom with the biggest bed.

Everyone seemed to be tearing at everyone's clothes, until they were strewn all over the floor. In moments, the floor was covered, like a chest of drawers had exploded.

Then we were all on the mattress, Elenna in the middle of the rest of us. I kissed Orion for a while longer before rolling over to kiss her.

"Orion, get the lube out of the drawer beside you," Aidan ordered.

Orion nodded and pulled the drawer open before reaching in for the tube and tossing it to Aidan.

Aidan left the tube on the pillow. He scooted down to part Elenna's legs with his hands and lowered his face down between them. His head bobbed as he licked and sucked her pussy and clit.

I sat up to watch and savour the way her back arched, her beautiful moans of pleasure. One of my hands idly dropped to Orion's lap, the tips of my fingers teasing his growing erection.

After an audible swallow and a few moments of hesitation, he did the same with my cock. With almost painful slowness, he ran his fingers from my tip up to my balls and back again.

He touched the bead of pre-cum that leaked from my slit, and smeared it as he slid his hand back up towards my balls.

His gaze dropped. He seemed fascinated by the way I felt both similar to him and different. My cock was slightly bent, longer but narrower than his. He seemed especially fascinated by the Prince Albert piercing decorating my head.

"Did that hurt?" He touched the ball on one side.

"At the time, yeah but it's worth it," I said. "Elenna loves it."

Elenna came, writhing and crying out Aidan's name to the whole building. Her eyes were shut tight, lips slightly apart as she focused on rocking her hips and grinding her clit against Aidan's face.

Watching her come, knowing she was in the middle of the wave of pleasure was both fascinating and arousing as hell.

She finally let out a whimper and flopped down to catch her breath.

"Such a good girl," I told her.

She turned her face towards me and smiled. She was so fucking gorgeous, she knocked the breath clean out of my body. So beautiful, sweet and smart.

Orion rolled his hips.

I turned back to him. He was also fucking gorgeous. Definitely not sweet, but his own brand of incredible.

I caught a moment of open emotion on his face, a look directed at Elenna, then at me. There was no need for words, I knew from that alone exactly how he felt. The same as I did, head over heels for her and him.

Aidan cleared his throat and the moment passed. He lay on his back and pulled her onto his cock. "Orion, lube her up. Elenna, lean forward and let him do it."

She leaned forward eagerly, glancing back over her shoulder as Orion squirted lube onto his finger and smeared it around her rear hole.

I didn't know which ached more, my balls or my cock. Holy shit.

Orion slowly, carefully eased his massive dick into her ass.

She groaned. "Oh, my—that feels… amazing. I've never felt so full."

"Finley." Aidan regarded me.

I raised an eyebrow at him. Whatever he had in mind, I was game for it.

"Orion's mouth looks empty," Aidan said.

Hell yeah, I was definitely game for that. If Orion was.

I knelt beside him and worked my cock a couple of times.

Orion gripped Elenna's hips and turned his face towards me. Tentatively, he opened his mouth.

Watching him the entire time for his reaction, I pressed my cock between his lips. When he didn't pull away, I pushed in deeper. He swirled his tongue around my head, circling my piercing and sliding across the sensitive skin of my engorged cock.

"Fuck, that feels good," I groaned.

Elenna turned her face to us. I almost came then and there from the expression in her eyes. She left no doubt in my mind that she liked what she saw.

Without thinking, I smiled at her and said, "I love you."

She didn't look surprised, nor did she hesitate to say, "I love you too."

Aidan started to move, thrusting up into Elenna's pussy. Like with everything else, he was the one who set the pace for the rest of us to keep. Slow and steady at first, but gradually becoming faster and faster.

Between Orion's mouth on my cock, and watching his sliding in and out of Elenna's ass, I was right on the edge, hanging on by my fingernails.

I didn't want to come too quickly. I could happily have stayed right here in this moment in time for precisely an eternity.

"I'm going to come again," Elenna said. Her voice was high, breathless. Fucking arousing.

"That's my slut," Aidan said approvingly. "Come for us like the whore you are."

"Such a good girl," I told her. And then to Orion, "Good boy."

Orion's dark eyes darkened further. He was right on the edge himself. He tumbled over when Elenna did, slamming his cock into her ass and filling her with his cum.

Aidan followed a moment later, pounding up into her body.

I hung on long enough to come a heart beat or two after him, squirting my hot release into Orion's mouth. His eyelids jerked upwards in surprise, but he took his mouth off my cock, looked right at me and swallowed.

"That was so hot," Elenna said breathlessly.

"We definitely need to do this again," I agreed. Every night until the end of time would be just about perfect.

CHAPTER 35

ELENNA

"If the team keeps up their momentum, they may be in contention for the Goodall Cup," Aidan was saying to a reporter right before the game.

I was only half-listening. My attention was on making sure the players had all the equipment they needed, and doing runs back and forth from the washing machines and dryers to make sure the guys had clean, fresh towels.

Finley was right, it wasn't glamorous, but I didn't mind. I liked working with him and the other guys. I loved watching my guys do what they did best, organising, leading and kicking ass. Their confidence was hot and contagious. If they could stay calm, then I could.

"What's your reaction to rumours that your wife is dating two other men?" the journalist asked.

Aidan laughed. "I thought we were here to talk about the Demons?"

"You're their head coach, so I'd think it's Demons related." The journalist laughed, like she was trying to lighten the mood and put Aidan at ease. "Wouldn't you agree?"

I walked past with an arm full of folded, dry towels and resisted the urge to wrap one around her throat when she smiled at him, obviously attempting to flirt.

Aidan caught my eye and rolled his towards the ceiling. He was definitely not impressed with her efforts.

I made a face before hurrying on, into the locker room to move the towels from the trolley and place them on a shelf near the showers. I barely glanced at the semi-naked men around me before hurrying back out with dirty ones in need of washing. The hamper wasn't full, but I wanted to walk past again and make sure I didn't need to rethink my temptation and strangle her after all.

I trusted Aidan, it was the journalist I didn't trust not to put her hands where they shouldn't be. If she wanted to keep them, she better be careful.

"No, I don't think my personal life is relevant here," Aidan was saying. "I'd rather talk about the team's performance this season. If you're not here for that then I can—" He started to step away.

She rallied quickly. "Of course, would you say Orion Scully-Evans' addition to the team has had a positive impact on their performance as a whole?"

"Definitely," Aidan agreed. "He's been a big asset, as

has the increase in team unity. As you know, no team is all about one player. The Demons have pulled together this season and they're playing like a well-oiled machine. There's always room for improvement, but it's a step in the right direction."

"Yes, I'm sure it is," she said. "Well, all of Dusk Bay is cheering you on tonight."

She sounded disinterested now she knew she wasn't going to get any dirt from him. She or someone else would try again later. At some point, we'd have to discuss our relationship with the world, if only so we could control the narrative.

I smiled to myself and hurried past. If she noticed me there, I might be bombarded by personal questions, and I wasn't ready for that yet. So far, Finley and I managed to keep out of the limelight, happy to leave that to Aidan and Orion.

"She's relentless, isn't she?" Sinclair trotted to catch up with me. "I swear she lies awake at night thinking of ways to get me to spill the beans on the players. She knows full well I have an ironclad NDA. Even if I wanted to talk about them, I'd be fired and sued so hard my grandchildren would still be paying off the debt."

"I have to give her bonus points for persistence," I said. "What's her name?"

"So you know who to take the hit out on?" Sinclair teased. She glanced back over her shoulder. "Naomi Higgins. She works for the local television station, but I suspect she's angling for a job in Sydney or Melbourne. One juicy story here could make her career."

"She's not going to get it from me," I said darkly. "She seems like the kind of person to change a story to make it seem…more salacious than it really is."

"Definitely." She glanced at her watch. "Ten minutes until game time." She seemed preoccupied.

"Is this about after or during the game?" I asked, careful to keep my voice down.

"Believe it or not, it's both," she said. "I can't tell you what or who, because of my NDA, but I have a feeling you'll find out soon enough." She gave me an apologetic look and a nod before heading to the entrance that led into the rink.

I wished I could do something to help, but no doubt she had the matter in hand well enough. She was good at what she did, including putting out Demons-sized spot fires. Because of her, the team had a good reputation within the AIHL community.

If only they really knew what went on around here.

I hurried to throw the towels in the washing machine before I also headed towards the rink to watch.

"Orion is off his game tonight," Finley remarked, his mouth near my ear, eyes on the ice.

"He does seem distracted." Which I totally understood. I'd be distracted as fuck too.

He'd already missed taking control of the puck when the opposition centre almost handed it to him. He'd stopped short of bashing his stick into the boards in frustration.

Aidan pulled him off the ice for a couple of minutes to give him a chance to regain his cool. By the time he went back out, he was slightly calmer, but still on edge.

The rest of the team was a lot more focused. Ever since the first puck drop, they'd virtually skated over the opposition.

I couldn't remember ever seeing Tiger so aggressive, which was saying something.

Coast seemed to be everywhere.

Phoenix hadn't let a single goal get past him, although one came incredibly close. He'd snapped his arm out at the last second, stopping the puck maybe a finger width from the inside of the post.

Now, he knelt in front of the goal, legs apart, leaning forward, ready.

Bray, Javey and the rest of the team sat on the bench, cheering and shouting, while Aidan yelled out directions, telling Bray to be ready to get on the ice in a minute or two. They switched out so often I didn't know how they didn't get whiplash. It was all part of the game, and I admit, added to the excitement.

The atmosphere in the arena was both tense and electric at the same time. The whole audience was on the edge of their seats from the start of the first period.

Mostly cheering for the Demons, but many supporting the opposition.

Some of these people probably never went to an ice hockey game before this season. The sport was still growing in Australia, but it was growing quickly.

The horn sounded for the end of the first period and the guys skated to the edge and stepped off the ice.

Aidan said something to Orion that had him shaking his head and looking furious. I couldn't make out what they were saying, but neither of them looked happy.

Orion stomped away and grabbed a drink of water.

"Wild guess that Aidan noticed Orion's head isn't in it," Finley said.

I snorted. "If I noticed, then he definitely did. Maybe he's thinking about last night." I glanced sidelong at Finley.

He grinned. "I know I am. I also noticed you had trouble walking this morning, before you had a bath."

"I have no regrets," I declared. Last night was amazing. Having Aidan and Orion deep inside me, while watching Orion suck Finley off, was memorable.

We'd all showered, more or less together before meeting back on the bed for a second round. This time with Finley in my pussy, Aidan in my ass and Orion's cock in my mouth. And in Finley's too, for a while.

I thought Aidan might tell them to fuck each other, but it was as clear to him as it was to me they weren't quite ready for that yet. When they were, I wanted to be there.

"I didn't think you did," he said. "You seemed to be enjoying yourself very much."

"I did, but my favourite part was hearing you say you love me," I said. And saying it back to him.

"I do love you," he said. "Very much." He kissed my cheek. I didn't look around to see if the journalist or anyone like her was looking or taking pictures. A kiss on the cheek and a quiet conversation could easily be construed as innocent. No one could prove it wasn't.

"I love you too," I said back. I crossed my legs at my knees as the second period started. As I expected, Orion was sitting out on the bench. He looked like he could have chewed holes in the ice, but it was Aidan's call.

The second period went almost as well as the first, but the opposition snuck two goals past Phoenix. It ended with the Demons leading by five points.

The third started with Orion back on the ice, looking like he was ready to spill blood to prove that he deserved to be out there.

"He's almost as hot as you," Finley remarked.

"He's much hotter than me," I argued. All three of them were, but that was okay. I loved all of them, no matter what, and I knew they all loved me, even though Orion hadn't said so yet. He would, when he was ready. Or I would. Either way, we'd get there.

"Not a chance," Finley said lightly. "I'm going to devote the rest of my life to making you realise how beautiful you are. And giving you more orgasms than you can count."

"I'm going to do the same for you," I told him. "You're beautiful too."

He pretended to fluff the back of his hair, and grinned, before we both turned our attention back to the game.

Orion was definitely back in his headspace now. People right at the nosebleeds seats of the arena probably saw the look of concentration on his face. The way he followed the puck, aggressively keeping it from getting past him, and stopping the opposition from regaining control.

In the first few minutes, the Demons scored another goal, increasing their lead. The opposition battled, played well, just not as well as the Demons. Any other night, they may have won, but tonight they were having their asses handed to them on a silver platter.

The audience was loving every second of it. They were on their feet, stamping and clapping as Javey snuck the puck in around the goalie by feinting to the left and charging to the right at the last second.

Ice sprayed up behind him, scraped by the suddenness of his movement. He was like a dancer out there. Strong and nimble.

"I give credit to them for not giving up," Finley said. It was only a minute or two until the end of the game and, in spite of a last-minute goal, they couldn't have caught up to the Demons.

The final horn sounded and the whole place erupted in cheers and shouts, and a rough rendition of the Demons' adopted anthem, a song by Wolf Venom.

Half the people didn't know the words, but no one seemed to care very much. They'd remember even fewer of them after a few celebratory drinks.

I clapped and cheered as loud as anyone else, before catching Orion's gaze and grinning.

He actually smiled back.

"Will miracles never cease?" Finley said. "He does know how to smile." He raised his hands and clapped for Orion, who rolled his eyes and sat down to remove his skates.

I elbowed Finley in the ribs. "Of course he does."

He laughed and rubbed his side. "It's good to see. He deserves to be happy. We all do."

"Yes we do," I agreed, letting him help me to my feet and heading away from the rink.

If Aidan's plan worked the way he hoped it would, we might even get the chance to do just that.

CHAPTER 36

I pulled on my coat and wrapped my red and blue Demons scarf around my neck.

Inside Finley's office was warm, but I shivered as though I'd already stepped out into the cold night air. I felt like my skin was covered in goosebumps.

Anticipation and fear of what was to come.

Footsteps sounded in the corridor outside. I turned, expecting to see Finley. Instead, Orion stepped into the room.

"You okay?" He'd changed out of his hockey uniform, showered and was now dressed in black jeans over old, black boots, and a faded grey T-shirt. What was the expression? Sex on legs. That was him.

He laced warm fingers into mine.

"Kind of," I admitted. Apart from the flock of birds flying around in my stomach. And the sweat on the palms of my hands.

"It's not too late to sit this out," he reminded me. "Go home and take a bath and we'll deal with it. Or go to Hazards and enjoy the celebration. We'll join you when this is done."

Both of those options sounded wonderful, but I shook my head. "I'm in this. I'm going to see it through to the end."

He took in my stubborn expression and nodded. "However this goes down, my cabin is still yours if I die."

"You're not going to—"

He pressed a finger to my lips. "Let me finish."

He lowered his hand to my cheek and inhaled. As he exhaled, he said, "I want you to know how I feel."

He huffed out the rest of his breath, heavy like he'd run a marathon. "I told you, the minute I laid eyes on you, I knew you were mine. Everything about you is incredible. Your heart, your spirit..." His knuckles ghosted down my cheek, to my neck. "Your body. Even your books."

He looked sheepish when I raised my eyebrows in surprise.

"Yes, I read them. How could I not?" He shook his head. "That doesn't matter now. What matters is that I need you to know I love you."

"I love—"

My words were interrupted by a boom. It sounded like it came from near the back of the arena. A moment later, it was followed by shouting and what sounded like gunshots.

"Fuck!" Orion pushed me into a crouch beside Finley's desk and dropped down beside me.

"What the hell?" I whispered.

He glanced at me but didn't say anything. We both knew the answer.

Geneva, or Nicholas and Celine, had come after us before we could go after any of them.

"I need to get to the equipment room," Orion whispered. "You stay here."

"I'm coming with you," I said quickly. "If they know the truth of what happened to Oscar, they're not going to stop until they find me. There's innocent people left in the arena. I won't let them get killed while they hunt for me."

"I'm not letting you hand yourself over to them." He looked ready to sneak me out another door, regardless of the consequences.

"I have no intention of doing that either," I said. "We need to find Aidan and Finley. And Sinclair and Wren if they're still tailing Geneva."

My heart squeezed. Had Geneva seen them? Were they…

I couldn't let myself finish that thought. My friends would be okay, they had to be.

Orion hesitated, verging on insisting I stay here or get out of the arena. I saw all of that on his face, followed by acceptance.

"Stay behind me," he said simply. "Do what I tell you to do and stay as quiet as you can." He rose and moved slowly towards the door.

More gunshots sounded, followed by screams. The silence that came after that was thicker than smoke.

Heavier than storm clouds.

The audience cleared out of the arena an hour ago, but staff and a lot of players remained for the press conference, or to start the cleanup.

Right now, it sounded like we were alone in here. If we were, then what happened to Aidan and Finley? I couldn't finish that thought either. I wouldn't accept that they were dead. Not even if I saw it with my own eyes.

We moved silently down the corridor and into the equipment room.

"Looks like the evening just got more interesting." Coast Riggs and Tiger Pennington, along with a couple of other players, were in the process of unlocking a locker in the back of the room and pulling out guns.

Orion grunted. "That's one way to put it. This anything to do with either of you?"

"Nope," Coast said. He tossed Orion a gun, then threw one to me. "Tiger and I saw about twenty of them swarm in after they blew the doors in. We recognised a couple of them."

"Fiorellis," Tiger said simply.

I checked over the gun in my hands. "Have you seen Aidan or Fin?"

"No, but knowing those two, they won't be far away." Coast held his gun out in front of him and peered out the doorway.

Tiger grabbed a couple more guns before closing the locker. "You never know if we might need extras." He shoved those into the back of his pants and stepped out behind Coast.

Coast glanced back at him. "Don't shoot me in the ass," he said to Tiger.

"Don't give me an excuse to," Tiger growled.

Coast grinned and turned away.

This was the kind of team unity Aidan hoped to see from both of them, but not under these circumstances. No doubt he would have appreciated the irony. He *would* appreciate it when I told him.

Orion rolled his eyes and followed them both out.

I quickly hurried to keep up with him.

The silence was broken by another couple of gunshots and a shout or two.

Up ahead, someone was running. I couldn't tell in which direction they were going. Not towards us.

We reached the end of the corridor.

It led out to a wide entry hall, wider now with the glass doors shattered, twisted metal hanging open. Shards littered the carpet, sparkling in the lights from overhead. A couple of bodies lay on the floor, blood pooled around them.

Neither was Aidan or Finley. Both looked to be players from the opposition team. I almost felt bad about the Demons having beaten them. They played so well and now, to end like this…

"I'm guessing they headed to the press area," Coast said. "That's where the rest of the team was last time we saw them." For the first time since I met him, his expression was grim. He gave both bodies a nod of respect before following Orion through another doorway at the back of the room.

"Stay in the middle of us." Tiger gestured for me to go ahead of him. He turned and walked backwards, covering the way we'd come.

For so many reasons, I wished Wren and Sinclair could see Tiger and Coast now. For one thing, if they could, I'd know they were alive.

They are, I told myself. *They have to be.*

The sound of a struggle came from up ahead, like feet scuffling on tiled ground.

Orion glanced back and nodded to Coast before they both broke into a trot.

I hurried along behind, sweat springing up on my forehead and under my arms. My scarf felt like a noose, but I had no time to remove it now. All I could do was keep up and look back every so often to make sure Tiger was still behind me.

He acknowledged me with a wave of his hand to keep going.

Orion and Coast drew to a stop beside the doorway to the press area. The door was open. Sound was coming from inside.

We were hidden from view for now, by little more than a flimsy wall.

My heart raced so hard it hurt.

Aidan and Finley were all right, they had to be. I felt like my whole world was teetering on the edge of an abyss. In the next few minutes, either we'd be dead or the attackers would.

Orion mouthed, "On three." He waited for the rest of us to acknowledge before starting the countdown.

One.

Two.

Three.

That was how many bodies lay dead inside the doorway. I recognised Naomi Higgins, the journalist who was asking Aidan about our relationship. Another was a junior coach. The third was one of the Demons' wingers.

They were all shot in the chest or stomach.

Beyond them lay a couple of people dressed in black pants and black hoodies. Both looked like they'd been struck hard on the back of the head.

At the rear of the room, near the door that led outside, Aidan, Finley and a couple of other Demons players stood over three people dressed in black. One man and a woman.

Both of my guys were visibly relieved to see me and

Orion alive and safe. As relieved as I was to see them.

"There's our beautiful woman," Finley said with a grin. He waved his gun at one of the men. "Have you met Jamison Fiorelli? He thought he'd pay us a little visit tonight, along with some friends of his."

"I thought he looked familiar," I said more easily than I felt. Two attackers dead and three held at gunpoint still left a lot.

I recognised one of Jamison's companions from our meeting with Nicholas and Celine. The other I didn't know at all.

I could come to so many conclusions right now, but we needed to deal with what was in front of us.

"Jamison was just about to explain why they're here," Aidan said. He pressed the gun to Jamison's temple. No one in the room was under any illusion that he'd hesitate to pull the trigger.

"We want Oscar's killer," Jamison growled.

"You found me." Orion stepped towards him.

"We know it wasn't you." Jamison glared up at him, then turned to me. His expression made my blood turned to ice.

"What do you *think* you know?" Aidan pressed the gun in harder.

Jamison tried to jerk away, but Finley had his gun on the other side, near his temple.

"We know Aidan Draeger had Oscar caught and taken to the location where he was killed," Jamison said.

He must have known he was fucked anyway, he

might as well come clean. If he was incredibly lucky, he might walk away from this alive.

"That's right, I did," Aidan said. "Someone had to deal with the prick." There wasn't even a hint of apology in his tone. If he ever had regrets in his life, engineering Oscar's death wasn't one of them.

"He was my brother," Jamison snarled.

"Ike was mine," I snapped. I was done with this pretence. It was time I admitted what I did, to myself, and to everyone else. "Oscar killed him, so when Aidan had him brought to me and gave me the choice to kill him myself, I took it. I held the gun to his head and blew his brains out."

Jamison flinched. "*You* did it."

"You thought it was me," Aidan guessed. "Or you didn't know, you just decided you'd figure it out as you went along."

"We knew enough," Jamison said to his own chest. "You as good as killed him. It didn't matter exactly who pulled the trigger."

"Are you here on behalf of Nicholas and Celine, or Geneva?" Finley asked.

"Or all of the above?" Orion added. "They might have pretended they had a divide to distract us from this." He gestured toward Jamison with his gun.

Jamison looked back at him, his lips pressed tight together.

"I'll take that as a yes," Aidan said. "It looks like open season on anyone named Fiorelli."

"It was Geneva," Jamison said quickly. "I was pretending to work with her until this was dealt with. This has nothing to do with Nicholas, Celine or Kaya." He looked desperate now. Wanting to keep his siblings safe.

Yeah, I knew how that felt.

"Oscar was working with Geneva," he added. "He was still my brother, but…" He shook his head.

"He betrayed all of you," Finley said.

"Yeah. I can prove Geneva is involved. She's in the building." His eyes begged to be believed.

I glanced towards Coast and Tiger, who stood near the door, acting as guards.

Coast shrugged. "I only got a quick look. One of them could have been her."

"If that's the case, we need to find her," Finley said. He lowered his gun.

Jamison sagged in relief, but it was premature.

"Shame you now know who killed Oscar," Aidan said. "We might have let you walk out of here, but that knowledge is something we can't let you leave here with." He nodded towards Coast.

"I swear I'll never tell—" Jamison's face froze before he slumped to the side, a bullet hole in the side of his head.

Coast turned the gun on his companions and put a matching one in both of them.

Aidan nodded his approval. "All right, let's find this bitch."

CHAPTER 37

ELENNA

"Where are the rest of the guys, as far as you know?" Aidan directed the question to Coast and Tiger.

"We all scattered when the door blew open," Coast said. "The rest of them must have gone the other way."

"Have you seen Sinclair and Wren?" I asked, my question directed at Aidan and Finley.

Both looked as though they'd forgotten my friends existed.

"No idea," Aidan admitted. "I presume you haven't tried calling?"

"No, just in case they're hiding out somewhere." I pulled out my phone and checked the screen. It showed no messages from anyone. No missed calls either.

I tucked my phone back in my pocket and unwound my scarf from around my neck. I scrunched it up and shoved it into another pocket.

"I'm sure they're fine," Finley said. He stepped over and gave me a squeeze and a kiss on the side of my mouth.

I wished I could be so optimistic, but all I could do was squeeze him back and take the comfort he was offering. I did the same with Aidan, who held on for a little longer before stepping back and directing everyone on where they should walk. Me, bang in the middle of the guys, beside Orion.

"I didn't get to finish telling you I love you," I said regretfully.

"You just did." He gave me a half smile before returning his focus to the doorway in front of us. "There'll be plenty of time later for us to tell each other."

"Yeah," I whispered under my breath. I kept my gun in front of me while we moved slowly, eyes and ears open for sound and movement.

Every so often, Aidan or Finley would move ahead to check through a doorway, or inside a bathroom.

Each time, they'd wave us on, my nerves becoming more and more frayed.

"Fuck," Aidan said softly.

"Looks like it," Finley agreed.

I frowned at them both until I realised what they were implying. We were close to the entrance to the rink.

If you were going to do something terrible to a hockey team, you'd attack them where it hurt them the most. On their very own ice.

"Now it's personal," Coast growled. When I glanced back at him, he shot me an apologetic look. "You're right, it was already personal. This makes it *more* personal."

"Keep digging yourself a hole," Tiger told him. "I won't need to shoot you in the ass, they'll do it for you."

"I'll shoot you both if you don't be quiet," Aidan snapped.

"Save your bullets for the enemy," Finley said. He moved on ahead, to peer carefully through the doorway that led to the rink. He stepped back away and nodded, his expression dark. "They have a bunch of people on the ice. They're surrounded by approximately fifteen people. They look like they're all armed."

"We know you're out there," a woman's voice called out.

Geneva.

"You know what we want and we know what you want. It's a very simple exchange. No one else has to die here today."

"The fuck they don't," Orion snarled, his voice too low for her to hear.

Aidan looked appraisingly at all of us before gesturing for Coast and Tiger to circle around to the other entrance. He held up one hand, with five fingers stretched out.

Coast nodded and they headed off at a trot.

"If we don't give them what they want, a lot of people could die," I said.

Enough already had. I wasn't going to let any more of them lose their lives because of me.

"If we give them what they want, I will personally create a bloodbath from the blood of anyone even closely associated with the Fiorelli family," Aidan said. "We are not handing you over to them."

"You're not going," I said before he got that idea into his head. "The team needs you. I need you." I put a hand on his cheek and silently pleaded with him to listen to reason.

"I think it's a good idea," Finley said slowly.

I looked at him sharply. "You can't be suggesting Aidan should…"

"No," he said. "I'm suggesting *you* should. It's only a matter of time before they put two and two together and come up with four. If Aidan goes, they'll kill him and then they'll come after you when they figure it out."

I gaped at him. Blinked a couple of times. "No, you're right. That's exactly my reasoning."

I just didn't expect him to agree with it.

"Are you out of your fucking mind?" Orion snarled. "She's not going in there. We're not sacrificing her for ourselves or anyone else."

"Of course we're not," Aidan said. "But Geneva doesn't know that."

I closed my mouth and eyes and exhaled out my nose. "Okay, I can do it."

Aidan glanced at his watch. "That should be just

about enough time." He kissed my mouth and spoke softly in my ear. "I love you. You'll always be the sun in the centre of my galaxy."

"I love you too," I told him. "All of you. Daddy Aidan, Orion, my constellation, and sweet Fin. You're my everything."

Finley reached for me to pull me into an embrace. "You're such a good girl. Go and do what you need to do."

I nodded and stepped towards the doorway, gun dangling from my fingers. I stepped through and held up my hands before I let the gun drop to the floor.

"It's me you want."

Geneva was a handful of years older than Aidan. Where his hair had sprinkles of grey, hers was fully dark brown, a couple of shades darker than mine. Either she had good genes, or she coloured her hair.

I couldn't make out any lines on her face at this distance, nor any other details other than that she was entirely in black, surrounded by people dressed the same.

I saw no sign of Nicholas or Celine, potentially confirming what Jamison claimed.

"Is it now?" she said smoothly.

She took a few steps closer, around the outside of the rink. "Elenna Christakos, if I'm not mistaken. Where is your husband?"

"Aidan has nothing to do with this," I said. "I'm the

one who killed Oscar. If you knew that weeks ago, it would have saved a lot of trouble."

"That's true." She clicked her tongue. "You certainly have caused a lot of that. I know my stepson was a handful, but he was young and ambitious. Not unlike your brother, Ike. They were a lot alike, I think. Both always into things they shouldn't."

I wanted to snap at her to stop talking about my brother. She had no idea what he was really like. Yes, he was a handful, but his heart was always in the right place. He was the kid who rescued injured birds and animals and nursed them back to health. He was the kid who punched bullies when they harassed other kids at school. He'd own up to it every time, which got him suspended several times and expelled from one school.

On paper, he was a pain in the ass, but he was still my baby brother.

"Guys can be like that." I shrugged indifferently.

"So can girls, evidently," she said, giving me a meaningful look.

"I suppose so," I said in the same tone of voice. "Either way, Oscar killed my brother and I killed him."

"You must realise he did that on my orders," she said. "Were you working on Aidan's orders?"

I snorted. I scanned the guys who sat on the ice, looking freezing cold.

Bray and Javey sat to one side, Phoenix near them. Lex right behind him. They were all watching me intently.

I dropped my chin and raised it again as though in response to Geneva's question.

"Aidan doesn't tell me what to do," I said. That was almost the truth. He hadn't told me to kill Oscar. He'd merely encouraged me to do it.

"I see you have guts," she said admiringly.

I didn't need her admiration, but I stood my ground and waited without answering.

She continued on. "You even had the guts to hand yourself over to me, knowing what would happen."

"I couldn't let you kill all these people for me." I jerked a thumb towards the ice. "When they walk out of here, you can do what you want to me."

"Wouldn't that be easy?" She crossed her arms under her breasts. "On the other hand, if I kill you now, it's a message to them. A visible reminder of what happens if they attempt to cross or disobey me. In order to maintain control, once in a while someone needs to be made an example of. In this case, that someone is you."

"Lucky me," I said sarcastically. "Go on then." I held my hands out to either side. At the same time, I held my breath.

Geneva took a gun from one of her minions and aimed it at me.

All hell broke loose.

Coast and Tiger burst in through the door at the back of the rink. Aidan, Finley and Orion burst through the other. Javey, Bray, Phoenix and Lex jumped up and threw themselves at the armed people around them.

The rest of the team and the opposition players who were hostages with them, took a moment to realise what was going on. Then they too were on their feet, wrestling control of guns, or punching Geneva's minions in the face.

Javey slipped on the ice and fell. A bullet aimed at him flew over the back of his head and embedded in the boards.

During all of this, I was fixated on the gun in Geneva's hand. The muzzle flashed, right before I was pushed aside.

Aidan let out a grunt of pain.

The sound was almost in unison with a shot from Coast's gun that took Geneva in the back of the head. She barely had time to react before she was crumbling to the floor between the rink and the first row of seats.

Aidan's shove sent me to my knees. I landed heavily, but twisted and fell on my ass to see him clutching the right side of his chest.

His face was a mask of pain, his hand over a bullet hole already drenched in blood.

Finley leaped towards him and brought him down to the ground beside me.

Between us, we tried to stop the flow of blood, while Orion stood beside us, picking off any of Geneva's minions who thought to come too close.

Time stopped for a minute or two, but now it restarted.

Several of the would-be attackers lay dead, the rest were on their knees, their hands behind their heads, held at gunpoint by pissed off looking hockey players.

Whether they were Demons, or Wombats, they were in control now.

"We need to get him to a hospital," I said frantically. I whipped the scarf off my neck and pressed it against the wound.

"I'm all right," Aidan groaned.

"Bullshit," Finley snapped. "Elenna is right. Orion and I will take care of things, you get out of here."

Aidan looked like he wanted to argue, but I helped him to his feet and we made our way back out the door. He was clearly in a shit load of pain but trying not to show it.

I flinched at the sound of footsteps running towards us, until Wren and Sinclair barrelled around a corner.

"There you are," Wren panted. "We went where Geneva was supposed to go, but they must have already left. We guessed they might come here."

"Is everyone okay?" Sinclair asked. She looked around behind us as Coast and Tiger led out the last remaining couple of Geneva's minions. Finley and Orion were close behind.

"The others are going to start the cleanup in there," Finley said. "It's going to take some work to get all the blood off the ice. Personally, I'm all for melting it." He shrugged and moved around to the other side of Aidan, pulling his arm over his shoulders to help support his weight.

"What are we going to do with them?" I nodded towards the two men being held at gunpoint.

All eyes turned to Aidan.

"Hand them over to Ice Miller," he said finally. "They can answer a few questions for us."

One of the men looked resigned, but the other's eyes widened in fear. He leapt at Tiger, making a grab for his gun. He got a grip on his hand and struggled to wrench it from his fingers.

"Fuck off," Tiger growled. He tried to elbow the man away.

It was Orion who raised his gun and shot the attacker in the wrist, narrowly missing hitting Tiger as well. The man screamed out in pain. He let go of Tiger to grab onto his furiously bleeding wound.

"Good shot," Finley said approvingly.

"Any fucking closer," Tiger grumbled.

"You're welcome," Orion said dryly. He and Coast shoved both of the attackers forward toward the doors leading out of the arena.

Most of my attention was on Aidan, but I didn't

miss the appreciative looks from Sinclair and Wren toward Coast and Tiger.

"Did you assholes take care of Geneva?" Aidan asked.

"I did," Coast said proudly. "Got there just in time. I have to say, Elenna has some balls, standing there like that. I would have pissed myself."

I managed half a smile. Honestly, it was a miracle I hadn't done that. When Finley first suggested I use myself as a distraction, I was certain I wouldn't pull it off. I was equally certain Geneva would shoot me on sight, or the moment she knew I killed Oscar.

Instead, I gave the guys time to get into place and be ready, while letting the players on the ice know there was a plan and they'd be needed to execute it.

Later, when all of this sunk in, I was going to be a puddle of jelly.

In the meantime, we helped Aidan into the back seat of his SUV, while Finley slipped into the driver's seat.

Wren and Sinclair followed in Wren's tiny hatchback.

Orion went with Tiger and Coast to deal with the two minions.

I almost felt sorry for the injured one. He'd obviously gone for Tiger's gun in the hope someone would kill him. I didn't blame him, I'd choose death over being tortured any day of the week.

"Hang on for a couple of blocks," I said to Aidan.

"You're not getting rid of me that easily." He managed a faint smile.

"I know I'm not," I said, my voice choked with emotion. "But that's got to hurt." Not to mention the scarf was more red than blue.

"Just a little," he lied badly. His brow was creased and beaded with sweat from the pain. "But I'm proud of you. Coast was right, I would have pissed myself too. You didn't even look scared."

"I was terrified," I said. "I just did what had to be done. That was all."

"It was more than that and you know it," he said. "If it wasn't for the tiny graze on my shoulder, I'd take your clothes off and fuck you silly here and now."

"I know you would," I told him. "Just relax. We're almost there." He looked like he was about to pass out from the pain.

"I love you," he whispered.

"I love you too," I whispered back. I kept my hand firmly over his wound as we drew up in front of the hospital.

"Ice Miller is having the time of his life with both of them." Orion pulled up a chair beside Aidan's bed and sat.

Aidan insisted he didn't need to lie down, but the doctor disagreed. He'd lost a lot of blood and needed to rest, at least overnight. The bullet went right through, without hitting anything major, but he'd needed to be stitched back together and would have to take it easy for a while.

That would be easier said than done.

"I've never seen anyone look so excited about torture," Coast said from the corner. Every so often he glanced at Sinclair who stood with Wren near the window. He was trying to be subtle, but I noticed, even if she didn't.

"He's a sick fuck," Tiger declared. He wasn't trying to hide the fact he was looking at Wren. She was looking back at him too.

"If anyone can get them to talk, it's him," Finley said. "He's very good at what he does."

"Why did Geneva attack us?" Tiger asked bluntly.

Everyone looked to Aidan, who shrugged, then grimaced at the stiffness in his right shoulder and chest.

"We were going to deal with her," he said. "It seems she decided to get in first. A bit more dramatic than anything we would have done."

Tiger grunted. "I figured it was something like that. What about the rest of them?"

"The Fiorellis? Either Jamison was lying and Nicholas and Celine were working with Geneva after all," Aidan said slowly, "or he was telling the truth and he was working with them and not her. Either way, they're going to be pissed off."

"Nothing we can't deal with." Coast pushed himself

off the wall. "We took care of Geneva, we'll take care of whatever else comes at us." He levelled a finger at Aidan. "Don't try to tell me we're not involved. When they attacked Demons Arena, they involved all of us."

"And you were the one who killed Jamison. And Geneva," Tiger said. "In front of a whole arena of people."

Coast grinned. "Let them come at me then. Nothing I can't handle."

"Getting too cocky will get you killed," Aidan told him.

"Lucky I have you to kick my ass when I get too cocky, Coach," Coast said.

"I think I should have shot you in the ass when I had a chance," Tiger said.

Coast flipped him off. "Love you too, bro."

Tiger grimaced. "Fuck off."

"I think it's time for everyone to go and let Aidan rest," I said. "We don't want him too tired to kick all of your asses."

"Yes ma'am." Coast saluted me and stepped towards the door. "Sinclair, do you need a ride to the after party?"

She glanced at Wren, who waved her away. "Go, have a good time. I might see you there later." Wren was eyeing Tiger, who was doing the same to her. I had a feeling they'd be occupied for a while.

I waited until they left to sit down on the side of the bed and lean my forehead lightly against Aidan's.

"I can't believe that's over."

"Those guys are a handful," Aidan agreed.

I laughed softly. "I meant Geneva, but them too." We'd dealt with Geneva. I'd admitted to everyone I killed Oscar. For the first time, I didn't feel dirty about it. I felt…nothing. That was in the past. It was time to concentrate on the future with my three, incredible men. Past time for us to get some rest and enjoy our lives and each other.

If the rest of the family went after Coast, we'd do the best we could to help. The Demons always looked after their own.

EPILOGUE

ELENNA

"I put it on, now I get to take it off," Aidan said to me. He took my hand and slid my wedding ring down off my finger.

I felt naked without it.

"If you keep saying things like that, we're not going to get out there," I told him.

"Yes, we are." Finley stopped to peer into a mirror and fix his tie.

He looked gorgeous in his black suit and red and blue tie. The same shades as the Demons' colours.

"What he said." Orion jerked his head towards Finley. He was dressed the same, but his dark hair and eyes contrasted starkly with Finley's red hair and blue eyes.

"If I didn't think you might shoot me for messing up your hair, I'd ignore them both." Aidan rolled his shoulder.

So many months on, it was still stiff and giving him the occasional discomfort. Like he always did, he tried to pretend it didn't. He fooled exactly no one, but fussing over him drove him crazy, so we kept a close eye on him instead.

"Good point," I agreed. I scooped up my bouquet from the table and waved it in the direction of the door. "I'm pretty sure none of you are supposed to see me beforehand."

"Too late," Finley said with a grin. "Besides, I think that only counts for an actual wedding. And if it doesn't, too bad. We like to do things our own way."

"Looks like an actual wedding to me," Orion remarked.

"We'll all be fashionably late if we don't get out there." I stood back while they hurried out the door, each giving me a kiss on the cheek as they passed.

Only because I might shoot them if they messed up my lipstick. I was almost certain they had some kind of competition going on to see whose cock it would end up decorating.

I followed them out, stepping onto a long strip of black carpet that ran between rows of chairs. Each one was packed with Demons players, staff, friends and family.

My father waited just outside the door to take my arm and walk me up the centre of the aisle. He smiled proudly and kissed my forehead.

This was unconventional, but he hadn't blinked

when I asked him to give me away to my three guys. Not once I explained the situation anyway.

Instead of the Wedding March, we walked up to the sound of a ballad from Ice Blue Roses, one heavy with saxophone and keyboard, and lyrics about love overcoming everything.

"Is this where I'm supposed to ask you if you're sure and tell you I can drive the getaway car if you want to run away?" Dad teased.

I laughed. "Probably, but I'm not going to run away. They'd hunt me down anyway and bring me back."

"Don't make me tie you up and stuff you into the back of my car," Aidan said loudly enough for most of the people in the room to hear.

A few people laughed, but most didn't think he was joking about it. They knew both of us better than that. Our relationship was complicated.

"Don't make me do that to *you*," Dad said pleasantly before he stepped back and went to sit down beside Mum.

Aidan didn't look particularly intimidated. He could handle my father if he had to. Wearing a suit that matched Finley and Orion, he was even more handsome than he had at our first wedding.

The guys arrayed themselves around me while the celebrant spoke of love and us making a commitment to each other.

I couldn't legally marry Finley and Orion, but I

could make the same commitment to them as I had to Aidan.

"You have a ring?" the celebrant asked.

"I have it." Wren reached into her pocket and pulled out a box. She and Sinclair were stunning in black dresses, each tailored to their taste and body shape.

Wren held out the box for Orion to take from her hand. He opened it and pulled out the ring.

Made from yellow, rose and white gold, the ring was made with three interconnecting circles. One for each of my guys.

Finley reached over and picked up the ring. He slid it onto my finger, up to the first joint. Aidan pushed it up to my knuckle, before Orion pushed it the rest of the way.

That was the compromise they'd reached after arguing about who was going to put it on my finger. When I say argument, I think rock, paper, scissors came into play. It was better than having a gunfight to settle the matter.

"I declare you, Elenna, to be committed to Aidan, Finley and Orion." Spoken in alphabetical order to avoid that argument before it started. "Congratulations." The celebrant stood back.

The guys took it in turns to kiss me, each deeper than before. Apparently any conversation about lipstick on cocks was forgotten.

I didn't know how I got so lucky, but here I was,

with the three most amazing guys on the face of the planet.

Finley here. If you loved this book as much as we love having a story told, go ahead and leave a review. If you're wondering where the anal is, you'll find it in the bonus scene here.

If you want to read the story of Sinclair and her guys, you'll find that in Breakaway. You'll also find Wren's story in Power Play.

ABOUT THE AUTHOR

Maggie Alabaster writes reverse harem romance.

She lives in NSW, Australia with one spouse, two daughters, one dog, and countless birds.

Jo Bradley writes contemporary romance.

Sign up for Maggie's newsletter! Sign Up!

Join Maggie's reader group! Join here!

Follow Maggie on Bookbub! Click here to follow me!

Check out Maggie's website- www.maggiealabaster.com

Sign up for Jo's newsletter

Book 1 Pitch

Book 2 Pound

Book 3 Session

Book 4 Muse

Book 5 Rhythm

Book 6 Encore

Novella Venomous

Saving Abbie books 1-4

Saving Abbie books 4-6 + Venomous

Ruthless Claws

Book 1 Ivory

Book 2 Crimson

Book 3 Elodie

Harmony's Magic

Book 1 Summoned by Fire

Book 2 Summoned by Fate

Book 3 Summoned by Desire

Shifter's Vault

Book 1 Discarded

Book 2 Deceived

Book 3 Disgraced

My Alien Mates

Book 1 Star Warriors

Book 2 Star Defenders

Book 3 Star Protectors

Academy of Modern Magic

Book 1 Digital Magic

Book 2 Virtual Magic

Book 3 Logical Magic

Complete Collection

Summer's Harem

Book 1: Shimmer

Book 2: Glimmer

Book 3: Flicker

Complete collection

Short reads

Taken by the Snowmen

Jingle All the Way

Also by Maggie Alabaster and Erin Yoshikawa

Caught by the Tide

Book 1–Pursued by Shadows

Book 2 Pursued by Darkness

Book 3 Pursued by Monsters

ALSO BY JO BRADLEY

Dusk Bay Sharks

Prequel Novella Sidelined

Spike

Punt

Intercept

Snap